all the
DEAD LIE DOWN

KYRIE McCAULEY

all the

DEAD

LIE

DOWN

 KATHERINE TEGEN BOOKS
An Imprint of HarperCollins Publishers

Katherine Tegen Books is an imprint of HarperCollins Publishers.

All the Dead Lie Down
Copyright © 2023 by Kyrie McCauley
All rights reserved. Printed in the United States of America.
No part of this book may be used or reproduced in any manner
whatsoever without written permission except in the case of
brief quotations embodied in critical articles and reviews. For
information address HarperCollins Children's Books, a division of
HarperCollins Publishers, 195 Broadway, New York, NY 10007.
www.epicreads.com

Library of Congress Control Number:
ISBN 978-0-06-324298-2

Typography by Molly Fehr
23 24 25 26 27 LBC 5 4 3 2 1

First Edition

For those who worry too much and sleep too little,
cluttering up midnights with their many thoughts.
I hope these pages serve as a proper distraction
from all that catastrophizing you are doing over there.

And for my grandmothers, Helen and Doris.
I'll spend my whole life trying to be
for others what you've been for me.

PART 1

Morning Bells and Death Knells

❧

One need not be a chamber to be haunted.
　　　　　　　　　　　　　—Emily Dickinson

The Sleeping House really did look as though it was at rest. Its windowed eyes were long shuttered shut. The ivy was so overgrown that it covered the house like a mourning shroud. Every so often its wooden bones shifted, settling deeper into the bed of dark soil on which it was built. But that was the first deception of the manor: its name. The Sleeping House was very much awake.
　　　　　　　　　—Alice Lovelace, *The Sleeping House*

1

A Bird in the Hand

———————— ❧ ————————

The mourning dove's bittersweet call was cut short, strangled into a silence that was even more unnerving than the birdsong itself. It was the first sign that all was not well at Lovelace House, and like most early signs of sickness, it was subtle. Easy to miss.

Marin Blythe barely noticed the sound at all. She certainly didn't notice its abrupt end. Marin was preoccupied, still thinking about the strangeness of the driver who had dropped her off at the gate, refusing to take her all the way to the house.

Place is cursed, the man said.

He didn't slam on the breaks or act hysterical. His voice didn't convey fear, despite the distance he insisted on keeping from the mansion, but rather something more like boredom. *It's cursed, of course, everyone knows*—his tone had been dry, humorless. A calm acceptance of fact, like he was telling her to carry an umbrella because it looked like rain. And while he may not have known Marin's business with Lovelace House, he didn't care to keep her from it, either. So out Marin went, onto the gravel path.

But a few minutes later, as she rounded the last bend of the driveway, Marin looked up, her curiosity blooming.

It was just a house.

A large house, and an old one. But just a house.

Marin rather liked the ivy that climbed one side of it, all the way up to its rounded turret. She liked the weathered gray stone peeking out from underneath the greenery. She liked the front steps, wide and grand and welcoming. She liked that there were windows in surplus, which told her that the inside of the house would be filled with streaming sunlight during the day. Marin couldn't stand dark, cramped spaces. Not anymore.

She lifted her suitcase, shifted her backpack from where it was slipping off her shoulder, and approached the house.

Cursed, the driver had said.

Stories, thought Marin. *And not even very good ones.*

Marin stopped to rearrange her skirt. The cheap polyester tights she'd worn were itchy, and their static cling had harassed her the entirety of her cross-country flight. *When I finally take these off, I'm burning them*, she vowed. When she looked back to the house again, a woman stood at the top of those wide front stairs.

She was easily the most elegant woman that Marin had ever seen. She must have been nearly six feet tall and wore a long dark blue dress that pinched at her narrow waist. The navy was stark where it contrasted with the woman's skin, light as porcelain, as though she avoided sunlight altogether, locked away inside the house behind her. High cheekbones graced her face, which was framed by dark blond hair cut like a razor's edge just below her chin. Marin recognized the woman from her author photo. It was printed on the back of the tattered paperback that Marin had read almost to pieces before shoving it into the side pocket of her backpack and getting on a plane to come meet Alice Lovelace herself.

Marin's awe was quickly replaced by a feeling of inadequacy so strong that she had to dip her face to hide the red flush she knew was blossoming across her own very low and rounded cheeks. Her gaze went to her brown oxfords, dusty from her walk up the gravel driveway. She focused on the precise place where those oxfords pinched her toes—half a size too small, but they'd been on sale.

"Ms. Lovelace." Marin spoke to her feet. "I'm—"

"Marin, of course," Alice said, and Marin looked up to see the woman's arms spread wide. "Welcome to Lovelace House."

Marin climbed the stairs and stepped into Alice's embrace, which was stiff and awkward but only lasted a moment before Alice was ushering her inside. The foyer was open and bright. The floor had wide-planked hardwood in a deep walnut color, and the walls were white, but one of those shades of white that Marin was sure had a special name, like *French Cream* or *Ivory Bone* or *Pearl Kiss*. The color was warm and earthy and reflected the sunlight coming in from the bay windows in the next room. There was art hanging on the entryway wall. It wasn't the kind Marin's mother had put up in their apartment. It wasn't something torn from a magazine and placed in a frame from the thrift store. This was an actual, real piece of art, with swirls in the paint that the artist themself had left there.

Marin wanted to touch it.

"My god, you look just like her," Alice whispered, and Marin turned to find Alice Lovelace studying her profile with the same scrutiny and wonder that Marin had felt while admiring the art.

Marin pictured herself as Alice was seeing her, for the first time. Marin's preference was jeans, a T-shirt, and sneakers any day of the week, but she'd wanted to make a good first impression, so she'd worn a burgundy corduroy skirt—her only skirt—and the itchy tights, and the shiny shoes, even if they did hurt her feet and had gathered dust on the driveway.

Marin herself had always been a gentler reflection of her mother. She had the same long, dark hair, wavy and thick. Today she'd twisted it up into two buns at the nape of her neck while she traveled. Her mother used to call it her *Princess Leia* look. Marin's breasts and belly and thighs were soft and rounded in the same places as her mother. Curves that always made men and women alike turn and watch her mother walk by them.

Unlike her mother, Marin's face featured constellations of brown freckles across her nose and cheeks, stark against white skin that blushed too easily. In fact, she felt the heat rising yet again under Alice's scrutiny. Marin's mother used to say that her emotions flickered like a movie across her face. All she had to do was watch to know all of Marin's secrets.

Marin also had her mother's wide mouth and full lips, and Marin liked to draw attention to them by wearing dark red lipstick, which she had done today.

Marin lifted her chin a tick higher at Alice's comparison. She was very much her mother's daughter and proud of it. "Yes," she said, "everyone said we were like sisters."

Alice had lifted one hand but dropped it now, seeming to remember that it was her long-lost friend's *daughter*, and not the friend herself, standing in front of her.

"No, not sisters," Alice said. "I was the closest thing to a sister Cordelia ever knew."

Marin opened her mouth but closed it again, unsure of how to respond. She was saved from having to figure it out by the patter of feet on the stairs.

The girls.

They were the reason she was here, after all, and she'd almost forgotten, so caught up in meeting Alice Lovelace— *the Alice Lovelace*—the same woman whose novels Marin had coveted from the age of twelve. The same woman that Marin's mother had once called her best friend, long ago, when they were children themselves.

Alice met the children at the bottom of the stairs.

"I'm so thrilled for you to meet Marin, your new nanny. Marin flew here all the way from California to take care of you. She's a long way from home, so let's be welcoming, all right?"

The girls did not look much alike. One had brown hair streaked with golden highlights and bound into braids, and she was the taller of the two. She stepped forward, and her angular face scrunched up a bit as she obviously looked Marin up and down. "She's very . . . young."

"She's the same age as Evie," Alice said.

"It's nice to meet you," Marin offered, sticking her hand out.

The girl took it with all the confidence of an adult. "Wren Hallowell," she said. "Rowena, actually, but you may call me Wren."

"And I'm Thea." The other child spoke from where she lingered on the bottom step. "Theadora, actually," she added, her tone both mimicking and mocking her sister's seriousness. "But you can call me Thea. Please."

"Well, Wren and Thea, I'm Marin. *Just Marin.* And it's very nice to meet you both."

Thea grinned, revealing a smile that was full of teeth. The adult ones were coming in before some of the baby teeth had fallen out, and as a result she had rows of teeth, like a little shark. Unlike Wren, Thea was towheaded, and her bright blond hair was cut short like Alice's, though Thea's hair fell in curls. She was endearing from the jump with her bright brown eyes, alight with curiosity. She smiled at Marin easily, whereas Wren seemed less sure.

The children were dressed alike, in white shirts and blue cardigans and chino pants and shining shoes. They were homeschooled—Alice had mentioned their tutor in one of her emails—but they were dressed impeccably. Not a speck of dust in sight.

Marin had never had a sister—or even *the closest thing to a sister*—but she'd always wondered if siblings liked to be dressed alike all the time.

She doubted it.

The conversation lulled, and Marin stood planted to the walnut floorboards as though she'd suddenly grown roots.

When Marin had gotten that first email from Alice Love-lace, she nearly fell out of her chair. As far as she knew, her mother hadn't spoken to Alice in decades, and yet there was Alice reaching out with condolences within days of Marin's loss. And crucially, throwing Marin a life jacket in a sea of grief and uncertainty—an offer for employment. Alice knew Marin was alone, and not quite eighteen, and Alice needed a summer nanny, and well, *maybe they could help each other.* She offered Marin room and board in exchange for nannying the girls every day while Alice wrote.

Marin made herself do some research before agreeing— though she knew in an instant she would say yes. It was the only real option she had. Besides, Alice Lovelace was something of a legend. She was a bestselling horror novelist and would have been independently wealthy from that alone. But she was also a *Lovelace*. The family had a longstanding prestige in New England, a name that once paralleled Rockefeller and Kennedy. They had left Alice the manor as well as what was rumored to be a significant inheritance.

Standing in that foyer, the enormity of it all struck Marin at once, rendering her overwhelmed and awkward in front of them. *How would she take care of these girls?* They were from an entirely different world than the bare-step-above-poverty one she had occupied with her mother.

Alice had been convincing, insistent even, when she'd contacted Marin. And yet there Marin stood, silent and unsure of herself.

It was Thea who saved her. Finally venturing off the final step, she slipped her small hand into Marin's larger one.

"A tour," Thea said, and Marin saw her elbow her older sister.

"Of course," Wren said. "Mother, we'll show Marin the house and the estate."

Estate. The word, and Wren's formal tone, didn't help Marin's feeling that she had jumped into the deep end by accepting this offer.

But she gave a nod to Alice, who stood and watched them climb the stairs together.

"Your room is down this way." Wren turned left at the top of the wide staircase.

"Is the other wing forbidden?" Marin asked with a laugh, gesturing to the hallway that ran in the opposite direction.

"No," Wren said. "Of course not. Why would it be?"

"Oh, no, I didn't mean—it's just—well in your mother's books, someone often says something ominous early on, like 'Don't go in the east wing—it's forbidden.'"

"Of course they do." Wren rolled her eyes.

"That's silly, Marin." Thea piped up. "There's nothing wrong with any of the wings." Thea leaned over to conspire, dropping her voice to a whisper. "But I'd stay out of the basement if I were you."

Thea dropped Marin's hand then and pushed open a door. "You're here."

Marin followed the girls into her new room. Her new home. It was bright and pretty, with light green walls and furniture that all matched in a rich cherrywood. Marin went to the window and pushed it partially open. There was a small balconette outside, only just wide enough for some potted plants. Beyond the yard, Marin could see only ocean in front of her, and the Maine coastline, stretching in either direction. There was a tiny strip of land to the right—another peninsula on Casco Bay. The tide was out, and instead of huge swatches of sand like the California beaches, here there were layers of rocks and tide pools, and seaweed left exposed in large clumps along the muddy edges. In the distance, Marin thought she could make out the faint white tower of a lighthouse. Or maybe it was a cloud. Marin squinted her eyes, but she couldn't be sure. The sunlight on the water played tricks on her.

"Welcome to Lovelace House." Wren's voice had little warmth in it, and when Marin looked down at the girl at her side, Wren's eyes weren't on the ocean, but staring right at Marin, her gaze calculating.

Marin flinched and immediately regretted it when the side of Wren's lips curved up in satisfaction.

Wren turned away, tugging Thea along with her. "We'll let you settle in a bit, and you can meet us downstairs for the rest of the tour."

"I like her," Marin heard Thea whisper to her sister as they left the room. "I hope she lasts longer than the others."

Then the girls left Marin alone, and when she heard the door click shut, Marin perched in relief on the edge of her bed. But before she could draw her next breath, a muted thump sounded from the other side of the room.

Marin turned toward the noise, waiting and listening for it to sound again.

THUMP.

Marin stood immediately. She couldn't help but think of a passage from one of her favorite Lovelace novels, about a house possessed by something sinister. Something that "lived inside the very walls," as Alice had written it.

Marin steeled herself and walked swiftly to the closet, pulling the door open before she could think about it any longer.

Inside there was a bird.

Its feathers and beak were bloodied, and she could see where it had scratched at the hardwood floor, could see the bloody marks on the inside of the door where it had been hurling its body. Marin scooped it up without a thought and carried it to her open window, setting it gently on the sill.

A moment later, it flew out, and Marin took deep breaths to calm herself down, glancing down at the blood left on her palms from the ordeal.

And then there was a loud crack right beside her, and she leapt back.

The bird had come back.

Marin watched helplessly as its small body crumpled from its impact against the glass and fell to the balconette. It twitched once more before growing still.

2

Ring Around the Rosie

Marin slammed the window shut and stepped back into the room, her stomach rolling. *It's only a bird. It's only a bird.*

She fled to the small bathroom that adjoined her room and turned on the cold water full blast. She first scrubbed the blood off her palms, her movements rough. Then she dunked her entire head under, letting the chilling water wash over her. Cold water always helped her come back to her body when she was on the brink of a panic attack. It grounded her here and now, pulling her back from her anxious tailspin.

If you are looking for something to be afraid of, you'll find it.

Marin's mother was gone, but her words lived in Marin's mind, echoing through at opportune moments. Memory was a kind of haunting in itself.

It was several more minutes before she felt the panic fully subside and shut off the water.

Just a bird. But the crumpled body was too cruel, provoking the grief she thought she'd buried with her mother in California. She remembered watching metal fold like paper. The feel of the cool rain falling through the broken windows until she was soaked and shivering. The smell of fuel and fire nearby.

Marin stripped out of her uncomfortable clothes and showered quickly. She changed into jeans and a simple black T-shirt and threw on some sneakers that were so worn she could see a glimpse of the sock at her toes. She hoped no one would notice.

Forget the rest of the estate, her new room alone was grander than any place she'd lived with her mother, often a studio apartment, the two of them living right on top of each other, sharing everything from the bed to the air. It used to frustrate Marin. Her mother preferred to move often, take them to new cities, nomad-like and poor, rather than be tied to some job she detested. Marin's childhood was marked by stress about paying the next bill or facing another eviction notice, and the seed of Marin's worry was planted early, with her often playing caretaker to her mother rather than the other way around. Cordelia never seemed to worry, so Marin did it for her.

But standing in this room, with all the privacy she'd ever wanted, Marin knew she'd trade it back in a heartbeat for more time with her mother.

Marin went downstairs to find the girls in the kitchen, waiting for her.

"Hello, you must be Marin," said a woman at the stove. She had an amber brown complexion and dark hair streaked with gray and coifed neatly at the back of her head.

"Welcome, I'm Neera." Her voice was soft and warm, with an Indian accent. She took Marin's hand into her own. "I help Alice manage the Lovelace estate. I've been with the family for years. But *lately*, I've been tasked with watching these two little heathens since they finished with their tutor last week and we were awaiting your arrival."

Neera winked at Marin and nodded toward the girls, who were at the table, currently pacified by milk and cookies. "Needless to say, I will be very glad to hand them off to you and have some peace and quiet in the afternoons."

The kitchen's swinging door burst open then, and a blur of rough movement caught Marin by surprise. Then an animal was on her, huge paws on her chest, and shaggy hair covering its eyes.

"Thisbe!" Wren shouted, jumping up from the table. "Down, girl."

She tugged the dog—the largest one Marin had ever encountered—down by her collar. "Sorry, that's Thisbe. She has rotten manners."

"Well, why don't you show Marin the rest of Lovelace, then?" Neera suggested. "And get this hellhound out of the kitchen."

Marin smiled at Neera and gave her a small wave good-bye. Her warmth was a welcome change from Alice's stiff greeting and Wren's cold one. It was spring in Maine, and there weren't many leaves on the trees yet, so when the wind blew in from the water it was unrestrained and bitter. Marin wished she'd brought a sweater. But then the sun slipped out from behind a cloud, and though a chill ran from the back of her neck down her spine whenever the breeze picked up, it was warm enough.

Instead of heading down to the water, the girls led Marin back to the front gate.

"The entire peninsula is called Winterthur, but it's only *technically* part of the town," explained Wren as they walked along the edge of the dark forest. "No one ever comes out this far."

Marin had never seen woods like these before. A hundred shades of dark green painted everything from the moss on the ground to the thick clusters of ferns. It was dark in the woods, and nothing moved.

A shock of bright purple caught Marin's attention, and she reached for the flower.

Thea's hand grabbed hers, squeezing hard and pulling it back.

"Those are wolfsbane," Wren said.

"These pretty purple ones? Like for warding off were-wolves?" Marin asked. "I thought that was fiction."

"No, it's real. It really was used to keep wolves away."

"Genus: Aconitum. Order: Ranancul—Ranincol—" Thea attempted.

"Ranunculales," Wren supplied the name for her.

"You girls know a lot about plants."

"Not as much as Evie," Thea said. "She grows all *kinds* of weird plants in the greenhouse."

"They're actually toxic," Wren said. "You shouldn't touch them."

"They don't look dangerous," Marin said.

"Dangerous things can be pretty too." Thea bared her own teeth at them for emphasis before skipping ahead on the trail.

"There aren't any wolves left, though every once in a while, someone spies a bear," added Wren. "Not many, and it's mostly safe thanks to Mr. Willoughby. He has his own cottage up the road."

The dog, Thisbe, bounded around them as they walked.

"What is she?" Marin asked, her hand reaching out to pet the dog's wiry fur.

"Irish wolfhound," Thea said. "And she was the runt. You should've seen her brother Pyramus."

"Pyramus?" Marin asked, trying to picture an animal even larger than the behemoth dog before her.

"Oh, she'll show you," Thea said, gesturing to Thisbe, who had picked up a large stick and was trotting proudly ahead of them. "Wait. Look at this."

Thea pulled Marin toward a row of trees lined neatly along the edge of what looked to be an old cemetery. Thea ducked into an opening at the bottom of one tree.

"Come on, Marin!" she shouted from within.

Marin crawled into the tiny gap and was delighted to find it opened into a larger space. There were two rows of the evergreen trees, planted side by side, so there was a hidden corridor running the length in between them.

"This is our arborvitae den." When Thea whispered, her voice held a tone of conspiration.

When they crawled back out, they found Wren next to a grave marked by a large stone gargoyle, roughly the shape and size of a dog but with folded wings and marred features, including a rounded, caricatured face.

On the ground in front of the gargoyle were dozens of sticks, and Marin watched as Thisbe dropped the new one into the pile.

"She likes to bring him gifts," Wren said. She nudged some of the sticks aside to show Marin the name carved into the base of the gargoyle's platform. *Pyramus.*

Thisbe darted away then, and the girls ran ahead, chasing after her.

Marin rose from the dog's grave, intent on catching up with them, when a flutter in the wind caught her eye, and she stopped short. There was something else along the side of Pyramus's grave.

She moved in for a closer look but stepped back again just as quickly. Lined along the stone were dead doves, all their necks twisted at strange angles. There must have been half a dozen of them, dropped haphazardly along the dog's memorial. It was a broken feather fluttering in the breeze that had caught Marin's attention.

She likes to bring him gifts, Wren had said, and apparently she hadn't only meant the sticks. Thisbe was killing birds and leaving them for Pyramus too.

Only a bird. Like the one left for dead in her room, and suddenly Marin knew how the bird got into her closet upstairs. Thisbe must have left it for dead there.

Marin was struck by the violence of it. The bent necks and bloodied feathers. But she was struck by the beauty of it too. The blue-green glimmer on the edges of the feathers as they caught the sunlight. The flecks of crimson red on the birds' necks. The white glimmer of a hint of bone. She knew what it was to grieve—to wish you could leave messages for the dead. As Marin stood beside the grave—so elaborate, so expensive, and all for a dog—she felt her throat begin to burn from the threat of tears and the ache of loss. Her mother's plain plot, in a cemetery that had no meaning to them except that the church had offered a bargain of a funeral price, was the only thing Marin had been able to afford. She'd spent their humble savings on a quick burial and a one-way plane ticket.

And now here she was, thousands of miles away, imagining

her mother's grave bereft of gifts or flowers or even visitors. She gave the dead birds one last look, their small bodies twisted and broken by the snap of Thisbe's jaw, left to rot over a grave not meant for them.

At least Pyramus wasn't alone.

3

Horrid

Marin briefly hoped that a change of scenery would interrupt the torrent of nightmares she'd had following the accident, but she had no such luck her first night at Lovelace House.

This one was shrouded in darkness. She was frozen in place, forced to listen to the screaming brakes, the deafening roar of collision, the soft whimper from the compartment ahead of her, where her mother had been a moment before. And then, just as suddenly as the nightmare had seized hold, it released her, replaced by a different noise altogether.

Marin woke to the peal of little girls' laughter. It reminded her of chiming bells.

She opened her eyes to find a long rope swinging in front of her face.

No, that wasn't right. It wasn't rope at all.

It was hair.

Clutched in Wren's hand was a swath of braided dark hair, at least ten inches long.

They wouldn't.

Marin's panic attack rolled over her like a wave, familiar and terrible as ever. It always began the same: her heart would start to pound in her chest, almost violently, so hard it hurt; then it was like she'd had the wind knocked out of her, and her chest felt constricted, tight, her breaths became fast and shallow. At the same time her body slowed, her mind began to race. Why would they do such a thing?

But where else would the long, dark braid have come from if not Marin's head as she slept? She found Thea, perched on her knees at the foot of the bed, clutching a pair of long silver scissors.

Marin screeched, sitting up in bed and reaching behind her.

She ran her hand down the back of her head, and stopped when her fingers found her braid, intact on the back of her neck.

She curled the end over her shoulder and looked to be sure.

She slowly became aware of Wren, who had doubled over on Marin's bedspread, laughing so hard there were tears in her eyes, and Thea, watching the entire exchange quietly, but with a small smile on her face.

"What the hell?" Marin asked, reaching for the braid in Wren's hand. "Do you think this is funny?"

She tugged the braid from Wren and examined it closer. She supposed it could be from a doll, but the hair felt and looked very real. "Where did you get this?"

Wren sat up slowly, wiping her eyes. "You should have

seen your face," she gasped out, and then collapsed into laughter once more.

"Thea," Marin snapped, her eyes shifting to the other girl, who was still, the realization of how upset Marin was finally washing over her, chasing away any humor she'd found in their cruel prank. Marin felt some small reassurance at the tears that quickly formed in the little girl's eyes, her regret evident. "Show me where this is from."

Thea waved for Marin to come with her and began to walk away. Marin leaped from the bed, and Wren gathered herself enough to follow along.

Marin hurried to keep up with Thea, who wound her way quickly through Lovelace's labyrinth of halls and stairs. She was all too aware of Wren walking behind her, the patter of her feet interrupted by the occasional hiccup of lingering laughter.

Marin remembered a poem her mother used on the rare occasion that Marin lied or broke a rule as a child. Cordelia would swing Marin up into her arms, tickling her and reciting the words. *"When she was good, she was very good indeed. But when she was bad, she was horrid."*

Wren Hallowell might just be the living embodiment of that poem. The child had been very quiet the night before, but she'd never taken her eyes off Marin. Her scrutiny, her clear dislike for Marin evident, began to feel like a weight on Marin's shoulders as the night dragged on. She felt that gaze on her wherever she looked or moved, and eventually excused herself to an early bed, citing her long day of traveling as an excuse.

And then she barely slept anyway. It took ages to fall asleep—Lovelace House was so quiet. Marin had only ever lived in cities, and she longed for the honking of horns and voices passing by beneath her window. She rose around four in the morning to open her curtains and her window, breathing in the salty air, admiring her view of the dark ocean. Eventually she drifted to sleep in the windowsill, and at sunrise, she dragged herself back to her bed. The tiredness had finally defeated the newness of it all, and she had finally slipped unhappily into her nightmares.

"She doesn't mean it," Thea said as they walked, navigating the halls of the manor so fast that Marin lost track of where they were. At some point, Thisbe joined them, tail wagging. They went down a short flight of stairs, turned again, and then they stopped.

They stood in front of a painted yellow door.

"The attic," Thea explained, and tugged it open. The staircase was narrow and steep.

"Of course she means it," Marin said, and just then Wren caught up with them.

It was obvious that Wren didn't want her there. She couldn't have guessed she'd be cruel about it, though. But then again, children had always been cruel. They'd teased Marin as a small girl, for the shape of her body, or the fact that she didn't have a father, or her lack of pretty clothes or the newest toys. Children could be vicious.

Marin wouldn't underestimate Wren again.

"Stay."

For a moment, Marin thought Thea meant her, before she saw Thisbe dutifully sit at the bottom of the stairs. Thea unbuckled the dog's collar and took it with her up the stairs, with Wren and then Marin trailing behind her.

In the attic, Thea led Marin around bookcases and shelves, finally stopping at a large wooden trunk tucked in a corner. She pulled what Marin now realized was a skeleton key dangling from Thisbe's collar, and unlocked the trunk, lifting the lid. "See?"

Marin knelt before it and drew back the sheet folded over the top of whatever the trunk contained. Her hands brushed against something soft, and she lifted it, holding it up to catch the light of the single, swinging lightbulb above her.

"Oh my god," Marin whispered.

It was another long braid of hair.

No, it was *dozens* of them.

Marin dropped the hair, horrified.

There were golden braids and auburn ones, a few were ebony black and copper red. All of them long and sheared off at the top and bound by hair ties or, on some of them, ribbons that were falling to pieces they were so old. On the other side of the trunk were frames with tinier braids and swirls of hair pinned inside. *In Memoria* one plaque read, with a name and dates scribbled underneath, practically illegible.

Wren knelt beside her then and lifted the braid that Marin had dropped. She returned it to the trunk, laying it neatly in a soft indent in the sheet, where it had clearly been residing for quite some time before Marin disturbed it.

"I'm sorry," she said without looking at Marin. "I thought you would find it a little funny. Evie likes our pranks."

Marin doubted that.

"No she doesn't," Thea said, and Marin smiled at the confirmation.

"Fine. But she doesn't get *this* upset," Wren said, and Marin could practically hear her rolling her eyes.

"It was unkind," Marin said. "And this is my first day here. You went out of your way to be cruel."

"You're right," Wren said. "I'm sorry."

"I'll forgive you if you tell me what on earth your family has an entire trunk of women's braids for."

"It's a family tradition," Thea said. "We grow our hair out and then chop it all off at once."

"I did that once," Marin said. "But I donated mine. Why do you keep them?"

"I don't know," Wren said. "We've always done it. So did our grandmother, and her mother too. Forever and ever, we've kept our hair. Mother says it's what all of the women do."

"But why?"

Wren closed the trunk and ran her fingers over the top.

"*Everything stays at Lovelace,* Mother says, *down to the*

27

bone," Wren answered. "That's why we have our own family graveyard too."

"What do you do with your hair when you cut it?" Thea asked. She turned the key in the trunk, locking the braids away once more.

"Oh, I guess it gets swept up and thrown away," Marin said.

"In the trash?" Thea said. "You throw your hair in the *trash?*"

"Well, it's only hair," Marin said.

She wasn't sure how they had done it. But they had made her feel that she was the strange one in all of this. "That's what everyone does with their hair."

"Well, not us," Wren said, running her hand lovingly over the trunk. "We keep what's ours."

"Thisbe!" Thea called out. They waited a moment, and then heard the clicking of the dog's nails on the hardwood stairs as she bounded up them. Thisbe ran up to Thea, who pulled the small metal key from the trunk and hooked it onto Thisbe's collar, right where a dog's name tag would go. "For safekeeping," Thea explained, buckling the collar back on Thisbe's neck.

Marin shrugged at the oddity of it. It wasn't even the third strangest thing they had done or said since she arrived, and she was tired, grumpy, and hungry. The truth was, she simply didn't want to focus on how creepy the children she had to nanny were turning out to be.

So she didn't.

"Let's get breakfast," Marin said.

"Will you tell Mother?" Wren asked, and for the first time, Marin caught an edge of uncertainty in her voice.

"Will she be upset that you played a prank on me?" Marin asked.

Wren fidgeted, and Marin didn't hate that she was uncomfortable with her actions.

"I don't know. Maybe. But she'll be more upset that we've disturbed her."

"While she's writing?"

Wren nodded.

"Then let's not disturb her," Marin said, and saw the slight relief in Wren's shoulders, the ghost of a smile on her serious little face.

Maybe not so vicious after all, Marin thought. Perhaps just lonely.

Marin understood loneliness. She understood it as an only child. She understood it as someone who had remained mostly friendless due to their frequent moves throughout her childhood. She understood the way it settled into you, became part of you, so that even when you were around others you still felt set apart. Like you'd never belong no matter where you went or who you met. Like you were a deserted island in a great, wide ocean.

Unreachable and barren.

4

The Girl Who Cried Wolf

M arin had always been a worrier.

From the time she was small, she was more cautious than the other children. Most likely to hang back from the edge of the playground slide. Least likely to climb a tree and risk the fall.

Marin knew that her worry didn't live in her brain. It lived deep down, nestled into her gut. It was only a feeling. An instinct. And perhaps it kept her from danger, but it kept her from everything else too.

Too worried. Too cautious.

Marin was nothing like her mother in that respect. Cordelia was adventurous by nature. She'd traveled the world, been skydiving, cliff jumping, mountain climbing. There wasn't an opportunity she had ever turned down, certainly not out of fear. The only weakness in her mother's armor was the ocean—Cordelia Blythe did not care for the sea. But she'd sit on the benches of the boardwalk with Marin, and they'd watch the sunsets and the ships roll in.

Marin asked her once, why choose San Diego for their next home if she didn't like the ocean? Cordelia had laughed, shrugged, and offered Marin a taste of her bubblegum ice cream—Marin crinkled her nose in a gentle refusal. *The ocean is beautiful, but it's dangerous, Marin. I didn't make that up in my head*, Cordelia had said. *Acknowledging that something can hurt you isn't the same as being scared, Marin. Understand?*

But Marin didn't understand, and everything scared her.

Then again, Marin rarely understood her mother—who could be impulsive, which, from Marin's perspective, often felt deeply uncomfortable. In turn, her mother didn't understand Marin's careful calculations. Her adherence to the status quo. To safety.

Marin began to listen to her gut early. She'd ask her mom to cancel a trip because she had that twisting feeling inside that felt off. That something terrible was imminent.

Why take the risk? she'd often asked her mother, and for a while, Cordelia had ceded to Marin's wishes. Perhaps she thought Marin would outgrow it. But listening to those worries meant that nothing bad *did* happen, the inverse of a self-fulfilling prophecy, and soon it became clear that Marin was never going to stop being afraid, never going to stop hanging back from the crowd, no matter how cautious they were.

Eventually, Cordelia began to push back against Marin's bad feelings. *We can't put our whole lives on hold forever*, her mom told her so calmly, so reasonably, that Marin tried. She pushed her bad feelings aside, buried them down deep, and said yes to whatever whim struck Cordelia, no matter how Marin's insides twisted in worry.

Right up to the Saturday that Cordelia insisted they get out of town for a few days. Take the train up north for the weekend.

Marin relented, but when they boarded the train, she sat a few rows behind her mother. She lay against the window, head on a pillow and headphones on and blasting. She knew if she sat with her mother, Cordelia would want to talk, and Marin didn't feel like talking. Marin didn't *want* another adventure. She wanted to stay home, and make Saturday morning pancakes, and go to a book signing, and read on the beach.

Besides that, her anxious stomach had made her queasy all morning. When she was little, if she lied or felt she had done something wrong, she wouldn't be able to sleep. The guilt would make her physically sick until she'd go to her mother in the middle of the night, the minor infractions of her childhood spilling from her lips in a rushed confession. And that was how Marin felt that morning as they boarded their train. On the verge of confession. Like if she didn't tell her mother everything in that moment, she'd never have the chance again.

And then the train car had crunched.

Like a can.

Like a paper bag.

For hours Marin was trapped, caged in by twisted metal on either side. She couldn't see the other seats, couldn't see her mother. But it seemed as though that was because the front of the train car no longer existed, and as she lay there in the wreck, wedged between seating and steel, with rain pummeling through the cracks, waiting for the rescue workers to reach her, Marin reasoned that probably meant her mother no longer existed either.

Marin had thought for a moment that maybe that day was the end of her worrying—after all, the worst thing imaginable had happened. What else could she live in constant fear of beyond losing the person she loved most?

But it only took a few days at Lovelace House for that familiar sense of dread to creep into her once more. And this time it lingered.

Just like the morning of the train and a million other times in Marin's life, she couldn't explain her worry. It was nothing more than a pit in her stomach. A black hole swallowing her up. Invisible to everyone else, but the force that ruled her every waking thought.

It was exhausting, and Marin wanted nothing more than to crawl into bed and sit with her fear and grief undisturbed. But she couldn't retreat. She was responsible for Wren and Thea, and if the rest of the summer was anything like the first few days, it was going to take every ounce of her focus, and maybe every bit of her obsessive overthinking, to keep the girls out of trouble.

Marin joined Neera downstairs to help her with breakfast, and then made Wren and Thea hand-wash the dishes—penance for their prank.

While they cleaned, Marin sat with Neera at the kitchen island, their voices hushed.

"They aren't making this easy on you, are they?" Neera asked.

"Well . . ." Marin began. She didn't want to lie, but she also didn't want to put into words how uncomfortable she'd been since arriving at Lovelace.

Neera laughed gently, not mocking but in commiseration. "This is not a typical family, Marin. They will take some getting used to. Besides, like you, they've recently suffered the loss of a parent. Not everyone handles grief with the grace you are showing."

She placed her hand over Marin's.

"Be patient. You could find a home here yet."

Tears sprang to Marin's eyes at the words. Because of course, that was what she had wanted when she'd agreed to come here, even if she hadn't been honest with herself about it.

A place to live, she'd told herself. *A summer to figure out her next move.*

There were logical reasons behind her choice. But they weren't the truth.

The truth was she wanted to belong somewhere.

Marin thanked Neera and helped the girls finish up, handing a towel to Thea to dry off her sudsy hands.

"What would you like to do today?"

"Let's play. We like card games, and you haven't seen the library yet."

"You have a library?" Marin asked. She shouldn't have been surprised. Lovelace House was enormous, and Marin had only seen a fraction of it so far.

They played card games for a while, and Marin felt the tension ease from her body as they sat in the bright, beautiful room. There were large windows that streamed sunlight—nothing dusty or dark about it. And in the corner of the room was the grandest piano Marin had ever seen.

"Do you play?" she asked. They both shook their heads.

"It's Evie's," Wren explained, glancing up from the cards in her hands. "She hates when we touch it."

"How long has Evie been away at school?"

"Nearly two months," Wren said. "She was home for spring break."

"You must miss her," Marin said.

"Mother says we should treat you like our sister now."

From Wren's tone, Marin could tell exactly what she thought of that.

"Well, that's silly," Marin said. "I'm not your sister, and I couldn't replace her."

Wren laid a card on the table and answered without even looking at Marin. "That's right, you're not."

Thea's hand shot out to swoop the card up. "Ha!" she exclaimed and laid her cards on the table. "I win. Again."

"Wait," Marin said, checking Thea's hand. "You don't win. Your hearts go four, five, six, *queen*, eight."

"Right," Thea said. "But it's Wednesday."

"So?"

"On Wednesdays, queens are wild."

"Oh, come on. That's not a thing. Did you just make that up?" Marin asked, turning to Wren for confirmation.

"When will you understand, Marin? Lovelace House has its own rules," Wren said.

"Don't worry. You'll learn how to keep up in no time, Marin," Thea offered, cleaning up the cards and stacking them neatly in the center of the table.

"Or not," Wren said, pushing her chair away from the table. "I'm going to read. You can keep her entertained, right?"

"Yes," Marin and Thea both said in unison.

"I'm here to watch *you*," Marin told Thea. "What should we play next?"

"Oh, I know." Thea took Marin's hand in hers. "Follow me. You haven't met my dolls yet."

"Well, I'd love to meet them," Marin said, letting Thea lead her past Wren, who had curled up in an overstuffed chair with *Anne of Green Gables* in her lap.

"I'm not your sister, Wren, but I could be your friend," Marin offered.

"You say that now," Wren said, and turned ever so slightly in her chair, offering Marin her shoulder and a clear dismissal.

Marin turned back to Thea, who was smiling at her. *At least one of them likes me,* Marin thought as she followed Thea out of the library.

In the hallway outside, Thea began to tug Marin left, but she heard a noise coming from the opposite direction. A muted shuffling noise.

"What's that?"

Marin began to follow the sound, bringing Thea along with her.

At the end of the hallway, she paused, listening.

"I'm sure it's nothing." Thea's voice was tinny, thin and high-pitched.

But Marin pressed on. Curiosity getting the best of her, like a stubborn, doomed cat.

The shuffling began again, and Marin stopped in front of a closed door. "What's this?" Marin asked.

Thea shrugged. "Linen closet."

Marin yanked the door open. Alice was standing just inside, a large cardboard box in hand, and she screamed and dropped it at Marin's feet.

Marin screamed too, startled by Alice.

The closet had no light inside. Alice must have been in

total darkness a moment ago.

But then, to Marin's surprise, Alice began to laugh.

"Oh, you gave me a fright, Marin, dear."

Marin smiled, unsure, and reached for the box and its now spilled contents.

"Leave it," Alice said, the humor in her voice gone for a just a moment. Marin looked up to find a smile on Alice's face but a steel sureness in her gaze, and she lifted her hands from the items that had fallen. They were old books, wrapped in green leather with gold lettering stamped into the flesh. They looked a bit tattered and delicate.

"Marin, *dear*." Alice moved forward as she talked, blocking the books behind the folds of her skirt. She wore another long, elegant dress, this time a sweeping black satin that looked more suited to a night at the opera than searching an old linen closet. "I would appreciate if you stayed away from this branch of the house. My study is just there"—Alice pointed down the hall to a sliver of sunlight in the crack of a door—"and I prefer to be undisturbed."

"Of course. I'm sorry," Marin said.

"We're going to visit my dolls," Thea said, interrupting the stiff exchange.

"How lovely," Alice said. Her smile was warm once more, or at least warmer, when she faced Thea. "You girls enjoy your walk."

5

Some Things Are Better Left Buried

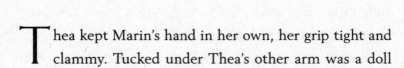

Thea kept Marin's hand in her own, her grip tight and clammy. Tucked under Thea's other arm was a doll that Thea had grabbed from her bed before tugging Marin along once more.

"Where are we going?" Marin asked.

"To see my other doll. I miss her."

Marin was surprised when Thea led her right out the kitchen door and onto the grounds. They passed by a huge greenhouse attached to the west side of the house, and then they were stepping into the woods that framed the property.

The temperature dropped by several degrees under the thick canopy of trees. They were mostly pines, but some birches stretched their ghostly limbs out to Marin too. Some sunlight broke through, leaving fluttering light on the ferns and undergrowth. Not enough to warm anything, but enough to give life.

Marin felt her sneaker squish through something and looked down to find toadstools, now smashed into the soil.

There were hundreds of them, small and red and black, snaking along the ground.

There was no trail.

"We'll get lost," Marin said, looking back for Lovelace House, finding it had already disappeared behind the dense woods.

"We won't," Thea said, and continued to pull her along.

A minute later, Thea finally released Marin's hand to unlatch a small gate. The wrought-iron fence formed a square right in the middle of the forest.

Inside there were more gravestones, only these were far older than those in the family graveyard that Marin had visited her first day. The stones here were illegible, worn down by centuries of exposure, aged dark stone covered in soft green moss.

Marin bent and brushed moss off of the stone nearest to her. She could barely make out the front end of the year. *Sixteen*—something. These stones were over three hundred years old.

"What is this?" Marin asked.

"This is where we buried her. Oh no, I was afraid of this. Sometimes they try to come back." Thea knelt at one of the graves. A startled scream began to crawl up Marin's throat before she could understand what she was looking at. There was a tiny, perfect hand, reaching out from the grave.

"It's all right, Marin. I'll fix her right away." Thea dug her hands into the soil. The ground should have been hard, but

Marin watched the loose soil slip through Thea's fingers as she dug around the hand.

The gravestone was very old, but the burial was fresh.

Thea dug in before Marin could get to her, and she pulled out a doll. It was covered in dirt, wearing a white dress now beyond saving, smeared in muddy stains.

"Thea—"

"This is my doll. She died. But I guess I didn't bury her properly." Her voice dropped down to a whisper. "I was hurrying. Mr. Willoughby doesn't want me to play in here."

"I can't imagine why," Marin said, not bothering to hide her sarcasm, which Thea ignored anyway.

Thea dug back into the dirt, determined to lay her doll to rest. Marin realized that the fastest way out of the graveyard was to help, so she dug her hands into the soil as well.

Please let whoever else was buried here be long, long gone, she wished.

Fortunately, her hands only touched dirt, and soon the hole was large enough—and now deep enough—to serve as a doll's eternal resting place.

Thea gently laid the doll back in, and together they covered her.

"You must say a few words," Thea said.

"A few words?" Marin repeated dumbly.

"For Cordelia," Thea said, gesturing to the small grave.

Marin's stomach turned at the doll's name—the same as her mother's.

It was a coincidence, of course, but it made her feel sick just the same.

A few words . . .

"We gather today, in memory of our dear . . . Cordelia. Our time with her was too short. But we take comfort in knowing that she's no longer in pain, having succumbed to . . ."

"Drowning," Thea offered.

"Drowning," Marin said. "May she rest in eternal peace."

Thea tucked her dirt-covered hand into Marin's.

"Thank you, Marin. Cordelia was a very good doll."

"I believe you," Marin said. "I'm so sorry for your loss."

They didn't linger in the graveyard—and Marin was grateful for that. She was grateful as well that Thea knew the woods so well because Marin would have gotten herself lost in just a few minutes out here. She could hear the ocean crashing against the rocks as the tide came in and might have tried to follow that sound. But as she walked the sound seemed to shift, from one side of her to the other, and other times it was lost entirely among the hum of wildlife and movement in the trees. But Thea never hesitated, her little footsteps sure.

They'd walked a quarter mile or so—it was slow without a path—when a sharp crack drew Marin's attention.

She stopped moving, and her hand reached to Thea by instinct, pulling her in close.

At first Marin thought it was a tree moving.

Surely those were branches, stretching out and up, reaching ten—no, twelve feet tall.

Then she saw the huge head that those branches were attached to.

It was a moose.

Marin recognized the animal, of course. She had seen pictures in books, and videos of them on nature shows. But she was wholly unprepared for the size of the creature. He was only a few yards away from them. If an animal that large startled, it could crush them in a moment, without even trying.

"He's beautiful," Thea said, but her voice had fallen again to a whisper. Maybe she understood that it could hurt them. Or maybe she was just in awe of the great beast.

The moose moved, his gait awkward, limping, and that's when Marin noticed his leg. It was broken, badly—the bone was protruding. And the area around the break looked inflamed and infected. It was hard to watch him move, putting any weight on it at all. His eyes were glazed over with a milky film, and it seemed his eyesight was impaired.

Marin felt a sharp pang of pity for the animal. She couldn't believe it was even alive with an injury like that.

Marin stood as still as the stone angels in the cemetery they'd just left, her grip tight on Thea's shoulder. They watched as the moose slowly passed by them, until he disappeared into the shadows of trees and foliage.

As good as dead.

The phrase rose to the surface of Marin's thoughts, tugged from some distant childhood memory. It was said in her mother's voice.

Marin had found a stray kitten once. It was entirely black, even down to the little bean pads on its paws, and days old at the most, its belly swollen with parasites. But what was shocking about the kitten was its little face. Instead of two eyes, it had one, in the center of its forehead, sealed shut by disease.

Marin had begged her mother to save it.

"Some creatures are beyond saving," her mother had said, but Marin refused to listen to her. She had emptied her piggy bank and brought the entirety of her savings to her mother, demanding a trip to the veterinary hospital.

In the end, her mother had been right.

When the kitten died anyway, Marin told her mother she didn't regret a thing because at least the kitten felt safe and loved before it died.

When they returned to Lovelace, Marin sent Thea off to sit with Wren while she handled the moose situation. *As good as dead.* Perhaps the creature was beyond saving.

But that didn't mean he was beyond mercy.

Marin decided to walk to the groundskeeper's cottage, but she stayed on the dirt and gravel road and kept a lookout for the injured animal.

Creatures in great pain could be dangerous.

Marin hadn't met Mr. Willoughby yet, but she found his home easily enough. It was visible from the road, and she was soon knocking on his door.

She heard him shuffling around inside and stepped back when he opened the door.

Mr. Willoughby was a tall man, she'd guess several inches over six feet tall. He was older than she'd expected, with a gray-white beard and hair, and thick eyebrows that were furrowed deep when the door first opened, though he quickly relaxed them when he saw Marin. She had to crane her neck to look up and meet his gaze. With her Leia buns and her cardigan on, she felt all of ten years old again.

"Mr. Willoughby, I'm Marin Blythe, the girls' new summer nanny."

"Marin Blythe," he said, stretching out a hand in greeting. "All the way from California."

"That's right," she said with a warm smile.

"How do you like New England?" he asked.

"It's cold. And cloudy. And there's no sand on your beach."

He laughed out loud.

"Very astute, Marin. Well, welcome just the same," he said. "What can I help you with?"

Marin quickly described the injured moose, and Mr. Willoughby assured her he would contact the game warden and take care of the hurt animal. He thanked her for telling him.

She was walking back down the path to his cottage when his voice called out behind her.

"Be careful in the woods, Marin, especially with the little ones. It's likely the moose broke its leg on its own, but just in case, stay sharp and let me know if you see anything," Mr. Willoughby warned.

Marin gave an awkward thumbs-up in agreement and hurried back down the path to the main road. She knew it was silly to be afraid of the woods. She had spent the whole afternoon in them without seeing anything dangerous. And she'd walked out to Mr. Willoughby's place safely not ten minutes before. It was nothing but Mr. Willoughby's warning in her head as she walked along the road, making her uneasy. But she felt the entire time like she was being watched.

Marin was glad to reach the yard and hurried up the stairs, closing herself back inside Lovelace House, where she was safe.

6

Mary Had a Little Lamb, What We've Got Here Are Demons

By the time Marin Blythe arrived at Lovelace House, the Hallowell girls were half-feral.

They'd put on a good show of it for their introductions, Wren with her soft wariness, Thea with her cherubic grin. But Marin learned quickly that it was just that: a performance, with all the motions memorized, down to the dimple on Thea's cheek as she pulled Marin through the house.

In truth, the girls were monsters.

Of course, the swinging braid had scared her, but once she'd calmed down, Marin had realized that it had been totally harmless.

Creepy but harmless.

The problem was, the girls didn't stop there. The pranks continued, and at first Marin didn't even realize they were escalating. They were such small infractions that Marin dismissed them as their strange sense of humor, shaped by years of loneliness, home tutoring, and having to entertain themselves for long hours in an isolated place.

It was a kind of hazing, and Marin decided quickly that it was easier to play along.

She screeched right on cue when she found a toad in her bed the third night, and then she winked at Thea as she carried him outside and set him free in the dark soil beneath the blueberry juniper that surrounded the house.

A few days later she discovered that all her bags had been rummaged through. But nothing had been stolen (in truth, there was nothing of value to steal), so Marin chastised them half-heartedly and moved on, hoping that was the end of it.

When her phone went missing, she threatened to tell their mother. But even that threat was empty. She didn't really care about the phone. She'd moved too often to have any close friendships from her old life. And there was no service at the end of the peninsula anyway. When it ran out of battery her second night at Lovelace, she hadn't even bothered to charge it again. And then it was gone.

It wasn't until Wednesday of her second week at Lovelace House that the girls tried to kill her.

They arrived early that morning in Marin's doorway. Thea wore a straw pith hat, and from what Marin had seen of the objects in Lovelace House, the hat was probably very old and genuine and had actually tracked a lion across plains at some point in history. Wren's hat was Western, wide-brimmed, with a tie tugged up to her chin to hold it in place on her too-small head.

"We're going to the jungle," Thea said in a rough Australian accent. "Gear up, Marin."

Marin pulled on her sneakers—really, what else did they expect of her?—and followed them through the winding halls of the mansion. They reached a double set of doors, and when Thea pushed them open, Marin's jaw dropped in awe.

It really was a jungle.

In actuality, it was the greenhouse. But it was huge—nearly as tall as the house itself. It was caged in by a metal framework and green glass, and it was large enough that Marin couldn't see the far end through the thick foliage.

"It's a little overgrown," Wren said. "Evie usually takes care of it."

"Let's go," Thea said, impatient to begin her game.

Marin chased the girls through their jungle for an hour. She'd been cast as the jaguar. She ran, weaving between exotic plants and bright pink flowers, until she was sweating. The greenhouse was warm and humid, the opposite of the New England spring weather she had dressed for this morning.

Finally, she caught them, throwing her arms around Thea's little waist and whipping her around in a circle. Thea's scream pierced the air so loudly that it nearly startled Marin into dropping her. For a child so soft and unassuming most of the time, Thea was loud when she needed to be.

"Time for a snack," Wren said, swinging her backpack to the floor of the greenhouse, and pulling out some fruit, bread, and cheese. They ate in relative peace for a few minutes, and then Wren pointed just past Marin's ear.

"There are berries behind you," she said. "Can you pick a few?"

Marin turned and eyed the purple fruit. They looked like blueberries, but they were smaller, and darker, shiny and nearly black. She plucked a few from the branches and held them out in her palm.

"Try one," Wren said. "They're so good."

"But, Wren, they're—" Thea began, and Wren dug her elbow into Thea's side.

"—tart," Thea finished. "They're very tart."

"I don't mind tart," Marin said, and was lifting her hand to her mouth when a voice rang out across the greenhouse.

"I wouldn't do that if I were you."

Marin turned toward the voice.

There was a girl at the entrance to the greenhouse. She looked to be about Marin's age, but she was tall and willowy, and she had thick blond curls tumbling past her shoulders. She wore a white collared shirt tucked into a plaid skirt that crisscrossed forest green and navy blue.

She looked like she had stepped through time, better suited as the heroine of a Brontë novel than the present day.

"Evie!" the girls shrieked in unison and leapt to their feet, dashing across the greenhouse and tackling the girl to the ground.

Evie.

The eldest Hallowell sister was home.

Marin made her way over to the sisters. Evie let Wren and Thea smother her in hugs and then rose and straightened her skirt, smoothed her hair back into place, letting her curls fall in such a way that they curved over the sides of her face, not quite obscuring her eyes.

"They're pretty enough but deadly." Evie gestured to Marin's hand, where she still held a handful of dark berries.

"Those are nightshade," Evie said. "Belladonna."

Marin, who knew next to nothing about plants, shrugged.

"Poison," Evie clarified, and reached out her hand, palm up.

Marin looked at Wren. Up to this point, their pranks had been teasing. Annoying but not dangerous. Marin dropped the berries into Evie's hand, who put them into the pocket of her skirt.

"I wasn't going to actually let her eat them," Wren mumbled.

"I'm gone for a few months, and I come back to you nearly committing murder? What's been happening here?" Evie's voice began with warmth, but by the end it felt strained. "Wren, your last letter worried me."

"I didn't think you'd really come," Wren said. "Everything is fine."

Evie crouched down and took Wren's hands in her own. "I'll always come. Besides, I was failing geometry and the headmistress was about to have my head. And even worse than that—look! *Pleated skirts only.* A travesty. How is mother?"

Wren smiled. "Mother is . . . on deadline."

Evie looked to Marin, as though she'd forgotten she was standing there.

"Why don't you let me clean up and change and we will go for a walk, hm? Just the two of us?" Evie said to Wren, who nodded her agreement.

Mother is . . . what? Marin was sure that Wren was about to say something else before she remembered Marin was there.

The truth was that Marin had seen little of Alice since her arrival except for the encounter at the linen closet. Alice joined them for dinner most evenings and sometimes during the lunch hour. At night, Alice relieved Marin of her duties and tucked the girls into bed herself. Besides meals and the handoffs, they had barely spoken at all.

She's writing, Thea had said when Marin asked, and *not to be disturbed.*

But now Marin had seen the concern etched on Wren's face the moment her older sister returned—the moment she let down her guard. Something felt wrong.

Then again, thanks to Marin's anxious brain, which seemed hardwired with fear, something almost always felt wrong.

Marin shook her head as though it could clear the webs of worry strung inside.

The Hallowell girls were just odd. They would take some getting used to.

"We'll clean up our picnic," Wren said. "Sorry again, Marin, for the berries."

"For nearly killing me?" Marin clarified.

"We wouldn't have let you eat them!" Wren insisted. "It was a test. We wanted to see if you trusted us."

"I *did*," Marin said, emphasizing the past tense.

Wren and Thea ran to go clean up, disappearing into the dense foliage of the greenhouse.

"Hopeless," Evie said, and Marin wasn't sure if she meant the girls or the overgrown greenhouse. Perhaps both.

"I'm Marin." She introduced herself, feeling awkward in Evie's own home.

"I know." Evie's eyes still fixed on the place the girls had vanished to. "Wren wrote that you're her favorite nanny yet."

"She didn't," Marin said with a startled laugh. "I think she might hate me."

Evie turned then, facing Marin head-on, and Marin had to stop herself from stepping back. Evie had Thea's dark brown eyes—eyes that seemed to know everything but gave nothing away in return. Eyes that made Marin feel vulnerable and exposed, like all her secrets were in plain sight across her face. Marin found herself wishing she could hide away from Evie's dark gaze.

Evie looked a lot like her mother, though her features were softer. Her nose more buttoned than long and straight like Alice's was. Her complexion was almost translucent in places, and Marin could see the blue lines of her veins in Evie's wrists and at the base of her throat. Evie's chest swelled as she took a breath, and Marin forced herself to look back to Evie's eyes, trying to remember what they were just talking about.

"If I'm her favorite, she must have abhorred everyone else," Marin said. "I overheard Thea say she hopes I last longer than the others."

At that, Evie laughed. Marin liked the sound of it. It wasn't delicate, like Evie's features suggested it might be, but full and loud and as unconstrained as Thea's.

Evie pulled a tin out of her other skirt pocket and flipped open the lid, offering a mint to Marin, and she took one. Cinnamon flooded her senses, and she watched Evie take two, placing them delicately on her pink tongue.

"Well, they've set the nanny-life-expectancy bar quite low," Evie confided. "They've had four or five since father died last year. Mother even considered choosing a school for me that wasn't year-round, just so I could be here to watch the girls in the summer at least, but *we mustn't neglect our studies*, as Mother says. So back to Arcadia Arts Academy I went."

"But not anymore?" Marin asked.

Evie wandered over to a plant blooming vibrantly nearby—brilliant red flowers sprouted in clusters, small fireworks of color. Evie cradled a handful of flowers in her hand. "No, no more Arcadia. I wasn't doing well there anymore. Besides, my sisters need me more. So does Mother, though she'd never admit it."

"So . . . you just left?" Marin asked.

"Technically, I failed out. I was on academic probation before, and I seem to have sealed my fate this spring term," Evie said with a wink. Marin felt herself warming to Evie so easily, which was odd after how difficult everything else at Lovelace had been.

"Math is the devil's handiwork if you ask me," Evie continued. "And useless too. If I want to study anywhere, it would be a conservatory, not college."

The girls rejoined them then, hats held in hand and the closest thing to a look of actual contriteness that Marin had ever seen on their faces. Evie quickly cried off to wash up and promised to find Wren for their walk in a bit.

It wasn't until Marin was tucked in the library playing a round of gin rummy with Thea that she realized that the feeling of dread—the one she'd felt hanging over her from the first day at Lovelace—had lifted, however briefly.

She'd been too distracted to worry.

Distracted by Evie's arrival.

Now the feeling returned like a stomachache.

Marin didn't know much about Evie. She hadn't been worried when her online searches had yielded little about the family—Alice Lovelace was known as eccentric, reclusive. Deeply protective of her children and their privacy. But that meant that Marin had agreed to come here on nothing more than instinct, and desperation, and the knowledge that her own mother had once known Alice.

She'd thought that was enough.

Marin glanced at the paperback book perched on the edge of the table. She was rereading one of her favorites by Alice, the thriller about the house that was not haunted, but alive in its own right and slowly picking off its inhabitants.

Despite the warmth of the afternoon light streaming in through the large library window, Marin shivered. And when she picked up the book and flipped it to study the woman on the back of it, she remembered the day she was twelve and brought home her first novel by Alice Lovelace from the library.

Her mother had lifted the book from the table and sighed heavily at the name on the cover before turning it over to Alice Lovelace's photo on the back. Marin was loving the book and was subsequently delighted to learn her mother had known Alice when they were children. Her curiosity piqued, she peppered Cordelia with at least a dozen questions. All of which Cordelia gave vague, uninspired answers to, about having known Alice and grown up with her, been friends with her even. But that it was long ago. At the time, Marin had shrugged it off so easily, her mother's reaction to the book. After all, people grow apart.

But now Marin had met Alice.

Now Marin was the one sitting in Lovelace House, trying to shake the feeling of dread that followed her room to room like a nervous dog, impossible to escape or ignore for long. Always just there, underfoot, tripping her up.

Maybe there was a reason that her mother, always so talkative and forthcoming and optimistic, had been quiet that day. Maybe Cordelia had been caught up in some memory of Lovelace that washed over her like a wind off the ocean, chilling to the bone everyone it touched.

7

Lying Like a Tombstone, Silent as a Grave

Within an hour of Evie's return home, Marin was summoned to Alice's office. For the office of a horror novelist, Alice's workspace was surprisingly bright and warm. It was a sunroom, with floor-to-ceiling windows. Marin paused at the door, knocking even though it was open, and waited for Alice's sharp "Yes, come in."

"You asked for me?" Marin asked.

Alice was perched at a small writing desk, with only a notebook in front of her and a handful of pens lying within reach. She didn't turn around; she just kept her pen poised above the page, dancing, as though she was practicing her words in midair before committing them to the page.

"I want to hear how it's going. With the girls."

"Oh. It's great. They're . . . very sweet. Wren has made an effort to make me feel at home here."

"Well," Alice drawled out, finally setting her pen down. She smiled at Marin. "That's a lie."

Marin shifted back and forth on the balls of her feet. Should she apologize for lying? Try to reassure Alice that her small children weren't little monsters? Quit on the spot?

Marin said nothing.

"You've met Evie," Alice said. It wasn't a question, but Marin hadn't responded to the last thing Alice had said and was starting to feel rude.

"Yes, I did," Marin offered. "She's very pretty."

God, what a strange thing to say.

Part of Marin wished she could die on the spot just to not have to finish this conversation.

"Nice, I mean." Marin tried to correct it. "Evie was very nice."

"Pretty and nice," Alice repeated softly, pulling off a petite pair of gold-rimmed reading glasses and turning to Marin. "Well, one of those is true. You get half credit."

She scanned Marin up and down. Gone was the skirt and the tights and the shoes. All replaced by her normal, comfortable clothes. Meanwhile, Alice Lovelace wore another sleek dress—this one a dark red—and Marin wondered who she bothered to dress up for, here on the end of the peninsula, when she barely even left her room all day.

"Evie has made the executive decision to take a leave of absence from school. Evangeline had been accepted into a prestigious summer continuance program, an intensive in music composition, but she took it upon herself to withdraw from the program and book a flight home, making everything quite . . . awkward."

"Awkward?" Marin asked, confused.

Alice gave Marin a look like she was something to be pitied, then returned her glasses to the bridge of her nose.

"Well, you are a bit redundant, sweetheart. Now that she's home, however unexpectedly, Evie could watch her sisters on her own. However, since I know you have no one and nowhere to go, of course we will keep you here, as planned. All I ask in exchange is that you tutor Evie. She failed geometry—and she already was in the easiest class they offered and a grade behind to begin with. She needs to get a decent score on her college entrance exams if she wants Harvard and Yale to overlook her weaknesses. I know you scored quite high on yours a few months ago, didn't you?"

Marin nodded, unsure how Alice could possibly know her test scores.

"So . . . am I *not* watching the girls?"

"No, you will do that too. Together. God knows they could use an entire team, so I'm sure you and Evie will have your hands full. You can trade off, mornings and afternoons, or watch them together all day." Alice waved her hand through the air. "However you like."

"Watch the girls all day and tutor Evie at night?"

"That's right."

"In exchange for room and board?"

"That was always the agreement, Marin."

"But—"

"Marin, darling, can I be honest here, for just a moment? You strike me as a very intelligent, capable young woman. You are here because I once cared very much for your mother. You are here because you are useful to me, maybe even more useful than I thought, if you can salvage Evangeline's school prospects. And you are here because, frankly, you are broke. And that means you couldn't afford to say no to me. Not when I invited you here and not now. I hate it when people say no to me."

Marin stood frozen in the doorway. No one had ever spoken to her in that way before, and the coldness of Alice's words, paired with the smile painted on her face, made Marin suddenly feel as though she'd been dropped into the sea without a life jacket.

But as cold as Alice's words were, they weren't untrue.

Marin had nowhere to go. She had nobody to care for her.

"Very well," Marin agreed.

"Good girl," Alice replied.

Marin stood in the doorway, waiting for more.

"My dear, I think we are finished here, and I have quite a lot of work to do." Alice didn't even look up as she spoke, her pen already dancing over the page once more.

Marin rushed from the room and didn't stop until she had shut the door to her own bedroom firmly behind her. She sank down to the floor.

It didn't matter. Not really.

She was fine with tutoring Evie.

It was just that in that moment, standing before Alice, Marin realized how little control she had over anything. On a whim, in a moment, Alice could make her leave. She'd given up her mother's apartment. She had no family, nowhere else to go, and no one to turn to.

Marin felt like a rabbit in a snare. Caught and powerless.

And yet, nothing Alice had done or said had been that grievous. She wasn't being cruel, only honest. If Marin's mother were here now, she would wrap her arms around Marin's shoulders and tell her that she worries too much. There were so many nights that Marin had spent sleepless with anxiety, layering her fears like blankets on top of her until the weight was unbearable.

You're drowning in it, Marin, her mother would say when Marin's anxiety got the best of her. *You need to come up for air.*

Marin breathed deeply now, knees pulled tightly to her chest. She listened to the rush of blood in her ears and lapping of waves on the rocky coast outside. She imagined all of her worries as a tiny speck of dust inside of her, irritating her from the inside out. Then Marin imagined layers forming over it, again and again, until it wasn't an annoying bit of dirt anymore but a round, shining, perfect pearl.

Then Marin buried that pearl down deep and tried to forget that it existed at all.

8

Sugar and Spice

On Sundays at Lovelace House, everyone dressed for dinner.

It was a tradition that Marin became aware of only after she sat down to the table in mud-streaked jeans her first week there, earning a look of tired disdain from Alice.

Tonight, Marin was determined to not make the same mistake. She only had the one skirt, which she'd worn when she arrived, so instead she chose the singular dress she'd kept. It was simple and black and fell to her knees, but if you looked closer, you could see that it was embroidered with delicate black vines and flowers weaving up and down the length of it. She bought it just two months ago. She had needed something to wear to her mother's funeral.

Marin reached for her favorite lipstick, a deep Bordeaux red, its finish like velvet.

She knew exactly how to do her hair, weaving it back and forth until one long, thick braid curled around her neck to hang down her front—a reminder to Wren that the pranks were not forgotten.

She didn't think Wren cared much if she forgave her.

Marin was early, so she and Neera set the table together.

"How long have you been here with the family?" Marin asked as she circled the table.

"Oh, my goodness, it feels like forever sometimes. Nearly thirty years now. Originally, I came on to help Alice's mother, Theadora—little Thea was named for her. Alice was sixteen, maybe seventeen then."

"It's hard to imagine her my and Evie's age."

"Oh, well, same for me. She never acted her age. She was always so put together. So austere. That's why we knew Charles was her match the moment she brought him home. He made her . . . lighter."

Marin had seen Neera in fleeting moments at Lovelace, each of them busy with the house and the girls, and sometimes Neera was closed away in a small office off the kitchen, door shut tight, and Marin could hear the occasional soft murmur from within when Neera took calls.

But Marin always felt better knowing that Neera was there. Like she had a partner who was on the outside looking in at the strange exhibit that was the Lovelace family.

"Lighter how?" Marin was curious about Charles Hallowell. But even more than that, she was curious about that version of this family. The one that was intact.

"In every way. She'd laugh. They loved to dance. And Charles, well, he didn't bend toward the will of the Lovelaces' legacy. He wasn't bothered by their money, didn't care for this house. When he was alive, he insisted on driving the girls into town for school every day."

"Oh? I'd assumed they've always had tutors."

"Only for the last year. He was quite adamant they grow up around other children. Be part of the community. It was . . . healthier, I think."

"Would Alice go back to that eventually?"

"It's doubtful. Sometimes the worst happens, and people grow, they adapt. But Alice? She just sort of broke. She's struggled to write. Her health declined quite a bit over last winter, though she seems better now . . ." Neera's voice drifted, and she'd paused in setting the table, lost in thought. She shook her head once, decisively. "Listen to me, droning on."

"No, don't be silly. I asked you."

"Well, Marin, you've brought some light—some levity, dare I say it—back into this house and into those girls. I haven't seen Wren so animated in months."

"She's very motivated in her mission to drive me away."

"Don't let her win." Neera laughed. "She needs you here, whether she'd admit it or not."

Marin smiled. It felt good to be needed, felt good just to hear someone say it, even if she wasn't sure it was true.

"You look very nice tonight," Neera said, gesturing to the

dress as she passed Marin silverware wrapped in a napkin— cloth, not paper.

"Thank you," Marin said, holding on to the napkin a moment longer than necessary. It was the same soft ivory material that had been layered in the attic trunk, tucking in long braids of hair from generations of Lovelace women's past.

"And I take it you have met Evangeline?" Neera asked, and Marin got the sense she was being watched closely for her response now.

"I did. She's lovely."

"That she is," Neera said, and moved to set the far end of the long oak table.

When she circled back again, her shoulder brushed against Marin's, and her voice dropped to a whisper. "Be careful with her," Neera said. "Remember, everyone's grief looks different. Things changed for all of them after Charles died."

"What do you mean—" Marin began to ask, but Wren and Thea burst through the dining room door, and Marin turned to marvel at them all cleaned up.

Any more questions she had for Neera would need to wait.

She'd spent the afternoon in the tidal pools on the shore with the girls, shin deep in the thick gray mud that marked the Maine coast. Wren had reached right into the pools, pulling out starfish and hermit crabs, letting them rest on her hand while she studied them up close. But Thea had held back, kneeling beside Marin and letting the cold salt breeze whip through her loose curls as she searched for sea glass, which Marin had noticed was her favorite. She was constantly pocketing little rounded bits of cloudy blue and green.

"I'm glad you're here, Marin."

"Thanks, Thea. I'm pretty glad too."

"Wren isn't," she added, shifting a handful of mud and silt back and forth between her palms.

"I've gathered that."

"I was always excited for you. It felt like I waited for ages for you to get here. But Wren didn't want you here. That's why Wren made her come home. Because of you."

"Wait, do you mean Evie? What do you mean because of me?"

"Thea." Wren was standing just a few feet away, staring at her younger sister. "I think that's enough chatting Marin's ears off. Come help me find a starfish."

Thea leapt to her feet, eager to be included, and took off across the rocks. Her bare feet caught on every memorized curve of stone that she'd likely been running on since she learned to walk. Marin didn't know how Thea could stand it—to be barefoot on the barnacle-covered rocks.

Then again, given enough time and exposure, a person could get used to just about anything.

When the sun began to sink on the water and Marin called them to clean up for dinner, the girls were more mud than children and had to hurry inside to shower.

The chance to ask Thea what she was talking about had

passed. It was easy enough to believe that Wren didn't want her there—she'd made her feelings rather obvious from the start. But had Wren really asked Evie to come home, just to get Marin to leave?

The feeling of not belonging only grew sharper over their shared meal. Marin felt she was missing some crucial piece of information, as though everyone else in the room was in on some joke at her expense. And if she intercepted one more *meaningful look* between Evie and Neera, or Alice and Evie, or Wren and Thea, she might just scream.

"Are you angry at that carrot?"

Marin was startled from her laser focus on her plate.

It was Evie asking, with the hint of a smile on her face.

Marin looked down again, to find her knife gripped too tight, and her fork spearing the carrot like she meant it.

"No." Marin instantly relaxed her choke hold on her utensils. "It's just all so delicious. Thank you, Neera."

And then the painfully silent meal continued. Why bother with a fancy family dinner every night if no one wanted to spend time together? Gone was the constant chatter of the girls that Marin had grown used to. When Alice had joined them, she was already in a sour mood, muttering something about the words not finding her that entire day.

"They'll come, Mother," Thea chirped. "They always do."

"They do not," Alice said. "I must find *them*. And they are stubborn, willful things. They have so much in common with you three. Maybe you four." Alice nodded in Marin's general direction. "This one's true temperament has yet to reveal itself."

After that, the table hushed once again. The girls didn't volunteer any of their usual questions, and Marin actually missed their voices in the void that was left. Marin suspected that Alice was upset with Evie for leaving her summer workshop and returning home without warning, though it seemed no one wanted to actually discuss it.

That at least was familiar to Marin.

Avoidance had been her mother's specialty.

Just when she thought she couldn't bear the quiet any longer, interrupted only by the occasional sharp scratch of cutlery across a plate, Thea Hallowell set down her glass of milk, folded her hands in front of her on the table, and cleared her throat.

"So where *do* babies come from?" Thea asked.

Neera laughed aloud. Evie choked on her water. Alice slammed down her knife, but Marin caught the flash of a smile before she remembered she was in a bad mood.

Wren only tilted her head at her sister's game.

Thea knew exactly what she was doing.

"That sounds like an excellent question for your new nanny." Evie's voice was saturated with wry humor, and Marin glared at her across the butter dish between them.

Marin waited for Alice to intervene, but her employer only gave her a brief glance that seemed to say, *well, on with it.*

"Well, Thea," Marin began, and felt the hot rush of blood

blooming across her cheeks. *Damn her for this*, she thought but refused to make eye contact with Evie while she was answering the question. "When a mommy and a daddy—"

"But sometimes it's two mommies or two daddies," Thea said.

"Well, yes, of course. When two people are in love—"

"But you didn't have two parents, did you, Marin? You had one," Wren asked.

"That's true. Well, then I guess when *someone* really wants to be a parent, they, um, they ask for a baby, and sometimes they get one."

It was the worst explanation of anything ever. But absolutely no one at the table called her out because doing so would mean volunteering a real answer to the question.

"Oh, okay," Thea said, and dug into her mashed potatoes with a smile still on her face.

Marin suspected that Thea knew *exactly* how babies were made. But she'd done the impossible. She'd broken the terrible silence of the table.

"Oh, Evie, wait until you see Agatha. She's grown so much," Neera said.

"Has she?" Evie asked, her dark eyes alive with excitement. "I'll visit her after our meal."

"Who is Agatha?" Marin asked.

"Agatha is a flower," Neera said. "A very rare one. I am secretary for the Winterthur Maine Horticultural Society, and Evie and her father and I plotted several years ago to bring Agatha here to the greenhouse at Lovelace. It took ages for us to get her."

"What is so special about the flower?"

"There are only a handful in private collections like ours," Evie explained. "And she isn't really ours. She's on loan, via the Horticultural Society. So technically she belongs to the entire town. But lives here. While we wait for her to bloom."

"And when will that happen?"

"Oh, it can take decades. But usually within eight years or so. And we think this summer might be it."

"Decades?" Marin asked. "That's unbelievable."

"Have the ladies been by to see her lately?" Evie asked between bites.

"No, not since . . ." Neera paused to clear her throat, her glance falling briefly on Alice before returning to Evie. "Not since last year. I thought we'd bring them out soon to see how it has grown, once you get the greenhouse back in tip-top shape."

"I'd love that," Evie said. "Marin, have you seen much of it? Would you like a little tour after supper?"

"Of course," Marin said. "If that's all right."

She directed the second half of her statement at Alice, looking up for permission. Alice often put the girls to bed herself, reading with them until they fell asleep.

"That's fine, Marin," Alice said. She wasn't exactly cheerful but seemed distracted enough from her frustration with her writing. "But once the girls are asleep, I think I'll try to work some more. Could you stay upstairs tonight in case they wake? Thea has been having nightmares lately—Thea, my dear, finish your peas."

"Of course." Marin gave Thea a reassuring smile and then pretended not to notice when Thea's peas disappeared under the table. Pretended not to notice Thisbe's tail happily thumping against the leg of her chair. "If you need me, I'll be right down the hall."

"I'll be next door too," Evie said.

Marin hadn't known where Evie's room was until that moment. If she was just beside the girls, that meant she was in the room directly across the hall from Marin.

She didn't know why this information irked her like a pebble in her shoe; she only knew that it did. But when Evie met her eyes again across the table, the hint of a smile on her lips, she felt almost as if Evie was laughing at her, just a bit. It was as though Evie knew it bothered her and knew the reason why and might let her in on the joke someday.

As it was, under the direct gaze of Evie's all-knowing eyes, Marin felt much like a bee drawn in by ambrosia, unknowingly resting in the maw of a Venus flytrap.

She also felt that she might not mind being caught if it was Evie Hallowell doing the catching.

9

Ruby Lips Above the Water

———————— ❧ ————————

Evie and Marin cleared the table together, with Marin rinsing the dishes and Evie drying them, while Neera and Alice herded the girls upstairs for bedtime.

Then Marin followed Evie to the greenhouse. The sky above the glass ceiling was still streaked with bright pink and orange clouds chasing after the sun as it began to sink below the horizon. "It's beautiful," Marin said, mostly to herself.

"It's my favorite place in the world," Evie said. Marin turned around to find her looking out over the plants and flowers and blooms of the greenhouse. She was dressed impeccably again, in a soft, flowing sage dress that tied in a bow in the back and buttoned all the way up the front. Every golden strand of her hair was shaped into a perfect curl, swept and pinned behind her ears to show off the large, round pearls on her earlobes. Evie was elegant, poised, and polished.

"Shall we?" Evie asked.

They circled through the paths of the huge greenhouse. It was an enormous extension of the house. "How long has this been here?" Marin asked.

"Only since my parents married. Twenty years or so? It was my mother's gift to him when they moved into the house. He never wanted to live here."

"Why not?" Marin asked, running her hand across a perfect pink rose as she walked past it.

"Too stuffy. Too old. Too *traditional*. He didn't really care for the Lovelace family, but Mother really wanted to raise her family in the house she grew up in. She insisted on it, he told me once. So the greenhouse was his. A home outside of Lovelace. And he really does love it out here." Evie hesitated a heavy beat of a moment before adding, "I mean, did. He did."

They walked in silence for a bit and then rounded to face a roped-off area of the greenhouse. In the center of it was the largest, ugliest plant that Marin had ever seen in her life.

"Marin, *this*"—Evie's hands gestured widely—"is Agatha."

"Oh," Marin said. "It's . . . um . . ."

"Hideous?"

Marin looked at Evie apologetically. "It's dreadful. What is it?"

"A corpse flower," Evie said, but the look on her face was anything but dread. She was terribly proud of the awful plant, and it showed.

"Well, the name suits it," Marin said.

"When it blooms, it smells like death," Evie told her.

"How lovely."

Evie then dropped to her knees, right into the soil, light green dress and all, and began ripping out weeds that had begun to sprout in the earth below Agatha.

It was the first mar to Evie's pristine appearance that Marin had seen.

It was delightful.

Evie seemed too excited at the thought of weeding to notice she was ruining her skirt, and Marin wasn't about to tell her.

"Marin, in the corner of the greenhouse is a sink and faucet and underneath is an old wooden bucket. Would you grab it for me, and we can clear this area out tonight?"

Marin quickly retrieved the bucket, and despite never having an interest in gardening and having accidentally murdered every single plant her mother had ever brought home, Marin enjoyed the work. She liked the dirt under her nails. But even more than that, she liked Evie. Working next to her, Marin could smell the cinnamon she'd noticed the day Evie arrived home. She wondered if it was a perfume.

After several minutes working side by side, Evie paused, reaching out to a branch on a neighboring plant.

"Look," she said, cradling something in her hand.

Marin leaned over to see a cocoon. It was a brilliant green gold, shimmering in the light of the setting sun, so bright it seemed to glow.

"It's a tigerwing," Evie said. "They are beautiful when they transform. Russet orange with cream spots on their wings.

Did you know that during a caterpillar's metamorphosis, when it enters its chrysalis, it essentially disintegrates?"

"Like, caterpillar soup?"

Evie laughed. "Yes, exactly. And then it takes an entirely new shape as a butterfly. But what's really interesting is scientists believe that they retain some memories from before."

"That can't be true," Marin said.

"Really, it is. I was just reading about it." The joy in Evie's voice was contagious.

Evie released the cocoon to dangle on its branch. This close, Marin could see just how dark Evie's brown eyes were. They nearly matched her pupils.

When they had finally cleared out the soil surrounding the corpse flower's section of the greenhouse, it had grown dark, and Marin needed to clean up and get upstairs. She didn't want Thea to wake from a bad dream and have no one there.

They walked the bucket back to the sink together, dumping the weeds into a compost bin.

"I'll head up and take over for mother," Evie said, not bothering to even rinse her hands before she pushed a stray curl out of her face, leaving a streak of dirt across her cheek.

"I'll rinse up here and then join you," Marin said, and Evie left.

Marin tucked the bucket away and then searched for some soap. There was a cabinet beside the sink, and she tugged it open. Inside was soap, which Marin quickly grabbed, but beside it was a thick book, with the words *Hallowell's Botany* inscribed on the front.

Marin washed and dried her hands quickly and then reached for the book. She flipped it open to find pages of drawings. They were the plants of the greenhouse, but the drawings were dated back over two decades. Evie's father's handwriting was distinct block lettering. But eventually there was another set of handwriting, in a small, slanting script, that was far nicer than any child's handwriting that Marin had ever seen before, and she knew without question it belonged to Evie.

Marin flipped to the back of the book. The last drawing was Agatha herself. The corpse flower. It was clear in these pages that the greenhouse had been a project Evie and her father had shared in. Lovingly sketched and crafted over years. Marin carefully tucked the book back the way she'd found it.

Upstairs, Marin rounded the corner and almost ran into Evie, who was standing outside of the door to the girls' room, which was slightly ajar. The sound of Alice's voice drifted out. She was still reading to the girls, who shared a room and slept in twin beds beside each other. Thisbe was sleeping across the end of Thea's bed.

Evie must have showered. Her hair was wet, swept into a neat bun at the nape of her neck.

Gone was the streak of dirt from her cheek.

This observation irritated Marin, until finally, she recognized the keen feeling of loss. She *missed* that streak of dirt, which had made Evie seem utterly human for once.

Marin couldn't help it. Her gaze swept over Evie, looking for another flaw to cling to.

She was wearing a nightgown, of all things. Marin's pajamas were usually some fleece pants that had been her mother's and a shredded old band T-shirt. But Evie was fashionable even to bed, her nightgown paired with a matching navy silk robe, tied at her waist, and dotted with dainty blue cornflowers. Evie turned to find Marin and raised a finger to her lips.

"Let's not disturb them," Evie whispered, and tiptoed past the door, Marin trailing behind her.

They paused at their respective doors for a moment, and Marin felt Evie's eyes trail across Marin's black mourning dress and back to her face.

"I like your lipstick," Evie said. "What's it called?"

"Oh, um, I think it's called Snow White's Folly."

"It's perfect on you." Evie's lips curved into half smile, so similar to Wren's, but it wasn't mocking in the slightest. There was also a warmth in Evie's dark eyes, flashing for a moment before it was gone, and Evie disappeared into her room.

Marin placed her fingers over her mouth, where it felt like Evie's compliment had left a physical impression on her. As though she'd been touched, not by kind words, but by fingertips.

Or lips.

10

Are You Sleeping?

———————— ❧ ————————

In the dead of the night, Marin was startled from sleep by the sound of Thea screaming. She was out of her bed in an instant, pausing only long enough to untangle her feet from her sheets, and then she was dashing down the hall.

Wren was already beside her sister, shaking her gently to wake her from the nightmare. Thea was curled into a tight ball, her hair and clothes soaked in sweat.

"Thea, Thea!" Marin lifted the small child into her arms.

Thea's eyes opened, and she clung to Marin, her little nails cutting into Marin's upper arms. But Marin didn't pull away. It was a clear spring night, and light from the moon streamed through the sheer curtains to illuminate Thea's face, still awash in terror at whatever she'd dreamed of.

"It's only a dream. Only a dream," Marin murmured again and again, soothing Thea by rubbing small circles on her back.

A moment later Evie arrived, crossing quickly to the bed and stretching her arms out to take Thea. But Thea's hands still clawed at Marin's arms, and she was afraid to startle her by shifting her away.

"It's okay," Marin said. "I've got her."

Evie perched beside her, and together they assured Thea it wasn't real.

"Do you want to tell us about it?" Evie asked.

Thea shook her head decisively.

"I'll sleep next to her," Wren offered, crawling into the twin bed beside Thea and wrapping her arms around her.

Thea quieted, snuggling in closer to her sister. They were only ten months apart in age, but Wren was so much taller and acted so differently that the age gap sometimes felt much larger.

Evie retrieved Thisbe from her own room and patted the foot of Thea's bed until Thisbe jumped up.

"Stay," Evie said, and Thisbe laid her huge head across Wren's and Thea's tangled feet, dutiful guard dog that she was.

Once Thea's breathing had calmed into the gentle rhythm of sleep, the older girls slipped out into the hall.

"We'll stay out here until you are both back to sleep," Evie assured Wren, pulling the door only mostly shut, so that a sliver of hallway light landed as a beam across the room.

"Will your mother come?" Marin whispered.

"Oh, I doubt it. Mother sleeps like the dead," Evie answered.

They stood there in silence, but it was content, sleepy and serene, not uncomfortable. Their quiet was only interrupted a few minutes later, when Marin yawned, suddenly and hugely. She flushed, embarrassed, but then Evie yawned too.

"They're contagious," Evie said, and laughed softly when Marin couldn't help but yawn once more. "Here, I'll close my eyes, or we'll never stop."

Evie closed her eyes, leaning on the wall, and then she was quiet for so long, so languorous and peaceful, that Marin thought maybe she had drifted back to sleep standing there. For a few moments, Marin simply watched, studying Evie, who was closer and stiller than she'd seen her yet.

Marin's disquiet had grown daily in the wake of the little Hallowell girls and their compelling older sister. Now, standing here, past midnight in the hallway, just the two of them, her curiosity was practically pulsing, like a living, beating heart. Marin had never felt anything like it, and she couldn't explain it, except maybe to say that Evie was like a book that Marin couldn't wait to get her hands on, to read every page and passage and footnote until she'd memorized the words.

Evie slept with her hair in tight foam curlers, nestled all over her head like burrs. Some curls had escaped and created a halo of frizz around Evie's face. It was the least put together Marin had seen Evie yet: disheveled, unguarded, groggy with sleep.

A few minutes later, when she was sure both girls had fallen back to sleep, Marin nudged Evie. Her eyes flew open.

"You'll pinch a nerve in your neck, leaning like that all night." Marin paired the teasing with a smile, and Evie returned the gesture by wrapping her hand around Marin's wrist and squeezing it once, tight. A quick, quiet thank-you before she slipped back into her bedroom, shutting the door softly as she went.

An hour passed quickly. And then another. Marin lay awake, staring at the ceiling of her room. It was covered in tin squares, and even though she'd been at Lovelace for two weeks, she couldn't discern the pattern in the design. There was a shape stamped on the tin that repeated, again and again, but it was so small, and the ceiling so high, that Marin couldn't quite make it out. It had become her game at night to guess what it was, trying to distract herself long enough to fall asleep in a room so quiet compared to her cities. A room so large and cold compared to the warm, sunny rooms she'd shared with her mother in California.

So every night, she'd stare at the ceiling, listen to the ocean, and try to *not* remember. And every night, as she wavered between consciousness and sleep, the sound of the waves on rocks below shifted to rain on metal. The smell of salt water became the salty, metallic scent of blood. And as dawn broke outside, ushered in by seagulls, their cries melded with the sounds of her mother's last words, a plea for Marin to leave her and get herself out of the doomed train. *Let go, Marin. You have to let go.*

11

Merrily, Merrily (Merrily, Merrily)

———————— ❧ ————————

B right sunlight flooded her room.

Marin scrambled for the clock on her bedside table. It was half past nine. A few weeks had passed since Evie's return home, and the four girls had settled into a kind of routine together. They spent their days on the coast or in the orchard, or cleaning up the greenhouse with Evie. And while the pranks had ceased—Marin was sure she had Evie to thank for that small grace—she couldn't shake the feeling that Wren hadn't quite given up her mission to drive Marin away. However, in the time that Marin had spent living at Lovelace, there hadn't been a day that the girls had let her sleep past seven.

They're up to something. She just knew it.

Marin dressed quickly, throwing on jeans and tugging on her worn sneakers without even bothering to find socks or change out of her sleep T-shirt.

She wasn't surprised in the slightest to find the girls' bedroom empty, their beds tidily made without anyone telling them to do it.

She passed the wing that led to Alice's office, and she paused. Maybe she ought to ask Alice where the girls might be. But then a shadow crossed under the door, and she heard the creak of the floorboards as Alice paced, and Marin felt something like panic, so she slipped past the hallway as quietly as she could.

She doesn't like to be disturbed, Thea had said.

I would appreciate if you stayed away from this branch of the house, Alice had told her.

Alice's pace back and forth in her office had been brisk, as if she was lost in some vortex, either inspired or desperately stuck. Marin didn't know which of those she was more loath to interrupt, so she opted for neither and hurried down the stairs.

Besides, Marin was confident she could find the girls.

She'd taken a CPR class once, a swim team requirement at one of her schools, and during it they had emphasized the dangers of water and children. *If a child isn't where they should be, check the most dangerous place first. You can always circle back to the easier places later.*

So Marin headed straight for the shore.

As she walked, she tugged her hair into two messy buns. She hadn't brushed it and had to comb at the large, nestled knots with her fingers to get it to cooperate.

But all her worry dissipated the moment she reached the top of the wooden stairs behind the house, the ones that wound down to the shore.

She could hear the girls giggling below. The sound echoed off the rocks.

She found them ankle deep in mud, pulled down by the weight of the small dinghy they were carrying toward the water.

"What are you doing?" Marin asked. She tugged her sneakers off, abandoning them at the shoreline to chase after the girls. She reached them right as they were putting the little boat into the water.

"Well, we're running away," Thea said, and Wren elbowed her in the arm.

"It's only a game," Wren said. "We always play in the dinghy."

"What about life jackets?" Marin asked.

Wren reached under the bench and pulled out life jackets, handing one to Thea and starting to put one on herself.

"Marin, we've spent our entire lives here. Do you really think mother wouldn't teach us to swim back to shore from our dinghy?" Wren sighed.

"No, but—"

"If you are that worried, you can come with us," Thea offered.

Wren rolled her eyes and climbed into the small dinghy.

Marin couldn't exactly let them row off alone, so she lifted Thea into the boat beside her sister, and Marin sat on the bench facing them.

"Where are we going?"

"The bluff," Wren said.

"It's the best spot for buried treasures," Thea added.

Marin watched Thea struggle with the oar, which was twice her size, before reaching out to take over.

"So we're pirates then?" Marin asked. With Marin rowing in unison with Wren, they began to move swiftly through the water, winding around the coastline away from the stairs and house. It took just fifteen minutes or so to get to the bluff overhanging the ocean by the Lovelace family cemetery.

Odd place to play games.

The tide was out for now, but would shift soon.

They climbed out into the shallow waters and pulled the dinghy with them, all the way up onto the muddy shore.

Thea grabbed a little wooden bucket from the boat, and the girls were off, combing the exposed mud for their prizes.

Marin's mudlarking was less zealous. She found a sizable chunk of sea glass for Thea. It was the full neck of a bottle, intact but worn smooth, and saved it to give to her later. She toed at the mud, slowly lifting a rock only to be startled when a large crab zoomed out from beneath it, scurrying over the exposed toes of her other bare foot. She yelped and dropped the rock back into place.

Marin watched the girls climb across the shore, and she worried.

She hadn't left a note at the house. She'd been eager to find the girls and then she didn't want to leave them alone with the rowboat—she was sure they'd have left without her.

She knew her responsibility was right here in front of her, but Marin wasn't used to children. Certainly not stubborn, entitled children like the Hallowell girls. She should have put her foot down. Said no. Seized the small boat and dragged it back from the water's edge.

But now her anxiety spiraled. She imagined Alice and Neera worried.

She pictured Evie, the way her eyes would darken with fear and disappointment.

As that last thought entered her mind, she couldn't take it anymore. Marin went to collect the girls, who were examining something in the mud.

"What did you find?" Marin asked, bending down beside them.

An object glimmered in the mud.

Wren lifted it, brushing the muck off with her thumb. It was a small round bit of metal. It looked like a coin. But it was very old and mishappen and unlike any coin Marin had seen before.

They walked to the water, the tide now about halfway in after an hour combing the shoreline, and Wren rinsed the object in the ocean water, peered at it closely for a moment, and then handed it to Marin.

"I can't make it out," Wren said.

Marin held the coin up close.

"It says *Memento Mori.*" She flipped the coin over. "*Memento*

Viva? Memento Vive? I can't make the second word out."

Marin left out the fact that there seemed to be a small skull imprinted on each side as well.

"What does it mean?" Wren asked.

"No idea," Marin said. "Here."

"You keep it, it's creepy," Wren said.

Marin pocketed the coin and then put on the sternest face she could muster. "We need to get back now."

"Of course, Marin." Wren smiled, her agreement too fast, too easy.

The tide rolling in made rowing back harder. They were fighting the current with every stroke of the oar. It wasn't until almost a half hour later that they rounded the last bend of the rocky shoreline.

They could hear the shouting before they could see them.

Someone was yelling the girls' names. Several someones.

They rounded the outcropping of rock and spied Alice, Neera, and Evie on the shore at the foot of the stairs.

"Oh my god," Alice said, splashing out into the water to grab the edge of the dinghy. "What were you thinking?"

Marin began to stutter in response. "They insisted—"

"I don't remember putting them in charge," Alice snapped, lifting Thea from the dinghy and clasping Wren's hand to pull her out too. "You know better," Alice said, directing the last bit to Wren.

Alice was gone before Marin could defend herself, sweeping the girls up the stairs and back into Lovelace House. Neera gave Marin a soft smile and then followed them.

Finally, Marin looked to Evie and found nothing but anger in her eyes too.

"They can't swim," Evie said, snapping the long rope that was used to tie off the dinghy, and quickly knotting it on the bottom of the stairs. "They could have drowned. How would you have gotten them both back here if something happened to this old thing?"

"They were in life jackets. And why on *earth* can't they swim?" Marin demanded. She replayed the conversation she'd had with Wren again, pausing on Wren's careful wording. She'd never actually said they could. "That's absurd. And dangerous."

Evie froze on the stairs above her, not turning around.

"He died last summer. He drowned. It was a boating accident."

Rain hitting metal, metal that had folded like paper, trapping Marin inside for hours. They couldn't see each other, but eventually Cordelia's hand snaked through a small opening, gripping Marin's hand so tight. Like she'd hold on to her forever.

The smell of soldering when the firefighters cut through metal to get to her. She didn't want to go. She wanted to stay there, holding on to her mom.

You have to let go, Marin.

"I'm very sorry for your loss," Marin offered. She knew the words weren't adequate for the flood of memories that Evie must have experienced when her sisters were missing and the dinghy was gone. She knew what it was like to replay your worst memory, like a horrible movie playing for eternity on a big screen and no way to escape the room.

"Yours too," Evie said.

"The girls aren't allowed in the dinghy," Evie said softly. "It's too soon."

"I understand. I'm sorry. I didn't mean to scare you. But the girls *do* need to know how to swim. I can teach them. I was on the swim team for years."

Evie considered for a moment.

"All right," Evie said, and began to climb the stairs.

Marin went to grab her sneakers, only to realize that she hadn't left them on the bottom stair like she normally did when she came down to the shore with the girls. She'd thrown them off while walking, eager to reach the girls before they pushed off from the shore in their boat.

The tide was now high.

Her shoes were gone.

Marin climbed the stairs behind Evie, her clothing soaked with water and her toes freezing on the cold grass in the yard. The day took so much longer to warm up here in New England.

Evie didn't say another word to Marin as they went inside to their rooms, making only the briefest of eye contact before they closed their respective doors.

As usual, Evie gave nothing away.

Marin changed out of her wet clothes. As she pulled off

her jeans, something clattered to the floor. It was the coin the girls had discovered down on the shore. She held it up to the light, running her thumb over the worn letters.

She had no idea what it was, but she knew where in Lovelace House she might find an answer.

When she reemerged from her room, there was a pair of shoes on the floor outside with a folded note card on top. The card had Evie's initials embossed on it.

I believe we wear the same size. These are yours to keep. I've never worn them.

Never worn. Well, that much made sense. Marin couldn't even picture Evie in running shoes. Evie wore oxford shoes or lace-up boots. Down at the shore, she wore leather fisherman's sandals, buckled neatly at her ankle. Evie's aesthetic was posh, polished, and vintage. Running shoes didn't exactly suit.

The shoes did in fact look brand-new, and expensive, and Marin didn't recognize the brand, but she slipped them on, and Evie was right. They did wear the same size.

Marin crept quickly through Lovelace House to the library, avoiding the sound of the girls' voices drifting up from downstairs. She'd collect them later.

Tucked safely in the library, she scoured shelves and titles for the better part of an hour until finally, perched precariously at the top of a rolling library ladder—a position that was far more romantic in theory than in actuality—Marin pulled the heavy tome she needed from its shelf.

Marin settled at the table by the window and ran her finger through the *M* pages until she found what she sought in the encyclopedia.

Memento Mori translated to "remember, we must die."

The entry had a picture of a coin somewhat similar to the one they'd plucked from the shore. The one on the page had a skull and crossbones and was only stamped on one side instead of both, but on the top it said *Memento Mori* and across the bottom, *Memento Vivere*.

The caption read, *Late 18th century memento mori coin commemorating the death of a loved one. Memento mori: Remember, we must die. Meant to serve as a reminder of mortality. Memento vivere: Remember, we must live. Meant to serve as a reminder to not take life for granted, to live it to the fullest.*

Marin scrolled down to read the rest of the entry.

First used by soldiers as a reminder of their mortality, the phrase Memento Mori resurfaced following the Black Plague, when a fascination with death and all things macabre swept through Europe.

And then there were more images accompanying the passage. There had been a popular art form called *danse macabre*, where people were depicted dancing with skeletons, embracing death.

But it was the next bit that really caught Marin's attention.

Memento mori totems became popular again in the Victorian era. At the time, all things gothic and macabre were in vogue, and people often held seances like they were parties, or even arranged for their dead loved ones to be photographed.

Sometimes they kept locks of the deceased one's hair, twisted into frames, and locked behind a pane of glass to form mourning art.

Sometimes they even kept entire braids.

Marin ran her fingers over the drawing on the page and remembered the softness of the braids bound and hidden away just a story above her. She wondered what other secrets might be hidden inside Lovelace House.

12

King of Cups

⁂

A few hours later, Marin sought out Evie. Her mission was twofold: one, to thank her for the shoes; two, to apologize for the incident with the girls. Marin ought to have known better than to take them at their word. Selfishly, Marin hated the thought that Evie might be mad at her. Just as she reached up to rap her knuckles on the thick wooden door to Evie's room, she heard voices drifting out. It was Wren's hushed whispers, frantically parring with Evie's.

"I won't say sorry," Wren said. "You and I both know, the sooner she leaves Lovelace, the better."

Marin dropped her hand, bending her head to better listen.

"I don't think that's the right choice here, Wren. She has nowhere else to go."

"That's not our fault. She never should have been brought here in the first place. We don't *need* a nanny. Not with you home where you belong."

"I'm not going to help you. I think she ought to stay."

"Evie, I'll tell."

There was a long beat of silence within the room.

"You wouldn't."

Wren didn't even respond, but Marin heard the squeak of one of her loafers against the hardwood floors as she marched across the room.

Marin was dying to hear what else they had to say, but she didn't want to get caught eavesdropping, so she moved quickly down the hall again, dipping back into her room just as Evie's door opened wide.

Marin watched through a sliver of open door as Wren walked down the hall, first with a scowl on her face, making her sharper features stand out even more than usual. Her dark brows were furrowed, and the point of her chin tilted defiantly up.

But then, just as she passed Marin's door, she saw it.

Wren smiled.

Marin couldn't make sense of the conversation she'd overheard. There were too many pieces missing. But it reminded her of what Thea had begun to tell her the other day—right before Wren interrupted. Evie came back *because* of Marin. And now Wren was trying to get rid of her.

Marin marched down the hall again, this time heading for Wren and Thea's room instead.

She knocked gently and entered the room when Thea chirped out "Come in!"

Thea sat crisscross on her bed, with her dolls spread out around her.

There were only half a dozen or so dolls, but Marin knew that many more than that were likely out in the woods, buried haphazardly between new roots and old bones.

"I have something for you," Marin said. "Can I sit?"

Thea grinned, revealing the fresh gap in her teeth from where she'd just lost another tooth, and nodded enthusiastically.

Marin sat and pulled the bottle neck from her pocket. Thea's eyes lit up at the sight, just like Marin had known they would.

"It's perfect," Thea said, her tongue catching on the *s* and giving her the sweetest hint of a lisp.

But then Thea looked up, and there were unshed tears in her eyes.

"I'm so, so, *so* sorry for earlier, Marin. It was cruel of us to trick you into going. Wren wanted to get you in trouble. She said she'd take Clementine if I didn't help."

For added measure, Thea pulled one of the dolls off her bed and clutched her tight. Marin noticed the doll's round cheeks and bright splash of pink on its cheeks. The smattering of freckles and the way Thea had twisted the doll's dark hair back into twin buns.

"Well, that wasn't kind of Wren, was it?"

Thea shook her head slowly.

"Well, Thea, it did hurt my feelings. But I forgive you."

"You do?" Thea sniffled and wiped her nose on the back of her sleeve.

"Of course."

Marin wiped a renegade tear off Thea's cheek and rose to leave.

At the door she paused.

"Hey, Thea?"

Thea looked up from her dolls once again.

"I was just thinking, we never got to finish our chat on the shore the other day. The one when you said you were glad I was here?"

"Oh, you're right."

"Well, I was wondering. Do you think Wren made Evie come home just so I would leave? Since she knew you girls wouldn't need a nanny anymore?"

"I don't *think* she did, Marin."

"Oh." Marin had told herself she didn't care that Wren hated her, but the relief she felt couldn't be denied. She reached for the door handle.

"I know it," Thea said.

Marin paused.

"It was her plan from the very start. Make Evie come home. Then you'd get sent away. Then things would be normal again. But I'm glad that didn't happen, Marin. I hope you stay here forever."

"Thanks, Thea. I hope so too."

Marin pulled the door gently closed behind her and paused in the hallway, leaning her head against the door. She fought the fiery pain that clawed at her throat, the threat of unshed tears burning in her eyes until she squeezed them shut.

Wren was just a little girl. It shouldn't matter if she hated Marin.

But it was more than that. Marin wanted to *belong* here. To truly feel like she was home.

The longer she stayed, the more the reverse seemed true: Marin wasn't yet part of this place, but this place was quickly becoming part of her, and she wasn't at all sure it was welcome there. It felt somewhat like an intrusion, a foreign body, irritating her from the inside out.

Lovelace House was a sliver of a splinter caught under her nail, and despite her unease, and no matter how it hurt, she kept pressing, letting it dig itself deeper.

This time, when she crossed the hall to Evie's room, Marin practically stomped her feet to make sure her footsteps were loud enough to be heard. She didn't think her ego could take another hit from Wren Hallowell today.

She knocked on Evie's door and waited.

A full minute passed, and she was about to leave when she heard shuffling inside. She knocked again, harder, and the door swung open almost instantly, startling Marin into taking a step backward.

Marin pretended not to notice the way Evie sniffled, ever so subtly. Or the way her eyes were a bit red and puffy. She wondered about the secrets Evie must be keeping, if she was crying just from the threat of it being spilled by Wren.

"That's a pretty headband," Marin said, directing her gaze to the bright yellow knotted head piece that perched on Evie's head like a crown, giving Evie a moment to wipe her eyes.

Evie reached a hand up, seeming to remind herself which one she'd worn.

"Thank you, Marin."

"And thank *you* for these," Marin said, turning her heel to show Evie how well the shoes fit her.

"Yes, of course. You're going to need them to keep up with the girls, aren't you?"

"I'm sorry, Evie. For what happened this morning. I thought they were safe. I never would have taken them out—"

"You listened to Wren. You shouldn't do that." Evie turned into her room, leaving the door wide to Marin in invitation, and Marin followed. Evie's room was even larger than Marin's or the one the girls shared. Her bed was covered in a black duvet that had flowers and plants embroidered across it. "Wren is very independent. She always has been, and she will try to convince mother to send you away. Try not to give her more ammunition."

"I understand. But I think they should learn to swim."

"I agree."

"Good. Then it's settled." Marin ran her fingers across the quilt on Evie's bed, tracing the embroidery.

The stitches were loose on the bottom of the blanket, the loops wide and messy, and the higher up the quilt, the neater they became.

Evie came to stand beside Marin and ran her fingers along the quilt as well. "I stitched these. That's why they are so terrible on that end. I started when I was Thea's age."

"That must have taken a lot of time," Marin said.

"Six years," Evie said. "I only ever worked on it a bit at a time, until I got bored. Which was very quickly."

Evie gestured for Marin to continue her exploration of Evie's room, and Marin took her up on the offer, her curiosity taking over, and circled to her bookcase. It was enormous, dark forest green, and filled with little paintings and shells and snow globes. Marin lifted a framed photo from one shelf. It was the entire family, Marin guessed, assuming the tall man beside Alice was Charles Hallowell.

It was Evie who stood out though. Her blond hair was dyed with streaks of purple, and she wore thick, winged black eyeliner and elbow-length black gloves. "Evie Hallowell, did you have a goth phase?"

Marin couldn't believe it was the same girl. Evie, who had only worn pristine skirts and sensible, natural makeup, and perfectly turned curls.

"All women have a goth phase, Marin. We all need to mourn. Some of us just choose to show it on the outside."

Marin giggled at the picture just the same. Evie looked about thirteen in the photo.

"I'm not really in a position to tease you. When I was this age, I watched *Practical Magic* and decided I was a witch. I set up an altar with crystals and everything."

"You didn't." Evie laughed.

"I did. I was trying to summon Paramore to come to my city. I was obsessed." Marin put the framed photo back on the bookshelf. There was a photo album on the shelf, leather bound and important looking. Marin started to reach for it, but Evie reached across her, grabbing the book and pulling it to her chest.

"I'm sorry," Marin said. "I thought it was more photos. I didn't mean to grab your journal."

"Not a journal. Just poems and some music I've written," Evie said, laying the book back on the shelf.

"You're a writer too?"

"Oh, no, nothing like mother. Just scribbles. I wasn't attending a typical private school. It was an art school. I studied music, mostly, piano and composition. And then I had regular academics, which I'm terrible at, which is why we have to study together." Evie gestured at the test-prep books lining her bookshelf, disdain dripping from her voice. "But I like to write for fun. For me."

"Well, if you ever want a reader," Marin said, and waved her hand, "I volunteer."

"Thanks," Evie said, and then she reached up and pulled down a small tin box. "Here, let me do something for you in return for the girls' swim lessons."

Inside was a deck of cards.

"No, no more cards. You Hallowell girls cheat," Marin said, stepping away.

"You just haven't learned house rules yet," Evie said, rolling her eyes, and for the first time, Marin saw the resemblance between her and Wren. It was much less obvious than what she shared with Thea, but it was there—a ripple of stubbornness beneath Evie's demure exterior.

"Besides, it's not a game. It's tarot."

"Oh, well, honestly, I don't really believe in any of that stuff," Marin said, shrugging in apology. In truth, Marin didn't know what she believed in. When her mother had seen that small altar Marin set up in the corner of the living room, she'd flipped out. It was about as angry as Cordelia had ever been. *These things aren't welcome in my home.*

Marin had never so much as mentioned a Ouija board again.

"That's all right. You don't have to believe in it. May I try anyway?" Evie asked, and when Marin resisted, Evie pouted her lips just slightly. "I'll forgive you for nearly drowning my baby sisters if you let me read your cards."

There was no counterargument, so Marin acquiesced, and the girls sat on the floor.

"We'll start with something simple."

"This is silly." Marin crossed her legs on the carpet in front of where Evie knelt. "But fine."

"Oh hush," Evie said, splitting the deck and shuffling the cards and laying two between them on the carpet. "The cards are all about the present. You, Marin, are preoccupied with the past, which you feel guilty about, and you are obsessed with the future, trying to avoid things that sometimes can't be avoided. It would be good for you to practice some mindfulness. Be *here*. With me. Now."

Marin looked up at Evie's sharp assessment of her. "How do you know all of that?"

Evie met her gaze. "You must know how expressive you are. Your face gives everything away. You know that phrase *wear your heart on your sleeve*? Well, you wear your heart on your sleeves, your cheeks, your eyebrows, your lips—"

Evie broke off abruptly, her eyes lingering on Marin's lips before meeting her gaze once more.

"Please? Let me read for you. You might even like it."

So Marin agreed. Only because Evie asked nicely. And because maybe, *maybe*, there was some truth in what she said. If Marin could spend her whole life believing something awful might happen just because she had a bad feeling, she could believe that answers might be found in reading cards. She could believe in things not known.

"Okay, so for this reading, the first card will be what you think you need. And the second is what you truly need."

Marin was watching Evie's hands. Her fingers were long and thin, and Marin could imagine them reaching for a piano, stretching up the length of the black and white keys.

"Oh," Evie said, and Marin's gaze shifted to the first card. "The King of Cups."

The card showed a man wearing a crown, sitting atop a throne that was floating in the sea. There was a cup in his hand, filled to the brim with water.

"You think you need emotional control. You are ignoring the chaos all around you, shutting it out, and nothing can bother your focus. Do you see? You want total control over yourself."

"I see a card," Marin offered.

"Hmm," Evie said, flipping the second card. "Interesting."

"Evie." Marin's voice held a tone of soft annoyance.

"What you *really* need is balance. This card is for temperance. Harmony. Patience. I think it means you need to be more forgiving."

"I'm very forgiving," Marin began to protest, but Evie lifted one of her hands to stop Marin.

"Of yourself, Marin. More forgiving of *you*."

"Well, that's nice coming from someone who just yelled at me for taking the girls out."

"I'm sorry. I overreacted. I should have known Wren was behind the whole thing. Sometimes the girls are . . . reckless."

"They are grieving. And bored," Marin countered. "But maybe swim lessons will help with that. Maybe they'll feel better about your . . . about what happened . . . if they aren't afraid of the water. Maybe they'll be less worried."

"*You* worry a lot, don't you, Marin?" Evie asked.

"Did the cards tell you that too?" Marin asked.

Evie reached out, grabbing one of Marin's hands in her own and holding it up. "Your nails are down to the quick. You bite them when you're thinking. And you pick at the skin here." Evie's finger brushed against the skin around

Marin's nails, which was peeling and red and raw.

"And you clench your teeth," Evie said. "It changes the whole shape of your face when you do it. And you do it whenever you get nervous. Or anxious. Which is often."

Marin shifted back, unused to this kind of scrutiny. Unused to being noticed.

"You're observant," Marin said.

"I'm not, Marin. Anyone really looking at you could see how hard you are trying to hide it."

"Says the girl who wears perfect hair and clothes every single day even though we never leave this house." Marin gestured at Evie's appearance. Today it was a dark blue dress that buttoned to the top with a white Peter Pan collar and capped sleeves. Her hair was pulled back into a neat twist that left her curls cascading in a river of gold down to the small of her back.

Impeccable Evie.

Unreachable Evie.

Like a doll that belonged on a top shelf, not to be played with.

Suddenly, Marin wanted desperately to pull her hair loose. Or accidentally spill something on the dress. Anything to mar Evie's perfect countenance. Anything to make her more human.

"I just . . . it helps me remember who I am. What's expected of me."

"What is expected of you, Evie?"

"Perfection," Evie said.

Marin looked down, somewhat ashamed that she'd been thinking of Evie that way too. It would be unfair to always feel the weight of those expectations.

"I can't help it. The worrying. It's always been there."

"And you've been told it's bad," Evie said.

Come up for air, you're drowning.

We can't put our whole lives on hold.

You have to let go, Marin.

"Isn't it?"

"Maybe, if it hurts you," Evie said.

"Or?"

"Or maybe you are seeing things others miss. Sometimes anxiety is intuition."

"How am I supposed to know which is which?"

"I don't know," Evie answered with a shrug. "But you should trust yourself, Marin. Trust those gut feelings. They are powerful. They could save your life."

They already did, Marin thought. *On that train.*

Marin reached for the cards. "My turn."

"I thought you didn't believe in this," Evie said, letting Marin take the cards from her.

"I don't," Marin said with a wry smile, "but you do."

Marin split the deck the same way she'd just watched Evie do it and then flipped over the card that was freshly on top.

"The four of swords," she read to Evie.

The card depicted a girl lying on some kind of bench or altar, hair streaming to the ground. On the wall above her hung four swords.

"What does it mean?" Marin asked softly.

"She's not dead. Not really, though it looks like it. She's only resting," Evie said. "She just . . . needed a break."

Before Marin could flip the second card—the one that would tell Evie what she really needed—Evie reached for the deck, pulling it from Marin's hands, and then sweeping up the card from the floor.

"Hey!" Marin protested. "We weren't done."

"You don't believe in it anyway," Evie said.

"Still, I let you read for me."

"Next time," Evie said. She twisted the cards in her hands, lining them up, but as she stacked them, one card went flying back to the carpet.

"Oh, a jumper," she said, and picked it up.

"What's a jumper?" Marin asked.

"A card that insists on being read, even if we didn't pull it," Evie explained, but then she looked down, and whatever was on the card made Evie's whole face turn ashen. She didn't say a word though, only slipped the card into the middle of the deck.

"Should we go find the girls? I'm sure mother has had her fill of them for the day," Evie suggested, standing and spreading her hands down the skirt of her dress, smoothing out any wrinkles she'd acquired while kneeling.

But then she paused, her hands stopped mid-motion as she became aware of what she was doing.

"You missed one," Marin said, reaching out to pull out a crease in the dress. She'd grant Evie her perfectionism if Evie would grant Marin her unrelenting anxiety.

It was like the danse macabre and the memento mori coin and the locks of hair, bound into a ring or a frame or tucked gently into a locked chest, to remember a loved one always.

It was like Neera had said when Evie first came home to them.

Everyone's grief looks different.

13

The Lost Girls

❦

They found the girls in the library. Alice had already left them to go write. Wren was reading her book in her usual chair, and Thea was in the chair's match, draped upside down on it, her little legs kicking in the air and her wild curls hanging down toward the floor.

She reminded Marin of the tarot card she'd just read.

Even Thisbe looked bored, sprawled on her back on the settee, though she sprang to attention when the door opened. Marin sighed and pushed into the room with Evie close on her heels. Why couldn't they have all been *here* this morning instead of in the damned boat?

"Thank goodness you're here. I'm so, so, *so* bored," Thea whined as soon as she saw Marin. "Please play a game with me, Marin."

"Sure. What game would you like to play?"

Thea grinned and raced to the other end of the library, pulling a wooden box off a shelf. She was halfway across the room when Wren looked up and cried out.

"No!" Wren was out of her chair and pulling the box from Thea's arms before Marin could react.

Wren was heading for the open window.

"Stop it, Wren," Evie said, and her voice brooked no room for argument. Wren turned, her face flushed with anger. Evie approached her slowly. "We won't play it. But I don't think defenestration is the answer either."

She slowly reached out, taking the box from Wren, and set it on the table behind her. Then she turned back and pulled Wren into her arms. "It's all right."

Wren shoved Evie away.

"Go ahead and play. I don't even care," she said, crossing the room to her chair to pick up her book once more.

"I didn't mean to upset you, Wren," Thea said. "I just miss playing."

"Do whatever you want," Wren said.

"Here," Evie said, gesturing for Marin to join her. "You can at least see what the fuss is about."

Evie opened the box, and inside was a board. It had a map carved onto it, and Marin recognized the shape of the peninsula easily enough.

"It's Winterthur."

"It was a gift from our grandmother," Thea said. "Here are the figures." She reached into the box and pulled out a few handfuls of small metal figures and began to line them up. There was a little winged fairy, a tall, slender elf. Grotesque monsters, a troll, a dragon.

"In our game, Winterthur is magic. Like Neverland."

"Our grandmother commissioned it for us. She knew how much we loved to play board games, so she had this made."

Marin studied the board. It was designed like a map, and it did look like Winterthur. She recognized some landmarks— the house, the wharf, the cemetery. But it was different too. There was a clearing in the woods, labeled Ghost Forest. There were secret chambers. Underground tunnels.

Little bits of mystery and magic woven into the landscape to lure out their imagination.

"What if we just set this one aside," Evie suggested, lifting one of the figures in her fingers and laying him gently in the box.

"That's Grey Hand," Thea said. "He's a zombie pirate. He was Dad's favorite to play with. Dad loved this game most."

Marin looked over at Wren. Her face was buried so far in her book that Marin didn't think she could even read the words.

The board was covered with wooden trees, painted intricately down to the last detail, and on the underside of each one was a clue. The figures had to weave around the board, collecting clues, before they could win the game. Adding to the complication, each figure had different rules for play. The dragon could move across the board on its turn ("He can fly," Thea explained), but the fairy could only skip a space or two at a time ("She can fly, too, but she gets tired").

They spent an hour explaining the game, and Marin

was only just barely beginning to understand how the rules worked.

"Enough," Wren said, finally approaching the table. "Can we play something else, please? What about hide-and-seek?"

Marin looked to Evie, who only shrugged.

"Very well," Marin said.

"Here," Wren said, handing a long strip of cloth to Marin and another to Evie. "We'll be in teams. The two of you have to find the two of us."

"No shore," Evie said.

Marin took the cloth. "What's this for?"

"So we don't cheat," Evie said, and twirled her finger for Marin to turn around.

Marin did so, and the strip of cloth was lowered over her eyes and tied around the back of her head. Evie's graceful fingers brushed the nape of Marin's neck, and she felt the goose bumps that prickled across her arms at Evie's touch. She silently, fervently hoped that Evie didn't notice them. Hoped that Evie didn't question why the sensation of her fingers grazing Marin's skin would cause such a reaction. Hoped that Evie wouldn't ask for an explanation when Marin herself didn't yet understand.

Marin reached her hand back to feel the neat bow now nestled at the back of her head.

Then Wren tied a second blindfold on Evie.

"No peeking!" Thea squeaked, and then they were off.

Marin listened as the sound of their footsteps faded into the heart of Lovelace House.

"How long do we have to wait?" Marin asked.

"Just a few minutes," Evie answered, closer to Marin than she realized. Marin reached her hands out, running one up Evie's arm before grasping her shoulder.

"Don't leave me like this," Marin said. "Your house gives me the creeps."

"Why is that?" Evie asked.

"Why does an old estate on the end of a peninsula, isolated from society and inhabited by one of our generation's greatest horror novelists give me the creeps?"

Marin felt the vibrations of Evie's laughter before she heard it.

"Well, when you put it that way," Evie said. "I guess that's fair."

Marin reached up and untied the bow on the back of her head, pulling off the blindfold.

Evie's was already off, and she was staring at Marin like she was amused.

"We didn't need these, did we?" Marin asked.

"I doubt the girls are even in the house," Evie said. "But it's part of their fun. Thea likes to do things a certain way."

"I can't *imagine* who she gets that from," Marin teased. "Hey, Evie, can I ask you something?"

"Sure," Evie said, putting the blindfolds away in a cupboard.

"What did the card say? The jumper?"

Evie made a long show of turning the key in the cabinet, locking up the board games—it seemed every door and cabinet at Lovelace House had locks and keys—before she turned around.

"It was nothing, Marin. The Ten of Swords."

"And what does the Ten of Swords mean?"

"It's all in how you read it. It can mean you've reached rock bottom, but then that means there is nowhere to go but up. That sounds fitting for us, doesn't it?" Evie gave Marin an encouraging smile, but it was a look Marin knew well. It was the one her own mother had used, when she wanted Marin to stop worrying about something.

"What else does the card mean, Evie?"

Evie stopped fidgeting and faced Marin head on.

"It can also mean betrayal."

They began their search in the greenhouse. Evie was confident the girls wouldn't choose anywhere in the house proper.

"It's just too obvious," she said.

"But there are a million places to hide in here," Marin said as they wound their way through the house.

"And who do you think taught them all of the best spots?" Evie said with a wink before pushing open the heavy doors.

So they searched the greenhouse first and, when they had no luck, moved out to the Lovelace grounds. They checked the gardening shed that Mr. Willoughby used. They searched in Evie's old tree house and in the orchard.

They were nowhere to be found.

"There are wild blueberry bushes," Evie said. "They are dense. Perfect hiding spots. Let's try there."

They ventured farther from the house, toward the woods, and sure enough, there were brambles of blueberries on the east side of the peninsula.

Marin could see glimpses of coastline and a long stone pier.

"What is that?" she asked Evie, pointing.

"The wharf," Evie said. "I used to jump off the end of it at high tide with my father."

It was low tide now, with water sloshing against stones forming the base of the pier.

Marin wandered down a row of blueberries.

"Don't these need to be cared for to grow like this?"

"They do. They aren't really wild anymore. Mr. Willoughby tends to them. Here." Evie stretched her hand out to Marin and had berries scooped in her palm that she had plucked as they walked.

"Actually blueberries?" Marin asked, remembering the other berries that a Hallowell girl had offered her not long ago.

"Actually blueberries," Evie said with a laugh, and tipped the palmful back into her own mouth.

She wrinkled her nose. "June is early. They're quite sour." But she picked a few more off the bushes for Marin.

Juice from the berries flooded Marin's mouth, so tart they made her eyes water.

"You weren't kidding," she said, and then watched Evie pick another handful from the bush to eat.

"I like them sour," she said at Marin's pointed look. They continued down the path that wove between the blueberry bushes.

Marin might have started to worry about the girls—it had been more than an hour since they'd last seen them in the library. But Evie didn't seem too concerned, and she knew them better than anyone.

But after weaving through all the rows, there were no girls.

"Now what?" Marin asked.

"Maybe they are in the house," Evie said.

"Or the cemetery?" Marin suggested.

Evie went still on the path ahead of her.

"They wouldn't go there," she said.

"They would. They took me there my first day at Lovelace."

"They didn't," Evie insisted, turning sharply. "Did they really?"

"Of—of course." Marin suddenly realized maybe it was wrong. A transgression of some kind.

"I can't believe them," Evie said.

Marin realized Evie wasn't mad at her but at the girls, for going to the cemetery.

"Then they can stay out here," Evie said. Without another word, she turned back to the house.

"Evie," Marin began, thinking she was only kidding. "Evie!"

Evie stomped away, her suede boots kicking up dust on the path they had walked. Her blueberry-stained hands folded across her chest.

Marin couldn't leave the girls out in the cemetery alone, so she headed that way.

She crawled into Thea's arborvitaes first, but it was empty.

The cemetery was different today. Fog had rolled in off the water, casting everything in strange shadows. A chill ran down Marin's body as she stepped into the old graveyard. *Damn them*, she thought.

It was only Evie's sharp refusal to enter the cemetery playing tricks on her, making her think there was something to really fear out here. And she knew it was likely nothing but grief that kept Evie from joining her. The knowledge that her father was in his final resting place inside.

But Marin couldn't see more than a few feet in front of her, and the effect was disorienting.

Finally, after several minutes, she could make out the shape of a girl ahead in the fog.

"Wren," she said. "Thank goodness."

But the girl didn't move.

Marin got close enough for the mist around her to clear and found a statue of an angel weeping over a grave, not Wren.

"Wren!" Marin called. "Thea!"

She searched the rows of headstones the same way they'd searched the blueberries, winding up one row and down the next, careful not to miss any. The girls should have heard her if they were out here.

Then Marin thought of the bluff. On a day this foggy, they might have been running. They might have lost track of where they were.

In her mind, Marin saw the girls laughing, playing, not seeing danger as they pitched over the edge of the bluff overlooking sharp rocks and water below.

Marin went straight to the far side of the cemetery.

Marin toed herself slowly to the edge of the bluff and peeked over the side, letting out a sigh of sharp relief when she found no injured children on the exposed rocks below.

At least the worst-case scenario wasn't realized.

Marin circled back the way she came. They weren't hiding in the rows of old gravestones. They hadn't plummeted to their deaths on the rocky shore below. Which only left the mausoleums.

Marin approached the stone temples, checking the pillars in each one, looking for someone tucked into the small niches on the steps.

Finally, she heard it.

A snicker.

It was soft, but it was close.

Marin stepped back into the front entrance of the mausoleum she had just checked. She frowned at the inscription in the stone overhead. There were a half dozen mausoleums, and this one looked oldest of all. But the others all had the name Lovelace carved into the stone edifice at their entrances. This one only had a handful of letters, *A-D-O-S-S-A*. Maybe there was another family name in these grounds.

Then Marin looked down and she saw it. The gate on this one had no lock, and it was slightly ajar.

Marin pushed her way inside.

Wren and Thea were sitting on top of a stone sarcophagus.

They screamed when Marin stepped inside, shrieks of joy, and Marin screamed in turn as well.

Not in joy.

"Unbelievable," Marin said. "You scared me to *death*. And Evie is so angry."

At this the girls had the decency to look somewhat ashamed.

"No more hide-and-seek."

"Like, ever?" Thea asked, voice thick with the threat of tears.

"Never again," Marin said, too angry and too relieved to feel badly for making her cry. "Let's go." Marin herded the girls back to the house, fuming the entire way.

"The graveyard is dangerous," Marin said. "You could fall. Or one of those ancient gravestones could break and crush you. Or you could have gotten locked inside the mausoleum."

"We're sorry, Marin," the girls said in unison, and Marin studied their repentant faces to see if they were mocking her.

She'd been with these girls for a month now, and she genuinely couldn't tell.

Back at Lovelace House, Marin sent the girls to apologize to Evie and went to grab a sweater from her room. Now that it was overcast, the entire house felt sepulchral and dark. Not unlike the tomb she'd just pulled the girls out of.

At her door, Marin paused. There was a roll of paper slipped into the space between the doorknob and the frame of the door and tied with a ribbon.

But before Marin could open it, a movement under the door caught her attention. She watched as a shadow crossed the floor in the thin gap underneath her doorway. It seemed to shuffle unsteadily, its gait awkward.

The shadow slowly retreated farther into her room.

If you are looking for something to be afraid of, you'll find it, Cordelia had often reminded her, the words a common phrase in their home by that point.

Cordelia had never understood Marin's fascination with horror novels. Why she would seek out the scariest things. But it was the same reason Marin's brain played through the worst-case scenarios in her head all the time. She'd convinced herself, like the opposite of an omen, that if she imagined the worst, most horrible possibility, then it couldn't come true.

So Marin played worst-case scenario now in a twisted effort to sooth her own fears. *Worst-case scenario #1*: the house really is possessed, just like in Alice's book, and when she goes into the room, the *thing* inside will consume her. *Worst-case scenario #2*: someone broke into Lovelace House, a serial killer, intent on harming her, lying in wait on the other side of the door. *Worst-case scenario #3*: a wild animal climbed in through a window that she forgot to close—something with a mouth lined with teeth meant for tearing flesh.

Maybe it was anxiety. Maybe this time it was just her imagination. Either way, Marin could stand in the hallway forever, dreaming up nightmares on the other side. Or she could just look inside.

Marin threw open the door, letting it swing wide.

There was a thin trail of blood on the floor, and Marin followed it. It led across the floor and up to her windowsill.

Her window *was* open, just a few inches, and Marin pushed it up the rest of the way to crawl out onto the Juliette balcony, where she just barely had enough room to stand.

There was nothing out there.

Marin put her hands on the railing to lean over so she could look down to the grass below, but there was nothing down below either.

It wasn't until she pulled her hands back to go inside that she remembered the paper, still clutched in her grasp. Marin unrolled the page.

I'm sorry for abandoning you out there. I hate the cemetery, and the girls should know better. Thank you for going to find them. —E

As Marin read, she traced the words with her fingers. Evie's penmanship was neat, distinct, and calligraphic—very *Evie*. Marin realized too late she was marking the page. Her hands were staining it with purple fingerprints from the berries she'd eaten with Evie. And in the corner, where her palm had touched it, a fresh streak of rust.

It was blood from the railing, from whatever had just crawled out of her room.

PART 2
Everything You Want Has Teeth

———————— ❧ ————————

There is something at work in my soul, which I do not understand.

— Mary Shelley, *Frankenstein*

In this place, long forsaken by God or any kinder deity, the line between the living and the dead was blurred. At night, she wandered the shore, eyes on the dark midnight sea, searching for something without a name. It was just there—at the edge of her vision. It was just there, at the end of her dreams, in that final moment before she woke. But when she took her daughter's small hand in her own and led her through the moss-covered gravestones, the child's eyes shone bright and curious, and she ran from the safety of her mother's grasp, content among the ghosts of her ancestors.

— Alice Lovelace, *Requiem for the Living*

14

If That Mockingbird Won't Sing

Let go, Marin.

In the soft shadows that predicted dawn, Marin stared at her tiled ceiling, frowning at the ambiguous pattern overhead. Marin suspected it was some kind of flower or fern, or a perhaps a fleur-de-lis, but she just couldn't make it out.

Her room was so quiet.

She'd shut her window to sleep, unsettled by the bloody trail that led across her room last night. Unsettled again by her nightmare. She could only remember fragments of it. Rainwater soaking her. The sensation of being trapped. The panic. The darkness.

Awake was better.

Marin squinted her eyes at the ceiling. Dammit, this would drive her mad.

She kicked off her quilt, possessed by the idea that the shape on the tin ceiling was familiar and if she could only get a closer look she would recognize it. She pulled her chair out from the cherrywood desk in the corner of the room and placed the chair on top.

She turned on the bedside lamp, illuminating the room with a soft glow.

Then she climbed.

Once she knelt on the chair, which was perched ever so delicately on the desk, its old legs ever-so-slightly uneven so that it rocked just a bit with every shift of her weight, Marin began to stand. She crept her hands up the wall one inch at a time for balance.

The plan was precarious at best.

More likely dangerous.

And yet, she rose until she was standing and then she craned her neck back to look at the ceiling, now only a few feet above her.

It was some kind of plant; she was sure of it now. The shape in each tin square was a stalk, with leaves and flowers shaped like bells etched on the sides.

But there was something else. Toward the base of each stalk, in lieu of the flowers, there was a different shape. Rounder, with hollowed out eyes and mouths.

They were skulls.

Pressed into the tin, surrounded by foliage and blooms, were a handful of little skulls on each stalk, on each tile, in a pattern that repeated itself across her ceiling a hundred times over.

Marin climbed back down, wishing she'd left well enough alone.

There was no chance that she would fall back to sleep. She wrote a quick note to Evie, telling her she got her note and there was nothing to forgive, and tying it with the same string Evie had tied on hers. She dressed quickly, slipped the note under Evie's door, and went down to the kitchen to start coffee.

She sat there at the large formal dining table that ran the length of the room and sipped her black coffee. Eventually, Thisbe lumbered downstairs, a signal that the girls would be awake soon. The dog often came down just before them.

Like a warning bell.

Here they come, Marin, Thisbe's sweet face seemed to say to her, *take cover.*

But when Marin heard feet on the stairs, it wasn't the girls or even Evie, but Alice.

"Oh. Good morning." Marin was surprised. She hadn't seen her since the incident down on the shore, and she didn't know how to act now. She was afraid to bring it up at all.

But it was possible she wouldn't see Alice for several days after this.

If her writing was going well, she barely left her office. Sometimes not even to eat. Lately she'd stayed up there more and more, leaving everything to Evie and Marin, including bedtime stories and tucking the girls in at night.

Which was fine with Marin. Sometimes it felt as though Alice was haunting the rest of them, working through the dead hours of the night, the only signs of her still living there were nothing more than a mug left in the sink or some slippers abandoned by the stairs.

"Coffee?" Marin asked, and Alice nodded.

Marin returned quickly, setting a cup in front of Alice, who was staring out the window, toward the sea. She looked tired—there were purple half-moons under her eyes, and her hair didn't have its typical straightened rigidity. In fact, it had some waves in it, and Marin saw that Thea and Evie got their curls from Alice after all.

But she must have been awake all night working.

"Ms. Lovelace? I'd like your permission to teach the girls to swim. I feel like they should know, and I'm qualified. It was the one thing my mother insisted I stick with even when we moved around so much, and I know CPR, and—"

Alice held up her hand, and Marin stopped talking.

"Your mother lived here, did you know?" Alice said. "From the ages of eight to eleven."

Marin knew they'd been friends, but she had no idea her mother had lived at Lovelace. Of course, she should have put it together. Alice likely had a tutor here, just like Wren and Thea did now. Where would she have met Cordelia except here?

"I didn't know," Marin said.

"I'm not surprised she didn't talk about it. We had a falling out."

"Over what?"

"Oh, I'm not sure I remember the details. We were still quite young. But her mother was our housekeeper for a while, and they lived on this floor, in the rooms just beyond the kitchens there." Alice gestured to the hallway beyond where they were sitting. "She loved the ocean."

At that, Marin looked up from her coffee with a frown.

"But she didn't," Marin said. "She hated the ocean. She gets seasick."

Alice was quiet for a long time, and Marin wondered if she'd said something wrong.

"She didn't always," Alice said. "We used to swim together. In fact, she was the one who taught me. My mother had never learned, always feared the ocean. And then once I was good, we'd jump off the wharf—that stone pier on the east side of the peninsula—and see who could hold their breath the longest. She always won."

"She hated losing games," Marin said.

"Yes, well, so did I." Alice then bent over, rubbing her temple.

"Are you all right?"

"This damned headache won't go away. But yes, Marin, you may teach the girls to swim."

The girls came crashing down the stairs then, with Evie ushering them in to the table for breakfast, and Marin was sad to have the conversation cut short. She wanted to know more about her mother's friendship with Alice. She wanted to know everything.

"Girls, you are with Mr. Willoughby this morning, helping with the road," Alice said.

"What?" Wren asked. "But why?"

"The cemetery is dangerous, the bluff is dangerous, and you know better than to go unsupervised."

Wren and Thea pouted through breakfast, but when Mr. Willoughby arrived to collect them, their grins couldn't be contained. Mr. Willoughby tried to maintain his stoic appearance, but Marin saw how his face softened when he faced the girls. *Softie.*

"What are we doing today?" Thea chirped.

Mr. Willoughby reached into the breast pocket of his flannel shirt and pulled out a small stack of index cards, consulting them for a moment.

"Filling in the potholes on the road with rocks," he announced.

And to Marin's surprise, the girls didn't argue with him once. They put on their boots and followed along, filling Mr. Willoughby in on their cemetery adventure the day before that had landed them in so much trouble.

"I have work to do," Alice said, her voice still strained from her pain. "Evie, I believe you have some studying to do? I left some test-prep books in the greenhouse—I thought it might be better to study out there, rather than the library. It's a beautiful day."

Marin could see that Evie wanted to argue about the studying, but she only bore a strained smile and said, "Yes, Mother."

After breakfast, Evie went to get some paper and pens,

and Marin slipped upstairs to Alice's office. She knocked softly, surprised when the door immediately whipped open. "What now?" Alice demanded.

Marin had carried a small hope with her upstairs that Alice might tell her more about Cordelia's time here as a child, but that disappeared quickly. Alice's disheveled appearance and the glassy look of pain in her eyes from her headache were warning enough, even before Alice snapped at her.

"I brought you—" Marin held out the contents of her hands.

A glass of cold water and some aspirin.

Alice stared down at it as though Marin were handing her a spider.

"Your mother was always the thoughtful one too," Alice said. The words might have been mistaken as kind, but her tone was cold. Alice took the glass and the medicine and closed the door in Marin's face.

15

Just Like the Movies

In the greenhouse, Evie was sitting on a blanket in the exact spot the girls had chosen for their picnic. Marin eyed the belladonna and chose a seat on the far side of the blanket, away from it.

"They aren't dangerous to sit next to," Evie said. "So what is the method of torture today?"

"Proofs," Marin answered. "They're fun."

"I assure you, they're not."

For the next two hours, Marin could honestly swear that she gave it her all. She'd tutored younger students at her last high school, and she knew how to go over a lesson and practice questions.

Alice couldn't possibly fault her diligence.

The problem was Evie.

Evie's attention lasted approximately eighteen seconds and then she was rising from the picnic blanket to point out a particular flower to Marin, or to find a better pen, or to get some water because the greenhouse was quite warmer than usual.

By the time Evie launched into the history of Agatha and the trouble the Winterthur Maine Horticultural Society had gone through to procure the rare plant, Marin was lying back on the picnic blanket in defeat with the test-prep book covering her face.

"Evie, did anyone ever screen you for attention disorders?" Marin asked.

"Attention? Well, yes. But Mother thought it was silly, so . . ." Evie shrugged.

"Of course she did." Marin sat up and closed the book. She was going to have to find some more creative ways to encourage Evie to study this material if they were going to be successful. But first, they needed a break. "How about a walk outside? Some fresh, cool air before the girls get back?"

It was too humid in the greenhouse, but Marin could hear the harsh ocean wind blowing outside. It sounded like a welcome relief from the clammy air inside.

"Yes," Evie said, rising instantly and letting her pages scatter. "Leave it," she said when Marin reached for them. "Let them rot."

Marin rolled her eyes and straightened the pages.

"Fine," Evie said, taking the papers from Marin. "I'll put these away."

Marin raised her eyebrows in judgment.

"I swear it," Evie said, offering her pinkie. "I'll put them somewhere safe."

Marin accepted the promise, hooking her pinkie around Evie's to make her swear it. The last thing Marin wanted to do was start over the next time they tried to tackle this test booklet.

"You go pull some of my sweaters from the entryway closet. It looks a bit chilly outside."

Marin hurried to the front foyer and pulled out two of Evie's cable knit sweaters. Marin chose the cream one and pulled it around her shoulders, shoving her hands into the oversized pockets.

She felt something in one of them and pulled out a slip of newspaper. She unfolded the delicate paper.

It was an obituary. For Charles Hallowell.

Marin read through the brief description of the man's life. Three daughters. Married to the renowned novelist Alice Lovelace. But it was the line at the very end that caught her attention. Charles Hallowell died in a boating accident. *After heroically saving his daughter Evie from drowning, he himself succumbed to the dangers of the ocean.*

Evie hadn't been away at school when her father drowned. She'd been with him.

Marin hadn't known.

She folded the article carefully and slipped it back into the pocket where she'd found it just as Evie appeared in the foyer with a warm smile on her face.

Marin felt guilty even though she hadn't meant to pry. She understood better than anyone why Evie wouldn't want to talk about that day. She didn't want to talk about her own mother or the train either. But something about the obituary just didn't sit right. Like a splinter under her skin, irritating her, despite how small and insignificant it seemed.

"That looks perfect on you," Evie said, nodding at the sweater Marin had chosen as she came into the hallway. "It's from the most charming little wool shop on the coast of Ireland. We went two years ago, for the holidays."

Marin's most expensive sweater was from a Gap outlet.

Evie pulled on a button-up cardigan that was crimson and contrasted her blond hair brilliantly. She looked like she belonged in a fairy-tale story. But when Marin caught a glimpse of herself in the wide mirror hanging at the foot of the stairs, she was surprised at her own appearance. She'd worn Snow White's Folly on her lips once again, telling herself it wasn't because Evie had liked it. Her hair was in her usual twisted-up space buns on the back of her head, but now the dark brown had streaks of light running through it from the sun. That same sun had brought out more freckles on her face so they stood out sharper than ever across her cheeks and nose. But that wasn't what had surprised her.

It took a moment, one where she almost didn't recognize her own reflection, to realize what was different.

She was smiling.

Marin cupped her own cheek to be sure the reflection

moved with her. To be sure it was still her in there. The grief that she'd worn since her mother's death had diminished. It wasn't gone, but it was less demanding. Marin was beginning to suspect the reason why.

Marin looked up at Evie just as she called for Thisbe, her voice somehow ringing soft and confident at the same time. When Thisbe failed to show, Evie shrugged, sending some of those long curls of hers falling over her shoulder.

Marin had to clench her fists at her side to keep from reaching to tuck them back behind Evie's ear.

"She's probably off with Willoughby and the girls," Evie said.

So they left without her and circled the house, ending up in the orchard. Evie was wearing a dress, as usual, but that didn't stop her from shifting her weight up into one of the apple trees and waving Marin up behind her.

Marin climbed onto the lowest, thickest branch and leaned against the trunk. She felt a tap on her shoulder and turned to find an apple so dark purple it looked black in Evie's outstretched hand. "Grandmother's Favorite," she said. "They're very good."

Marin accepted the apple with thoughts of fairy tales and poison apples only briefly crossing her mind before she sunk her teeth into the fruit. It was completely absurd, of course, but then again, it wouldn't even be the first time one of the Hallowell sisters handed her poisonous fruit.

"These were your grandmother's favorite kind?" Marin asked. The apple was extremely tart, flooding her mouth with a sour-sweet taste that made her purse her lips in response.

"No, that's just their name. Look." Evie pointed to the trunk of the tree, and Marin saw a line running up the center of it. "Did you know that two trees can grow right into each other? They abrade each other's trunks, sort of rubbing them raw from proximity, and then they begin to grow together, until they are just one being, sharing a single root system and nutrients, everything. It's called inosculation. Once they're joined, they can never be taken apart again."

"I didn't know," Marin said.

"That's what these are. My father tried this as a botany experiment, back before the greenhouse was built, and well, it worked."

"They're delicious," Marin said, taking another large bite. They ate their apples in quiet contentedness, the absence of the noisy little girls felt in every soft moment.

"Marin? I really am sorry for yesterday," Evie said. "I sort of abandoned you to find the girls on your own. It's just that I don't go into the cemetery."

"It's all right," Marin said. "I understand."

"You don't," Evie began, but Marin held up a hand.

"Evie, you don't owe me an explanation for your grief. I didn't mind going in to get the girls."

"Graveyards don't scare you, then?" Evie turned her head

137

to the side, studying Marin carefully, like she'd just admitted something important.

"No," Marin said. "Wren scares me."

Evie laughed and went back to eating. For a while longer, they balanced on their branches in the tree, crunching on their apples, enjoying the comfortable silence.

They were still for so long that Marin watched as a deer and her fawns emerged from the woods, and she elbowed Evie gently and pointed in their direction. The deer crossed into the orchard, making their way around, chewing on the soft, slightly rotten flesh of apples that had fallen to the ground, until they were right below the girls, so close that Marin could count the white freckles on the baby deer's backs.

She pointed the fawn out to Evie, who tried to move down to Marin's branch for a closer look.

Only her boot slipped on the branch.

The sudden movement startled the deer below, who sprang from the orchard toward the cover of the forest, and Marin reached for Evie, grabbing her arm and pulling her roughly back to find purchase on the branch.

Physically, their equilibrium was restored, but Marin felt unsteady. She was pressed up so tight against Evie that she could feel her heart. It was racing, Marin guessed from the scare of the fall. Evie was a head taller than Marin, and Marin had to crane her neck a bit to look up into Evie's dark eyes.

When they'd first met, Marin thought that her eyes gave nothing away, but she could see it now. It was subtle, her emotions masked, guarded like a treasure. But now Marin spotted the flickering evidence of Evie's fear, quickly replaced by warmth as she realized that she was safe, that Marin had caught her.

"Thank you," Evie whispered.

They were close enough that Marin could smell the cinnamon scent Evie always wore and make out the faint blush on Evie's cheeks.

Evie brushed a hand over Marin's cheek.

"That's Leo," she said. "The lion."

"And Ursa Minor over here," Evie said. Her fingers dropped to Marin's collarbone, where another thousand or so freckles led a path up and over her shoulder.

She was finding constellations in Marin's freckles.

Then Evie's dark gaze dropped to Marin's lips. "What was it?" she asked.

Marin furrowed her thick brows in confusion. "What was what?"

"Snow White's Folly. What did she ever do wrong?" Evie moved a fraction of an inch closer, and without thought or hesitation, Marin responded in kind.

"I don't know," Marin answered truthfully. "I guess she just . . . trusted the wrong people."

Evie shifted away so quickly that Marin almost lost her balance.

"We can't do this," Evie said.

Marin was so confused.

"We didn't . . . Evie, we didn't do anything."

Evie muttered some excuse about needing to go. It was half-hearted and inane, and Marin saw right through the crystalline lie, but Evie was already climbing down the apple tree, crouching on the lowest branch to grab it with her hands and swing down to the dewy grass below.

Marin leaned against the tree trunk, pulling Evie's sweater in closer around her body, and watched as Evie fled.

16

My Darling, Clementine

———————— ❧ ————————

"Y ou're doing great!"

Marin was waist-deep in water so cold that she couldn't feel her toes. Her hands were under Thea, who was floating—or rather, learning to float. Or rather, *trying* to learn to float.

When Marin had informed them they'd be learning to swim, the girls had been hesitant, to say the least. When Thea finally emerged from Lovelace House, she was wearing goggles that covered two-thirds of her face, complete with a snorkeling spout, and two sets of water wings, so large on her little stick arms that she couldn't put them down.

Wren put on one of the life jackets from the boat.

"Girls, I appreciate that you want to be safe, but you'll never learn in all that gear." It had taken Marin another hour to coax the girls out of their floatation devices, one bribed piece at a time until they'd finally made it into the water.

"Good job, Thea," Marin said. "Try to relax."

"Are you insane?" Thea demanded, her voice so loud with her ears submerged in the water that it echoed off the rocks behind them.

Marin helped Thea up. "Remember, the water is shallow. You can stand. And I'm right here. I won't let anything bad happen to you."

"I think it's Wren's turn," Thea said, shifting her feet underneath her and wading to shore.

Things went better with Wren, who gained confidence faster. Within an hour, Wren was able to use a rudimentary stroke to keep her head above water. Soon she was circling Marin, the brightest smile Marin had seen yet plastered across her face.

"Wonderful, Wren. You've got this." Marin swam beside her, and they even managed to cover the basics of the breaststroke.

Neera came down the stairs from the house, clapping enthusiastically when she saw Wren's progress.

"Good job, brave girl!" she called from the shore. She was wrapping a towel around Thea, who had been sitting there, teeth chattering, since she'd left the water.

Wren and Marin climbed out of the water and embraced the towels that Neera offered.

"Oh," Marin gasped when she pulled it around her body. They were fresh out of the dryer. "So warm. Thank you, Neera."

"Of course, Marin. Girls, let's give Marin a little break. Why don't you join me in the kitchen? We're baking banana muffins."

In the house, Marin left the girls with Neera and beelined up the stairs. She needed a shower to rinse the salt water from her hair.

But as she passed the library, she paused.

There was music playing inside.

Evie's piano.

Marin didn't have to look inside to know it was her playing. It was some classical piece, the music almost violent by the time it reached its crescendo. Marin imagined Evie playing. Did she lose some of her careful composure as she played?

Marin wanted to know.

But she hadn't seen Evie since that morning in the tree, when she'd fled at the exact moment when Marin thought they might—well, she wasn't exactly sure what she thought was going to happen. But she'd known what she *wanted* to happen. She'd known the feeling of loss when Evie had pulled away from it.

Marin leaned her head against the library door, listening to the final lingering notes. She could at least be honest with herself. She'd wanted to kiss her. And now she didn't think she'd ever dare cross that line with Evie again. She couldn't. Evie's flight—her clear rejection of what was growing between them—stung too deeply to repeat. But

Marin hadn't realized until the opportunity was gone just how badly she wanted it.

Marin heard footsteps in the corridor and stepped away from the library door just as Alice rounded the corner.

"Marin," Alice said. "Perfect. I was coming to find you. Could you—"

Alice stopped.

"Marin Blythe, why are you dripping water all over my floors?"

Marin looked down. She was still in her swimsuit, wrapped tight in a towel, but her hair had been steadily raining droplets to the floor.

Marin tore off her towel and knelt to soak up the water. "I'm sorry, I got distracted."

Evie chose that moment to begin playing again, and Alice tilted her head in understanding. "She's quite talented, yes?"

Marin only nodded, embarrassed to have been caught listening outside the door.

"Marin, I'm feeling unwell again. Can I bother you to handle bedtime with the girls once more tonight? I think I might retire early."

"Of course," said Marin.

"Thea likes the book with the cats that fly," Alice added softly just as she turned away.

"Yes, I know." More often than not, Marin and Evie were with the girls the entire day through bedtime now, and

Alice emerged from her office or her bedroom less and less frequently.

Marin showered and changed and then crossed the hall to Evie's door. She thought she heard Evie moving around in her room, but she didn't knock.

Evie never emerged for dinner.

Marin fell asleep in the girls' room halfway through her third reading of the book with the flying cats to Thea.

Let go, Marin.

She blinked her eyes open, glancing at the small clock on the girls' bedside table. It was past four in the morning. Marin groggily made her way to her own room and didn't even bother to change, simply pulling off her jeans and crawling under her sheets. She didn't fight sleep, succumbing once more to a nightmare that began the same each time, with the pitched shriek of brakes on train tracks.

The next morning, when Marin heard the squeak of her doorknob turning, she half hoped it would be Evie, coming to collect her to watch the girls, the incident in the apple tree put solidly behind them.

But it was Thea's little round face peeking through the open doorway. "SOS," Thea whispered. She'd lost another tooth, and the *s* sound slipped through the gap with a distinct whistle. "It's Wren. She's making pancakes. It's a disaster."

Marin groaned and sat up, slowly stretching her arms

above her head, reminding herself she wasn't trapped in sheets of metal like she had been in her dreams.

"It's kind of an emergency," Thea chirped from the doorway, where she was shifting on her feet impatiently. "Mother will be furious."

Those were the magic words to wake Marin fully and propel her out of bed, into sweatpants, and down the stairs toward the kitchen.

The last thing she needed today was an irate Alice.

SOS was right.

Marin stepped into the kitchen and her jaw instantly fell in abject horror. Every surface of the room was covered in dust.

No, not dust.

"It's flour," Wren confessed, a look of pure misery on her face where she stood on a stool, surveying the damage she'd inflicted.

"I—I—" Marin stammered, then shut her mouth.

Well, they'd finally done it.

They'd left her speechless.

Marin stepped forward, mindful of the footprints she was leaving in her wake. She swept a finger over the white powder coated table and lifted it to her lips. Flour. *Everywhere.*

"But—" Marin tried again. "How?"

Thea stepped forward and lifted the empty bag of flour. "Wren needed flour, so I got the bag—"

"The sealed bag," Wren interjected.

"And I sort of . . . threw it?" Thea said it like a question.

"You threw it," Marin repeated dumbly.

"And I did *not* catch it," Wren said.

"And it . . ." Thea mimicked a bomb exploding with her hands.

Marin drew a deep breath to calm down, regretting it when she sucked in a fine cloud of airborne flour.

"Wren, what's that smell? Something is burning," Marin said between coughs.

"Dammit!" Wren shouted and turned back to the stove. She flipped the pancake, revealing a completely black circle on the other side. "Well, Thea. I think that's that. Time to call it."

Thea looked at the clock on the wall. "Time of death. 9:43 a.m." Her face dropped in mock sorrow. "That's the fourth one we've lost today."

"Okay," Marin said, taking charge of the situation before Alice found them all like this. "Wren, turn off that stove top before you burn Lovelace down. Thea. *Towels.* Get them wet so they catch the flour. Start with the counters and table. We'll clean the floor last."

Marin barked out orders for another forty minutes.

At one point, Neera entered the room, took a glance around, and turned promptly on her heel to go back the other direction.

Marin didn't blame her one bit.

They salvaged exactly seven pancakes from the wreckage, and those needed a generous helping of syrup and cinnamon to make them edible. The girls gobbled them down, appeased by sugar and butter and some semblance of order to the chaos they'd unleashed in the kitchen.

"Thanks, Marin," Thea said, her mouth full of sticky, syrupy goodness.

Marin smiled. "What are nannies good for?"

Wren opened her mouth, and Marin braced for another one of her casually cruel retorts, but Wren shut it again, seeming to remember they still had to spend the whole day together and that Marin had just come to their rescue.

"Thank you," she said. "I'll clear our plates. And then we want to go for a walk."

"Where are we walking?" Marin asked.

"I'm afraid it's sad news," Thea told her. "Clementine died."

"Oh, not Clementine!" Marin said. "Well, I'm very sorry to hear that, Thea. We should probably lay her to rest, shouldn't we?" Marin tried not to think too hard on the fact that the doll that Thea had purposely made resemble Marin was now dead.

"You girls should go get dressed," she said. "I'll finish up here."

While the girls ran to change out of their pajamas, Marin went to bottle up water for their walk. Mornings on the end of the peninsula were still comfortably cool—there was always a breeze off the water. But knowing the girls, they'd be wandering in the woods for half the day. And off the water, in the June heat, it would be sticky and warm by noon. She packed the bottles and a picnic blanket and some snacks into her old backpack.

But when Marin took a sip from her own bottle, she spit the water into the sink.

It was salt water.

She tested the others and found the same.

Marin turned on the faucet, dipping her head down to drink. Sure enough, salt water was coming through the tap. She let the water run for a full minute and then tried it again.

It was fresh water again.

Marin dumped all the bottles and refilled them, checking the water between each one to make sure it was okay. She made a mental note to ask Neera if that had ever happened before.

When she found the girls on the front steps waiting for her, Evie had joined them. She wore the same crimson cardigan that she'd worn in the orchard, and Marin couldn't help but feel the choice was deliberate.

She waited for some comment or meaningful look, anything in reference to what had happened between them, but Evie only smiled.

"Time for a funeral?" Evie asked.

"Lead the way," Marin said to Thea. Thea carried her doll

wrapped up in a baby blanket and marched directly toward the woods with Wren by her side.

Evie and Marin trailed a few steps behind.

"So, what's with the dead dolls?" Marin asked, keeping her voice low.

"It started when I was home for winter break. All of a sudden, her dolls had myriad ailments. All fatal. All requiring a formal burial. We used to get invitations on black construction paper, but she got tired of the hassle. Neera and I think it is just how she's dealing with losing our father."

"How many dolls has she buried?"

"Dozens," Evie said. "And those are just the ones I know about. Mother forbade her from doing this in the family cemetery, the girls aren't supposed to go in there, but the little graveyard in the woods is even older than the Lovelaces'. There's no one left to mourn them or mind Thea there."

Marin nodded, but Evie looked nervous.

"Do you think it's wrong, Marin?" she asked. "To disturb the dead?"

"I think it would be more wrong to keep a child from processing her grief however she needs to," Marin said. "And I don't know about you, but I'd rather spend my time caring for the living than fearing the dead."

17

The Soil and the Rot

———————— ❧ ————————

T he woods of Winterthur were practically primordial.
Thick vines roped through the canopy. The trunks
of the trees were covered in layers of lichen that clung like
soft coats. Dark moss grew along roots and then burgeoned
across the ground, a quilted patchwork of green blanketing
everything it could reach. Sometimes it seemed to move,
a subtle expansion, like the forest itself was alive, asleep,
drawing a deep breath.

Like it might shudder itself awake at any moment.

There were speckled birches and spotted toadstools, and
it reminded Marin of that fairy tale, the terrible one, with
the house made of candy meant to lure children in.

Then again, thanks to the Hallowell girls, Marin could
almost understand why a witch might feel compelled to
eat them.

Thea's funeral service for her doll was quick. She'd brought
a garden spade to dig a shallow grave. This time when she

asked Marin to say something, Marin had thought it out a little more.

She knelt down so she was at Thea's level and took her little hand in her own.

"I know death is sad, Thea. We will all miss Clementine very much. But death is also natural. It's just another part of life. And our time being short is what makes our time together so precious. And there's something kind of beautiful in that, don't you agree, Evie?" At the last word, Marin looked up to Evie, who was staring at her so intently with those serious eyes of hers that Marin was afraid she'd said something wrong.

Evie had only just opened her mouth to respond when a horrible scream echoed through the trees, making every hair raise on the nape of Marin's neck.

"What the hell *was* that?" Marin whispered.

"Something dying," Evie whispered back. "We should go home."

Marin didn't need to be told more than once. She reached for Thea's hand, tucking it into her own. As they exited the wrought-iron fence around the tiny graveyard, another scream came.

"I think it's a monster," Wren said, unperturbed, as she began to walk through the woods toward Lovelace House.

Thea's boots crunched after her.

"I'd guess alien," she said, and craned her neck, scanning

the skies, her face almost hopeful, for some sign of an extra-terrestrial invasion.

"Aliens abduct. Monsters hunt," Wren said. "So we just have to answer one question."

"What's that?" Thea asked.

"*Is it hungry?*" Wren said.

Marin shivered, wrapped her arms around her midsection, and forged on behind the girls. "Well, *I* don't want to know the answer."

It took her a moment to realize that Evie wasn't with them, and she turned back. Evie was standing at the edge of the graveyard, staring off into the woods, into an area too thick for Marin to see.

"Evie?" Marin said softly. "What's wrong?"

"Sorry," Evie said. She shook her head and turned to Marin. "I'm sorry, I thought I saw something."

"It's the monster!" Wren hurried back to Marin's side, eyes sparkling with excitement.

"The alien!" Thea corrected.

Before Marin could say a word, the girls took off in the direction that Evie had been staring.

"No!" Evie shouted, but the girls had a head start, and no fear and absolutely zero sense of self-preservation as far as Marin could tell.

"Evie, what did you see?" Marin asked.

"I don't—it wasn't—" Evie stammered, and Marin ran

right past her, yelling for the girls to stop.

She found them standing in place just beyond the thicket, with Wren holding back a cluster of branches. Marin approached behind them and looked over their shoulders.

On the ground not ten feet away was a baby deer, likely one of the ones that Marin and Evie had seen in the orchard. Only now the deer was very dead. The white fur around the fawn's mouth and neck was dotted with pink flecks of blood. There were chunks of flesh torn from its belly.

Bite marks, Marin realized. Wren turned to look up at Marin. "See? I was right," Wren said. "It was hungry."

They regrouped in the library.

Instead of walking to visit Mr. Willoughby this time, Marin went downstairs to call him from the safety of the house.

She described the gruesome scene to him.

"Stay out of the woods. I'll take care of it," Mr. Willoughby said, his voice gruff.

The man wasn't nice per se, but he was kind.

Marin returned to the library, only realizing once she entered the room that there had been animated voices not a moment ago. Wren and Evie turned toward Marin as she walked in. Whatever they'd been arguing about, they had stopped when she entered the room.

Thea was on a chair, clutching a new doll tight, looking back and forth between her sisters and Marin.

"Just *tell* her," Thea said.

"No," Wren and Evie said in unison, their voices matching in sharpness.

"Tell me what?" Marin stepped toward them. "Tell me what, Evie? Tell me what you saw in the woods?"

Evie gave herself away, breaking eye contact with Marin to study her shoes.

"What was it out there, Evie? You saw whatever killed the deer, didn't you? Why not just tell me? Was it a wolf? A bear? A pirate zombie?" At the last, Marin lifted the piece from the Winterthur game on the table. Grey Hand. Charles Hallowell's favorite token.

Wren flinched, and Marin regretted her action immediately.

"I'm sorry, I just . . ." Marin set the piece carefully back down.

Wren looked up at Evie, who gave her a single, decisive shake no.

"That!" Marin shouted. "That right there. What was that *look*?"

Wren had moved to the bookcase, refusing to meet eyes with Marin. Now she was pretending to be preoccupied with some jar on one of the shelves.

They'd reached an impasse.

Evie couldn't answer, and Marin couldn't let it go.

For a long, drawn moment, no one spoke. And then something struck the library window with a resounding crack. Marin turned just in time to see a bird crumple against the window and fall outside. Another mourning dove.

Wren whirled at the sound too, dropping the bell jar from her hands. It smashed against the floor, shattering into a million pieces.

"Wren, don't move," Marin said. "I'll lift you out of there."

Wren was barefoot, surrounded by shards of glass like confetti.

"I'll go check on the bird," Evie said. She was out the door before Marin could respond.

Marin bent carefully over the glass to Wren, lifting her beyond the sharp pieces to safety.

"Wren, please go grab a dustpan and brush so we can clean up the glass," Marin said.

"What if I say no?" Wren said, testing Marin's *very* last nerve.

"You may have blackmailed your sister into letting you do whatever you please, but you haven't blackmailed me," Marin snapped.

"Not yet," she said.

But when she had gone, Marin knelt beside Thea.

"Theadora," Marin said. "What did Evie see in the woods?"

"I can't," Thea said. "You have to talk to Evie."

"I won't be mad, whatever it is."

"I know, Marin. But it's not my secret."

The door opened. Wren had returned with the pan and brush, and Evie was just behind her.

"The bird?" Marin asked.

"It was gone," Evie said. "Must have just been stunned."

Evie stared at the shattered glass, and Marin finally examined the mess as well. The jar must have had a small animal skeleton inside. Maybe a canary. There were a few such displays around Lovelace House.

"Girls, why don't you go play in the greenhouse. Or water the flower beds?" Marin suggested. "We'll clean this up."

They didn't hesitate for a second, practically fleeing from the library.

But Evie stepped away from the mess.

"What's wrong?" Marin asked. "Is it the bones?"

Evie nodded, retreating even farther across the room.

"It's fine, Evie. I've got it."

Maybe Evie was even more sensitive about death than Marin was. Or maybe she was just squeamish.

Marin considered Evie's manicured hands and shoes and bows.

It was possible that Evie just didn't like to get her hands dirty.

Well, that's exactly what she was hired for, Marin thought bitterly, and swept up the mess into a trash can.

"Can you take it right out?" Evie asked.

Marin wanted to tease her for it, but Evie's face was drawn and pale, and despite her frustration with her, Marin didn't press the issue. She took the entire mess of glass and bone downstairs and out to the trash.

When she returned to the library, Evie was curled up in

the large window with her legs tucked to her chest. Marin wasn't sure what was wrong until she heard a soft hiccup.

Evie was crying. Marin had pushed too hard. Whatever Evie had seen in the woods, it had clearly left her shaken.

Marin went to her.

But halfway across the room something sharp pierced through her sock into the soft ball of her foot. Marin cried out and sank to the thick plush carpet.

"Are you okay?" Evie sprang from the window, wiping her eyes.

"I must have missed a shard of glass," Marin said, and Evie reached for her foot, carefully tugging her sock off.

"Yeah, it's way in there," Evie said. "Stay still." And went to get a small case from one of the drawers in the wide walnut desk in the corner.

She opened a sewing kit.

"Can't you just pull it out?" Marin asked.

"No, it's all the way embedded. We could just leave it. It'll come out on its own, or your body will just form some protective scar tissues around it."

"And it will, what, stay there forever?" Marin asked.

Evie shrugged.

"Just get it out," Marin said, and lay back against the carpet. Marin closed her eyes while Evie carefully slipped the needle into her skin, working to get the glass shard to lift out.

"I'm sorry," Evie said, knowing she was hurting her.

"It's fine," Marin said.

Marin looked up at the ceiling of the library, recognizing the tin tiles that crossed her own room. More flower stalks.

Which meant more little skulls.

Perfect.

"Evie," she began. "Why are there tiles of skulls all over the house?"

"What?" Evie asked, glancing up from her task. "Oh." She craned her neck to study the ceiling and then smiled. "Your imagination is getting the best of you, Marin Blythe. Those aren't skulls."

Marin gasped as Evie's needle caught the edge of the glass, shifting it inside her foot.

"Sorry," Evie said. "Those are not skulls. I'll show you in the greenhouse when we're done here, okay?"

It was a few more minutes before Evie set the needle down and reached for a set of tweezers, and Marin felt the shard as it was tugged from her foot.

"Got it," Evie said, dropping the offending scrap into her hand. "Wait."

"What?" Marin asked, sitting up. The piece was bloody.

"It's not glass," Evie said.

Marin looked closer.

Evie was right. It wasn't glass. In her palm was a sliver of broken canary skeleton.

"It's bone."

18

Memento Mori

Evie led Marin through the winding rows of garden. They found Thea and Wren, who were aiming the spraying hoses at each other instead of Evie's flowers and were already soaked straight through.

"Technically the garden is watered," Wren said before Marin could even scold them.

Marin looked to Evie, who shrugged and said, "It's only water. And she's right."

"You're no help," Marin told her, but there was humor tucked in her cheek as she said it.

The Hallowell girls had made malicious compliance an art form.

"C'mon, this way," Evie said, tugging Marin along to the far side of the glass-domed room. "Look there." Evie pointed, and on the ground, Marin saw a small white . . . skull.

She lifted it up.

It was delicate and diaphanous—so paper thin she could almost see through it.

"What is it?"

"A dead snapdragon," Evie said, and gestured to the plant that blossomed in front of them.

Alive, they looked like regular flowers, a brilliant burgundy shade that Marin wanted to capture in a lipstick. It was vibrantly red with violet hues.

But dead and dried, the flower looked like a miniature skull in her hand.

"That pattern on the tiles is snapdragons. Not skulls. But you weren't wrong, they do look alike."

Marin found a flower stalk that was dead on the bottom half, tiny, dried skulls clustered among the leaves. Just like they looked on the tiles.

"I was starting to think that house was haunted," Marin confessed. "Like in one of your mother's books."

Evie picked up another stalk of dead snapdragons with a string of flower skeletons on it, passing it to Marin.

"I suppose the driver was wrong after all," Marin said.

"What driver?"

"The one who dropped me off when I moved here. He said Lovelace House is cursed."

"Why on earth would he say that?" Evie asked.

"Apparently the entire town believes it," Marin said. "Lovelace House has a serious PR problem."

"That's absurd. Lovelace House has never been haunted. Or cursed."

"Let them talk," Marin said. "Who cares what people think?"

But as soon as she said it, Marin knew the answer.

Evie cared.

Evie, who dressed impeccably and slept in curlers and wore flawless makeup even when Marin and Neera and her family were the only people she would see all day.

Evie seemed to care a lot about what people think.

Marin turned the skulls over in her palm. *Flowers*, not skulls. If she'd found these alone in a garden bed, she'd have thought they belonged to a fairy.

Evie reached out then, taking Marin's hand and squeezing it. It was the first time she'd touched her since the orchard. Marin waited for her worries to resurface, the ones that had overwhelmed her just an hour ago in the library. But the fear never came. With Evie's hand gripped tight in her own, Marin simply . . . wasn't scared. There was no monster in the woods. There were no skulls imprinted on the ceiling tiles.

Marin squeezed back, reassuring Evie and letting her keep her secrets.

For now.

Once again, Alice didn't join them for dinner, so Evie and Marin tucked the girls into bed and read them each a book.

The excitement of the day seemed to have finally caught up with them because they were both asleep before Evie even finished the first read through.

Marin carefully climbed off Thea's bed, trying not to disturb her, and Evie did the same.

Outside their room, Evie waved her hand for Marin to follow her, and they went back to the library.

"It's still early. Should we study?" Marin asked, reaching for their stack of notebooks and exam review guides.

"Definitely no studying," Evie said. "Let's just . . . hang out?"

"Relaxing? At Lovelace House? I didn't think I was allowed."

"I won't tell Mother your secrets." Evie wandered around the library, pulling random books off the shelves. "If you won't tell her mine. Aha!"

Evie pulled a particularly thick tome from the shelf and then she opened it up to reveal a compartment inside.

"Sneaky," Marin said, approaching her. Inside the book was a flask, and Marin gasped in mock scandal. "Evie Hallowell, drinking? I wouldn't have thought."

"I contain multitudes," Evie said before taking a swig from the flask. When she offered it to Marin, she took a quick sip too. It was strong, and Marin gasped after it went down, her throat on fire from the cinnamon whiskey.

She turned the flask over in her hands. It was leather and

engraved with the words *Memento Mori*. Marin traced the words with her finger and looked to Evie.

"I've seen this before," Marin said. "What does it mean again?"

Marin remembered. But she wondered if Evie knew it too.

"'Remember, we must die,'" she translated, and then shrugged. "I don't know, it belonged to Father. I stole it from his study when I was fourteen."

Marin returned the flask to Evie, who tucked it back into its hiding spot, on a shelf nearly out of reach for her and out of reach for Wren and Thea.

"Would you play for me?" Marin nodded her head toward the baby grand piano on the far side of the room.

"Oh, um, sure," Evie said.

Marin had listened through the library door, and even muted, Evie's playing had sounded impressive, but Evie hadn't played in front of her before.

Evie smoothed her skirt as she sat down on the bench, and Marin couldn't help but smile at the motion before sitting beside her.

Evie shuffled through a stack of sheet music on the piano—the paper so thin it was nearly transparent—and chose a piece. It wasn't printed music. It was written. And scrawled across the top in Evie's perfect script was the title: *Thea's Lullaby*.

"I wrote this to help with her nightmares."

Evie began to play, and it was like she had chosen only

the sweetest, most melodic light notes for Thea.

The song was soft, playful, precocious. It felt like Thea.

When Evie finished, she shifted the paper back and chose a new one: *Sonata in B Minor (Wren)*. This one didn't have nice notes. But they were interesting and compelling, and sometimes angry.

And Evie was magic. She soared through the music, her fingers slipping across the keys so fast it barely looked like she touched them.

What a waste of time, studying geometry, when Evie could play like *this*.

Now Marin understood what Evie meant about college. She would hate a traditional school. She belonged in a music conservatory, if she belonged anywhere but Lovelace House.

Right now, Marin couldn't imagine her anywhere else beyond this moment in the library, with her hair falling out of its pin on the side of her head, blond curls framing her face and then falling into her eyes.

Marin wanted to move them back so she could see, though it didn't seem to matter. Evie's eyes were closed sometimes as she played. She knew the music by heart.

But Marin reached anyway, like she couldn't help it, and tucked Evie's hair behind her ear, knocking her hair pin loose so it clattered against the keys before falling to the soft carpet below.

Evie stopped playing instantly and turned her face to Marin, so quickly that Marin's hand grazed her cheek before she dropped it in alarm.

"I'm sorry," Marin said. "That was beautiful."

"Thank you," Evie said, but she didn't turn back to the piano.

Marin felt the same pull again—whatever she'd felt in the apple orchard. She recognized it this time. Recognized the desire. She wanted very much to lean in toward Evie. Wanted to kiss her.

But she hesitated, doubt creeping into the tender moment.

Last time, Evie had run away. And Marin didn't want to risk that again.

Then a soft growl sounded beneath the piano. Thisbe crawled out, hackles raised, staring at the door of the library, which was slightly ajar.

"Is anyone there?" Evie called out, her voice ringing out clear as a bell.

There was only silence, but Thisbe didn't settle.

"Shall we go check?" Evie asked Marin, sliding off the piano bench.

"Do you always run toward the danger?" Marin asked, but she moved to follow Evie.

"Do you?" Evie giggled, walking across the room and pulling the door open wide.

Alice Lovelace stood at the door, but she was facing away from them, staring down the hallway.

"Mother?" Evie asked.

Alice ignored her.

Evie reached out, set her hand on Alice's shoulder, who jumped at the touch.

"My goodness, Evangeline," Alice said, turning toward her. "You scared me."

"I scared *you*," Evie said, peering past her mother to look down the hall. "What were you staring at?"

"Oh, it was nothing," Alice said. "I thought I heard something. But it's just an old house. Sometimes its bones need to settle."

Alice didn't look well. Marin saw dark circles under her eyes that hadn't been there a few days ago. She'd been locked away working for so many hours. Now that Marin thought about it, she wasn't sure exactly when she last saw Alice. Had it been two days, or three?

"Why don't I get you some tea?" Evie offered. "You need to sleep. You look exhausted."

"Thank you, Evie," Alice said, and this time she looked right at her.

Marin could see the moment Alice settled back into herself, stopped staring down the hall like she'd seen a ghost. It was the moment something guarded and cold slid into place. "But I'm fine. Just missing your father, as usual."

At that, Evie stepped back like she'd been struck and turned away from Alice. "All right. Good night, then."

Alice left without ever telling them what she had come

to the library for, but Marin didn't intervene and she didn't ask questions. There was something silent and awful in that exchange between Evie and her mother, and Marin didn't understand what it was. But it was the mention of Evie's father that had changed everything in Evie's body language.

Whatever was unsaid between Alice and Evie, it had something to do with Charles Hallowell.

19

Down by the Sea

———————— ❧ ————————

Marin loved teaching the girls to swim.

Every morning she would take them down to the shore to practice, and slowly, surely, they began to trust in their ability. Marin could count their progress in discarded accessories. Thea's spare set of floaties went first, quickly followed by her goggles. Wren's life jacket was next, followed by Thea's primary floaties. And then one morning, all that was left was the little kickboard Thea used to keep her head above water.

When Thea finally braved putting her head all the way underwater, Wren, Neera, and Evie cheered from where they were spectating on the rocks. For the first time since she'd arrived at Lovelace House, Marin felt useful. It became an easy habit for them—rise early, swim to the point of exhaustion. They'd call it a day whenever the tide turned.

High tide was best for swim lessons.

And low tide was best for clam digging.

The morning that Thea gave up her kickboard felt like a graduation of sorts, and afterward, Neera called them all into the kitchen, smiling like she had a secret.

She pointed to a large brown paper bag resting in the kitchen sink.

"Yes!" Thea shouted. "Oh, yum, yum, yum. My *favorite*."

"What is it?" asked Marin.

"Go take a look," Wren said.

Marin walked to the sink and peeked into the bag.

Several large lobsters were crowded inside. She'd never had lobster before, and right now all she could think of was that they looked like very large insects.

"Tonight, we are having a seafood *feast*," Neera announced. "Your mother says she is near the end of this draft, and she needs to get out of that room for a bit, don't you think? Besides, we are celebrating our newest swimmers."

Thea's toothless grin couldn't be beat, and even Wren got caught in the excitement, and Marin heard the rare sound of her laugh more than once as the girls helped prepare. She saw how Wren hurried to gather the things they needed. How excited she was for their mother to emerge and join them again among the living.

Instead of the formal dining room, the girls were sent to set up the conservatory for the meal. Like the greenhouse, it was a structure attached to the house made entirely of glass, but it was much smaller and just off the kitchen, letting sunlight flood both rooms.

"I love the conservatory," Thea said. "Isn't it perfect, Marin?"

Marin had to agree with Thea's assessment. The room was warm, inviting. Thisbe ambled in and collapsed right in a beam of sunlight. Within moments, she was snoring.

"I do. The only conservatory I've ever been in before was as Professor Plum."

Thea laughed, and even Wren smiled.

"We used to have dinner out here all the time before," Thea said.

Wren looked up from where she was carefully folding the napkins and sliding lobster claw rings to hold them in place. *Before.*

The word carried too much weight—for Marin and the Hallowell girls.

"Neera asked us to collect the clams." Marin checked a clock on the conservatory wall. It wasn't a normal clock. Instead, it showed the tides. "It's nearly low tide now. Should we head to the shore?" Marin asked, eager to distract Wren.

They gathered a bucket and two clam rakes—antique, rusted old things that were cumbersome to carry with their long spikes. Then they collected Evie from the library, where she was meant to be reviewing the exam booklet, but she was at the piano, fiddling with the keys and staring off into space.

"Clams!" Thea shouted from the doorway, startling Evie from her reverie.

They all wore pants they could roll up above their knees

and made their way down into the mud flats of the shore.

The low tide had exposed something new washed to shore: an entire pine tree, its remnants now driftwood that belonged to the sea.

Although right now, they just belonged to Thea.

She climbed right onto the tree trunk and leaned over the far end to peer inside.

"Hey, check this out," Thea called.

The others circled the large tree to see what Thea had found.

The entire inside of the tree had been eaten away by water. It was filled with dozens of inverted branches, the pieces left behind after the rotted wood had washed away. It looked like a deep, dark mouth, filled with teeth on all sides.

"It's a sarlacc," Marin said, delighted with the comparison.

"What's a sarlacc?" Wren asked.

"It's that sand pit monster, in *Return of the Jedi.*"

"What's a Jedi?" Thea asked from her perch on the trunk.

"Never mind," Marin said. "Let's find some clams, shall we?"

Evie led the way, pointed down at the mud.

"See the holes? That's where the big ones are. Careful, they spit."

And just as she said it, Marin saw an arch of water spring up from the mud up ahead. And then another.

"They *spit*?" Marin clarified. She'd seen the little water arches before, but she'd had no idea what caused it.

"Sort of," Evie said. "It's a defensive thing. But we don't want those. They are too large."

Evie led Marin and the little girls out farther, to a mud and sand bar that was only exposed in the low tide. That was where she swung her clam rake, sinking its claws into the soft ground. A moment passed and she was reaching in and holding up the clam to show Marin. "This is what we want. Littlenecks."

The clam was like a little white stone in her hand.

Marin joined Evie, digging her clam rake into the mud. It was harder work than she'd anticipated, and soon she was sweating in the summer sun, even with the cold Maine waters at her feet, and her arms began to ache. At one point, Thisbe joined them, and she began to dig furiously in the sand, shooting it up in every direction so that it landed in Thea's hair.

Thea ran away, giggling and splashing in the shallow water.

As Marin worked, she moved farther from the girls, looking for fresh places to dig.

She sank the rake into the mud and pulled again. But this time when she lifted it, there was a large clam crushed right on the end of one of the pikes.

Marin grabbed the ruined clam. When she turned it over, something glittered in the sunlight.

A pearl.

Marin set down the rake and pulled at the broken bits of shell. She'd never actually eaten clams before, and now that she was fingers deep in one, she wasn't sure she ever would.

Her finger reached something hard and round, and she pulled it out. She bent to rinse the pearl in the water and then examined it.

Marin felt a wave a nausea. The ocean waves lapped at her legs, and she felt like they were inside of her too, echoing through her body, deafening her ears with their roar.

It wasn't a pearl.

Marin was holding a human tooth.

She said nothing to Evie, who was working about ten feet away and hadn't noticed anything. Instead, Marin reached into her bucket of collected clams and pulled one out. She set it on a rock, and smashed it open with the rake. She dug through this one and found nothing at all. Too small.

She dug furiously back into mud and sand with her rake. Her muscles now burned, protesting her arduous movements.

She found another large clam

This time when she broke the shell open, the sharp edge of it caught her finger, slicing it open, but Marin kept going, and her fingers found something small and solid inside.

It was another tooth.

Marin felt tears in her eyes and blinked furiously. It didn't make any sense.

How would they have gotten there?

She dug again, ignoring the little clams in favor of the larger ones. This one was empty.

But the next one wasn't.

Another tooth.

And then another after that.

In a few minutes, Marin had collected half a dozen human teeth.

She gritted her own teeth as she smashed open another clam, and finally Evie noticed the ferocity of Marin's swings. Noticed what she was doing to the clams on the rocks.

Marin tried to quell her panic as she swung that rake, feeling it crunch against shell and stone, her thoughts a staccato of anger and fear.

What. *Smash.*

Was wrong. *Smash.*

With this damned house. *Smash.*

And then the rake was pulled from her hands, and she whirled to find Evie standing there in shock. This time, Marin could read Evie's expression perfectly clearly. It said *What in the actual hell are you doing?*

Marin held out her hand, fingertips bloodied and fist clenched, and opened it, showing Evie.

"Teeth. The clams have *teeth* in them."

Evie stepped back, horror crossing her face. "Marin," she began.

But Marin didn't want to hear it. There was something wrong. And Evie was keeping secrets from her.

Marin ran, handful of teeth clasped to her chest. She didn't know why she held on to them. Some part of her wanted the evidence, so when she doubted this was real later, she could hold them and be reminded.

Evie was calling for her, chasing after her, but Marin kept moving. Her feet sank in the mud, making each step a struggle, but when she reached the rocky part of the shore, she ran outright.

Her foot had just hit the bottom of the wooden stairs leading back to the house when she heard Evie cry out behind her.

She turned back.

Evie had tripped while chasing after her.

Marin could see the gash in her knee even from a distance.

Marin stopped running. She put the teeth into her pocket, her chest heaving, and went back to Evie. By now the little girls had caught up, and Thea gasped and turned away from Evie's injury.

"Wren, go get the first-aid kit from the house," Marin said.

She knelt beside Evie and reached for her leg. The gash was deep. Evie must have caught it just perfectly on an outcropping of rock.

"You'll need stitches, I think," Marin said.

She held Evie's hand while they waited for Wren to return, and then Marin sat in front of Evie and wrapped her knee tight.

The bandage was soaked with blood almost immediately.

She helped Evie stand, wrapping her arm around her own shoulders so Evie could hop up the stairs on one leg. It took ages, and Marin was exhausted when they finally reached the top of the steep staircase.

Neera greeted them at the top.

"She needs stitches," Marin said.

"I can do them," Neera assured her, helping Evie into the house.

"You can?" Marin asked.

"We are fairly well prepared for emergencies out here. It takes almost an hour to get to the hospital," Neera explained.

The girls were sent out of the room, but Marin stayed.

If the stitches hurt, Evie didn't let on. She was stone still, the only indication of pain was that she occasionally squeezed Marin's fingers.

Marin herself watched with a kind of grotesque awe as the curved needle slipped in and out of Evie's skin. Neera's fingers were fast and sure, and within a few minutes, it was over. She cleaned and wrapped Evie's knee.

"I'll take clams off the menu," Neera said, gently resting her hand on Evie's shoulder.

"Thank you, Neera," Evie said.

Marin sat across from Evie and reached into her pocket. She dropped the teeth between them on the table.

"Do you know where these came from?" Marin asked.

"No. Truly, Marin. I don't."

"Have you been lying to me?" Marin asked, leaning forward. Something was wrong. All her instincts told her something was wrong with this house.

You worry too much, her mother's voice urged from the depths of her consciousness. Words she had repeated to Marin so frequently in life that they now followed Marin from the grave.

But did she worry *too much*? Or was it just enough?

"No," Evie insisted, her voice almost pleading with Marin. *Stop asking*, it said *Let me be. Let go.* But Marin wasn't done.

"Are you keeping something from me?"

Evie dropped her head in shame.

Marin wanted to let it go. She wanted to sink back into blissful ignorance. She wanted to trust Evie implicitly. But she couldn't do it. Not when every time she tried, some new dark, terrible thing sprouted up in front of her.

"You aren't going to tell me." Marin already knew the answer. Evie couldn't even look at her.

Marin grabbed up the small pile of teeth, refusing to abandon the one piece of real proof that something was deeply wrong at Lovelace House, and she left Evie alone. Her secrets could keep her company today.

20

Children Shouldn't Play with Dead Things

———————— 🜸 ————————

A month before Marin's arrival at Lovelace and just days before Cordelia's untimely death, Marin's mother had woken her before school, hours early. She perched on the edge of Marin's bed, clutching something tightly in her hand.

"What is this?" Cordelia asked, her voice piercing and sharp in the soft morning quiet.

"That is what is commonly known as a piece of paper," Marin said, rolling away from her mother, pulling the comforter up over her head.

"Where did you get it?" Cordelia had pressed, tugging the blankets down. Marin finally sat up, responding to the urgency in her mom's voice, squinting at the paper.

"Library," she told her, flipping it to where the invitation was printed. "It's just a book signing, with that author you used to know. Lovelace. She's coming to San Diego this weekend."

Cordelia sat back on her feet, kneeling on the edge of

the bed. In the corner of the invitation was Alice's author photo, and she stared for a minute.

"No one mailed this to you?" she asked.

"No," Marin said. "The librarian gave it to me since I read all of her books."

"All right," Cordelia said, and Marin saw her relax. "What if instead we go up to Portland this weekend? We can take the train." Marin sleepily agreed, and Cordelia set the invitation by the bedside table and curled up next to Marin, wrapping her arms around her, kissing her forehead. "Sorry, baby, get some sleep."

Marin woke with a start in her bed at Lovelace House, the warmth of her mother's kiss still tattooed on her skin. It wasn't a dream this time. It wasn't *the* dream. It was a memory.

It was still the middle of the night. Moonlight streamed in from the windows and across her bed. Marin reached for the book that had been pushed to the edge of her mattress— the one she had fallen asleep reading the night before. She opened it to the last bookmarked page. This was the same book that she'd been in the middle of reading that weekend, and she'd tucked the invitation to Alice's book signing in to hold her page.

She'd loved this Alice Lovelace novel so much that she'd stolen it from the library, the evidence of her crime on its stickered spine. She read the book until that spine had cracked. Until a small chunk of pages at the front of the book could lift right out, and Marin had attempted to tape them back in with middling success.

She'd forgotten that conversation with her mom, and as hard as she tried now, she couldn't make sense of it. Her mother had been so upset.

But Cordelia had done so many things that confused Marin. Like insisting they get out of town that weekend, frantically pulling things into bags. It was the *over*packing that tipped Marin off. This wasn't a weekend trip. Cordelia was bolting again. Uprooting them on a moment's notice. Whisking Marin off to another new town, another new school.

A new destination they never reached after the train derailed.

Marin heard a scratching sound. She set the book down and listened. For a while, she'd kept her windows shut tight at night, afraid another animal would find its way into her room. But tonight it had been too hot to sleep, and she'd tossed and turned for hours before kicking off her sheets and opening the windows, desperate for the cool breeze off the ocean.

Maybe that had been a mistake.

There it was again.

The shuffling sound came from the floor, louder and closer than the first time. Marin looked around. She didn't have anything besides the book to throw at whatever made the noise, but her bedroom door was ajar.

For a moment, she thought of just bolting for the hallway.

Marin thought of all the horror novels she'd read. All the scary movies she'd watched with her mother, when they would scream and throw popcorn at the television when a girl decided to go investigate a strange noise.

Boo, Marin could almost hear Cordelia now. *Don't look. Run!*

Marin had to look.

She leaned over the side of her bed, book raised like a small weapon.

"Hi, Marin," Thea said from where she crouched on the floor beside Marin's bed.

"Thea!" Marin squeaked. She cleared her throat and tried again. "Thea. What are you doing? You scared me."

"Sorry, Marin. I'm just hungry."

"Thea, it's so late. What happened to your lobster feast?"

Marin herself had skipped the seafood feast in the conservatory. She knew she wouldn't be able to bring herself to eat anything after what had happened with the clams.

"We were uninvited. Wren and I got into an argument and Mother had a migraine and she got *so* angry, and she sent us to bed without supper."

"Wait, so you didn't eat anything at all?" The punishment seemed so extreme for a sibling argument. On cue, Marin's stomach protested, grumbling over the meal she'd missed too.

Maybe a midnight snack wasn't the *worst* idea.

"Let's go," Marin said. She swung her legs out of bed, ignoring the little brush of fear that tingled up her calves at the thought of the dark space under her bed. It was Thea. Only Thea. There was nothing else crawling around her room.

Not this time.

She placed her hands on Thea's little shoulders, directing her out into the hall, and as they passed the girls' room, Thea slipped in to see if Wren wanted to come too.

In the kitchen, Marin gathered the girls on stools at the kitchen island.

"So what would you like?" she asked.

"Pancakes!" Thea said.

"No," Marin answered decisively. "Oh, I know just the thing. My mom used to make this for me." Marin grabbed a loaf of bread and popped a few slices into the toaster. She put together her favorite comfort food in silence, with the girls watching her curiously.

Marin spread butter onto the toast and then sprinkled sugar and cinnamon on top.

"Cinnamon toast," she said, presenting it to the girls.

They stared at it.

"I know it's no fancy fresh-caught lobster, but come on, give it a chance." Marin nudged the plate closer.

"It does smell pretty good," Thea said.

"This was my dessert when I was growing up, when we

couldn't afford anything else," Marin explained.

There was a noise at the doorway, and Evie entered.

"Did we wake you?" Marin asked.

"I heard the pitter-patter of little feet pass my doorway." Evie climbed onto a stool beside her sisters. "I figured you two were starving."

"Would you like some?" Marin reached for the bread when Evie nodded. She made some toast for herself and Evie, and they perched beside the girls.

"What is it?" Evie asked.

"Marin was just telling us about how she was so poor they ate this for dessert."

"Thea, don't be rude."

Wren tried it first. "Mmm. I think I like struggle toast."

"Cinnamon toast," Marin corrected.

"I know what I said," Wren said with an impish grin.

"Fine. Struggle toast. But it's the best dessert. Or breakfast. Or midnight snack when your mother neglects to *feed* you."

"Fair point," Evie said, smiling into her next bite.

Twenty minutes later, they'd settled the girls back into bed and pulled their door shut.

"We should talk," Evie said. "I didn't mean to keep you in the dark, Marin. It's just . . . it isn't easy for me. To let someone in. Lovelaces aren't good at . . . this." Evie gestured to the small space between them, and despite her frustration, despite her fear and worry, Marin felt a surge of relief and hope at the movement. This. Us. Evie felt it too.

"What about Hallowells?" Marin asked. "Are they good at this?"

Evie smiled.

"Actually, yes. They really are. But it's late. Tomorrow? After breakfast? We can ask Neera to keep the girls for a bit, so we can really talk."

"Tomorrow," Marin said.

Marin never fell back to sleep. It was just as well because she didn't expect she'd get lucky twice in one night with regard to her nightmare. At dawn, she gave up on sleep and rose for the day, throwing back her curtain to find a shoreline drenched in fog, with gray clouds hanging heavy in the sky.

What a dreary day.

She slipped on her shoes, gathered Thisbe from the girls' bedroom for company, and wandered down to the water. It was still crisp and cool outside this early, despite it being mid-July. She expected rain clouds would roll in soon after the fog.

She still wasn't used to the kinds of storms they had up here in the northeast. She'd lived in places that had hurricanes and flash floods and even tornadoes, but nowhere with the violent thunderstorms that shook all of Lovelace when they arrived.

She wasn't used to them. But she loved them.

It would be a rainy day indoors, and she'd have to find new ways to entertain the girls, and on very few hours of sleep. The memory of her mother had left Marin longing for her. And she felt the distinct ache of wanting to be comforted.

Thisbe was oblivious to the chill in the air and splashed right into the cold tide pools. Marin laughed and slipped off her shoes, following the lumbering creature to play.

Marin had also learned she loved dogs. Or rather, one dog. *This* dog. She rolled up her pajama bottoms and went in after her, splashing in the shallow pools of water.

She spent over an hour on the shore, but the sun never rose—the sky was too overcast. And the fog was stubborn on the water, so much that Marin couldn't see ten yards out even as the tide retreated.

As the water left and rocks were exposed, they looked like tombstones rising from the ground.

Suddenly Thisbe began to bark and paw furiously at the water's edge. Marin walked over, her feet sinking in the mud with each step, and found water bubbling up where Thisbe was digging. An underwater spring, maybe, pushing water to the surface.

But Thisbe wouldn't let up. She kept digging and barking at the little pool of water until finally Marin gave up tugging on her collar and dropped to her knees to help.

They shifted through the mud and sand, casting aside clam shells as they went.

Finally, Thisbe stopped, sniffing at something white sticking out of the muck.

Marin grabbed the edge of it and pulled, but it was stuck tight.

She sank her hands into the mud, feeling around for the bottom of the object, and pulled again. It came loose with a sickening squelch. She rinsed the mud off it and held it up for a better look.

It was an entire mandible.

Marin dropped it back into its watery grave.

She stared at the water, debating whether to pull it back out. Instead, she scooped at the mud in great handfuls, sinking the mandible back down until it was buried once more.

She called for Thisbe and began to climb up the winding wooden stairs back to the house.

It was time to have that talk with Evie.

Marin swept through the house to her room. She was still in her pajamas and felt this conversation deserved more dignity than her mother's T-shirt and a pair of muddy sweatpants.

But her door was wide-open, and she heard the little girls before she rounded the doorway.

"Are you sure it's dead?" Thea's voice whispered, holding a tone of reverence that Marin had never heard before.

"Oh, it's dead," Wren answered, her voice also hushed.

Marin slipped into the room. The girls were sitting on

the floor at the foot of her bed, and in Wren's hand was a mangled, bloody mourning dove.

It was the exact same kind she'd found in her closet her first night at Lovelace.

And maybe the same creature that had flown out of her window and left a trail of blood behind more recently.

Marin had been blaming the dog. *She likes to leave presents*, Wren had told her. Marin assumed the dog was hunting birds, leaving them half-dead in her room occasionally.

But now she saw it wasn't Thisbe. Thisbe had been with her.

It was Wren and Thea.

"What is this?" Marin asked.

Wren gasped and stood, the dead bird still clutched in her hands. One of its wings was torn half-off. Its little feet were curled in, and its neck was twisted the wrong way.

"Wren, pranks are one thing, but *this*." Marin felt sickness churning in her stomach at the sight before her. The little girls were strange, and sometimes even mean, but this was entirely different.

"I didn't," Wren said, but Marin held up her hand.

"What are you doing with it?" she asked. She imagined them planting it in her room as another gruesome discovery.

"Practicing. But we didn't kill it," Thea insisted. "We just found it in here when we came to wake you."

"I thought it was the dog all this time. I thought Thisbe

was leaving birds in here. But it's been you."

"It hasn't!" Wren insisted, even as she clutched the dead bird tighter in her hands. Marin wanted to believe her. She really did. But the ease with which Wren handled the mutilated creature was stealing her reason.

"You said death is natural, Marin. You said it's just part of life," Wren pointed out. And it was true. In the woods, with the doll and then the baby deer's body. She'd told them that to reassure them. "You said it even has *beauty* in it."

"Well, it also has germs in it. Put it down."

There was a creak of a floorboard behind her, and just as Marin turned to see Evie approaching them, already dressed for the day in an ivy-colored dress with matching green boots, Wren stepped closer.

"Fine," she said defiantly, and reached out to her older sister.

Evie put her hand out before she even saw what it was, and the dead dove landed on her outstretched palm.

"*Rowena Hallowell*," Marin began. She knew how squeamish Evie was. How just the idea of going into the graveyard had sent her sprinting back to the house. Wren's unkindness was—

Marin saw a movement in Evie's hands.

The bird twitched. Its good wing fluttered, began to flap.

Its bones protruded from the wound on its side, and Marin watched as those bones shifted, pulled by small tendons that were lifeless just a moment ago.

Marin moved to take the monstrosity from Evie, but Evie was faster.

She dropped the thrashing bird onto the floor and brought the heel of her boot down on the creature, swift and sure and without hesitation, crushing its skull.

21

Sweet Lark, I Will Pluck You

B lood slipped out from beneath Evie's heel. It was thick, viscous, and congealed, and it seemed to move in slow motion, spilling across the floorboards.

There were flecks of it across the toe of Evie's other boot, the velvet sage green now marred by crimson dots that evidenced the violence of her actions.

"What was that?" Marin tried to control the shaking in her voice.

She failed, but it didn't matter. Evie didn't even look at her. Didn't acknowledge that she'd spoken.

"Wren, I'll need an old towel. And the bleach."

Wren shot off in an instant at Evie's request, and Thea just stood with round saucer eyes, staring at Evie's boots and the protruding corpse of the bird.

Marin moved to her, pulling her in and turning her in one movement. But any attempt to shield her from the moment was coming far too late.

"What the hell was that?" Marin asked again, and this time Evie looked up. She'd been staring at the floor, just the same as Thea, as though in a trance.

"I'm so sorry you had to see that, Marin." Evie's voice was steady.

"Evie." Thea looked up to her oldest sister. "You have to tell her."

"Yes, I know," Evie said.

Wren returned with some rags and bleach and one of the dog towels, and Evie took it and covered her boot before pulling it away from the bird. She quickly wrapped up the body, tucking the ends in when a few feathers stuck out.

"I've got it," Wren said, taking it from Evie.

"Don't be silly, I can do it." Marin stepped forward to take the dead animal from Wren, but Evie held up a hand.

"She's used to it, Mare, let her go." Evie's voice was soft but firm.

She'd never used a nickname for Marin before, and it hung in the air like an offering.

Evie dropped to her knees, just beyond the edge of the thickened blood on the wooden floorboards, and began to pour bleach over it, scrubbing it away.

Within minutes, the bird was gone, and the area was impeccable once more. If Marin focused very hard on the grain of the wooden floor, she thought she could see a slight variation in color where the blood had been.

Or maybe it was the light.

Either way, the girls had done a good job.

They were quick, efficient. Practiced.

She's *used* to it.

She's used to *it*.

The implication was that Wren was used to whatever had just transpired there. That she was used to cleaning up the aftermath. Disposing of the body. Washing bloodstains off floorboards.

"We'll be in the library," Thea said, and just like that, the girls were gone through the door, refusing to take part in whatever reckoning was rising between Evie and Marin.

For a heartbeat, Marin wanted to run too.

She wanted to forget what she had just seen. Forget the mandible and the teeth she discovered at the shore. Forget the monster in the woods that had been feasting on the baby deer. She wanted to forget that the last time she was alone with Evie; she hadn't confronted her about all the strangeness at Lovelace, all the secrets she knew Evie was keeping from her. All she had wanted was to be near her. To talk with her. Listen to her play piano. Maybe one day hold her hand. With Evie, none of it mattered, and somewhere along the way, Marin had leaned into that feeling, barely able to call it by name until now. Evie felt *safe*. And Marin was terrified that everything was about to change. Terrified that Evie's great secret would be a loose thread, ready to snag on something sharp and unravel their carefully woven tapestry.

But Marin was also afraid to turn away from Evie in this moment. She thought that if she started running from Lovelace, she'd never stop. Just like her mother. Running forever, rootless, homeless. And Marin was tired of that. Marin didn't want to be alone anymore.

Marin couldn't run from Evie, nor did she want to.

"Can we go somewhere else?" Evie asked. She toed the floor with a bloody boot, and Marin understood.

"Greenhouse?" She suggested Evie's favorite place intentionally, and Evie must have known, because for the first time today, she gave Marin a small, grateful smile and led the way downstairs.

The greenhouse was gray today, filled with shadows in the ferns and plants. At some point in the morning, it had started to storm outside. But Marin hadn't even noticed the rain until they stepped into the greenhouse and could hear every drop pinging off the glass. Through the ceiling, Marin could see the dark storm clouds above. It was dreary, an aberration of the greenhouse's typical bright light and color.

Lightning briefly illuminated every shadow in the greenhouse, but in the eerie light, the largest plants looked like creatures climbing out of the earth, their branches and leaves like extended arms reaching for her. The thunder crashed a moment later, rattling the earth, the glass, Marin herself, and she shivered, even though it wasn't cold.

Evie was suddenly there beside her, drying her hands on a dish towel.

She must have just rinsed off any blood left from the bird.

Seeing Evie like this—hair placed carefully back into place, and a thin nervous smile set ever so perfectly on her polite lips—it would have been entirely too easy for Marin to dig no further, ask no questions.

But they'd come too far to ignore it now, and they both knew it.

"It was never the house, Marin," Evie said. She was clasping her hands so tight together that Marin could see where the crescents of her nails dug into her own skin. "It isn't Lovelace that is haunted. It's me."

"Haunted?" Marin didn't understand what Evie was saying.

"Haunted. Cursed. I don't know. I never knew what to call it." Evie's small laugh was harsh, biting. "Mother calls it *a gift*. But it certainly isn't that either."

"So what exactly is it?" Marin wanted Evie to be clear.

"I bring things back. Dead things. We didn't realize until I was two. I found a dead mouse in the library. They said she screamed when she saw it in my little hands. And then she screamed again when it sprang back to life."

Marin glanced around the greenhouse. "Are the girls out here? Are they in on all of this? It's one thing for them to prank me, but for you to do it, too, I just—"

"Marin, it isn't a prank. I'm not lying. You *saw* it upstairs."

"I don't know what I saw upstairs. It was just—it was a dead bird. Thisbe has left them in my room before."

"You know that's not what it was."

She was right. And suddenly, Marin's chest felt too tight. She tried to suck in air but it only left her chest feeling hollow, numb, as she gasped for breath.

"I can't breathe," Marin said, doubling over, and Evie was there, starting to rub circles on the small of her back. It was so instantly soothing, but that realization only made Marin even more upset. The sudden comprehension that she needed Evie, followed by the immediate crashing fear of all that could entail.

It was too much.

"Please don't touch me." Marin snapped the words out, and the hand fell away.

Instead of leaving, Evie murmured to her, words low and soft, encouraging Marin to match her own deep breaths. After a few minutes, Marin's breathing normalized, and she opened her eyes.

She'd never gotten through a panic attack this quickly before.

"Does this happen often?" Evie's voice was so gentle.

Marin thought of her first day at Lovelace House and the wounded bird locked in her closet. Running cold water on the back of her neck to make it subside.

"It's been a little while," she answered softly.

Evie's boots were right there, ruined by bloody flecks. Marin *did* know what she saw upstairs. But it was impossible.

"Impossible," she echoed aloud as she stood upright again. She'd imagined a thousand impossible scenarios in her life. Every worst-case scenario. And even she couldn't have foreseen *this*, not by instinct or anxiety or imagination.

But she'd seen it firsthand. That dead bird came back to life in Evie's hands. She'd watched as Evie brought down a vicious heel to crush it dead once more.

Knowing what she saw and understanding it were two different things.

"You bring dead things back to life." It wasn't a question; Marin just needed to test the absurdity of it on her own tongue.

Evie was still standing a few feet away, giving Marin the space she had asked for. Marin wasn't sure if it was Evie who had changed, or if Marin just knew her better now. But this time when she looked at Evie, Marin saw the moment that her careful facade slipped into place like a mask. This time it was a fraction of a second too late, and Marin had already seen the naked fear on her face for a moment before Evie hid it away, a gesture as practiced for her as fixing her hair or smoothing her skirt.

But Marin saw it.

Evie was terrified.

Marin grabbed her hand and pulled her along, weaving

through the rows of the greenhouse until they were in the very back, among the snapdragons. Not far from the corpse flower, which seemed to grow faster every day, its single bloom huge, its stench permeating.

"Show me." Marin wanted proof.

"You've seen it."

"Again."

Marin knelt down in the soil, searching. She found a dead butterfly, delicate as a tissue, with a hole in one wing. She was about to hand it to Evie, and as soon as she moved closer, Evie reached out, but before she'd even touched it, Marin felt the change. The butterfly shook, tickling the palm of Marin's hand, and shivered back to life. It tried to flap its useless wing but couldn't fly. It was alive.

But also not.

"I used to have to touch something dead for it to work. That's why I had gloves on, in that photo? Father insisted I wear them. But now . . ." Evie gestured to the butterfly in Marin's palm. "It's changing. Now I just have to be near it."

Marin looked around the greenhouse.

Neera kept remarking that it was thriving now that Evie was home to care for it. But it wasn't just thriving. It was exploding in growth. It was as though nothing in there had died in weeks, and Marin could see how the branches overwhelmed each other.

Evie spent so much time in here. Her presence alone was

enough to spur this wild, spontaneous growth. To create a room so full of life it could barely contain it.

"It's unnatural," Evie said, even as Marin came to the exact opposite conclusion.

Evie took the struggling butterfly from Marin. She crumpled it in her hand. "'All that lives must die.' Besides, bringing it back doesn't make it well. I can't fix what's broken. It's just suffering. Like the bird. This isn't life. It's . . . something else."

"Is that why you killed the bird? The butterfly? To spare them pain?"

"They won't die again on their own. But the way they move? Their cries if they can still make sounds? They're so awful, Marin. They wake confused. They're in pain. I can't leave them like that."

Marin knew that this moment was crucial. This was what Evie had been hiding. What Wren had blackmailed her over—a secret so strange that Evie buried it away. And like the flowers budding all around her, this moment was ephemeral. Fleeting. She could either accept Evie, or she could run from her.

Marin shifted on her heels, studying the strange, ethereal creature in front of her. She could think of any number of words that might apply to her. Witch. Reaper. Necromancer.

But Marin didn't see any of those things.

All Marin could see was the worry trembling Evie's lower lip. The way her pearl barrette had slipped down the side of her head, hanging on a few loose strands of hair, ready to fall at the slightest provocation. It was the purple shadows under her eyes, telling Marin that even if Evie claimed everything was fine, something kept her up at night.

These little flaws were reassuring. They told Marin that despite her dark ability, even in the midst of this awful revelation, Evie was just a girl. A tired, lonely girl.

Marin reached for her.

22

Birds of a Feather

Evie sank into the soil beneath the snapdragons, and Marin followed her down.

"It's okay," Marin murmured, her arms wrapped tight around Evie. "It's okay. You aren't alone."

Marin's gaze dropped to Evie's lips. She leaned in, slightly, with a question filling the space between them.

But it was Evie who closed the distance.

Her lips were warm, and Marin was overwhelmed by cinnamon—first the taste of it on Evie's mouth and then the scent of it like a cloud hovering around her from her perfume.

Kissing Evie was everything Marin had imagined in the apple orchard. In the library. It was mesmeric, and Marin felt she was a moth drawn in by the promise of warmth and light. Helpless against its pull. Afterward, Marin couldn't have said who initiated the second kiss, or the one after that, but she was suddenly down in the dirt with Evie, hands tangled in her curls, twisting and unraveling them. It was thrilling to make a mess of them. Evie was pulling her closer yet, like the fraction of a centimeter separating them was still too much distance.

With Evie's lips on hers, Marin felt her mind go deliciously blank of the crowd of worrying thoughts that constantly harassed her. There was only Evie.

Outside the storm raged on, and the greenhouse was dark except for the lamps that lined the wall. But the looming plants no longer felt threatening. Marin felt like they were inside the green-gold chrysalis that Evie had shown her weeks ago in these same gardens, protected on all sides. And here, with Evie, Marin was melting down into something she didn't recognize. Something joyful, free, and alive.

They were caterpillar soup, and Marin laughed at the thought, and Evie chased the laughter on her lips, kissing her deeply, and for the first time in her life, Marin wasn't caught up in thoughts about the past or the future—she only existed now.

Maybe it was the dark magic in Evie's hands, bringing Marin fully back to life. Marin, who had felt grief like it was woven into her and fear ever present in her mind, dictating her every waking thought and choice. The words "what if" had been her constant companion and a constant threat to her peace.

All of that dissipated with Evie's touch.

And then everything went dark.

Evie broke away.

"That's the power going out," Evie said. "The girls will be scared."

"Damn, you're right." Marin scrambled to her dirt-stained knees and looked at Evie, who was—well, Evie was a mess. She had cried earlier, and her eyes were still red-rimmed, her hair tangled.

But she was smiling. And she looked lighter than ever as she took Marin's hand and stood beside her. She didn't smooth out her dress or dust off the dirt.

"Come on, they're probably desperate to find out if you stuck around or are halfway into town already."

Marin liked the way Evie didn't let go of her hand, only tucked it into a fold of her dress.

They hurried up the stairs, but halfway to the top, Evie pulled Marin in close and stole a few more kisses, their feet tangling together so that they tripped onto the stairwell with a thud.

When the older girls finally stumbled up the last stair, they saw Thea outside of the library. She was standing perfectly still, staring into the room, and she turned and put her finger to her lips to quiet them. Something in Thea's gaze sobered Marin instantly.

She crept forward, slowly peering around the doorway.

Alice was standing very still, directly in front of Wren,

who was sitting by the window at their board game table. The storm had darkened the room in shadow, but Wren was completely still as well, as though she'd frozen in place.

Then lightning flashed, and Marin saw a glint of metal.

Alice was gripping the belly of a hatchet.

"Thea, what's wrong with your mother?" Marin's voice was so soft, she wasn't sure Thea heard her at all.

"That isn't mother," Thea answered.

Evie reached the doorway, and Marin heard the sharp intake of breath when she saw Alice. Evie placed a hand on Marin's shoulder, wordlessly telling her to stay.

Marin wrapped an arm around Thea as they watched Evie slowly cross the room toward her mother.

"Thea," Marin whispered. "Where is Neera?"

They needed help.

"She left. She went into town to run a few errands."

Marin could only watch as Evie shifted her feet until she was finally between Alice and Wren.

"Mother." Evie's voice was so soft, whispered like a prayer, her eyes never leaving the blade. "Mother, what's wrong?"

Evie reached for the hatchet, but the moment her fingers touched Alice's on the handle, Alice startled and lifted it high above her head.

When she swung downward, Marin screamed, and turned away with Thea in her arms so she wouldn't see.

A loud thunk echoed across the library.

Marin peeked through her hair and saw that the hatchet was buried in the table, and Evie had pulled Wren away.

Alice stepped back, and a moment later, the lights flickered on.

"Evie?" Alice's chest was heaving, her breathing labored. "What happened?"

"You . . . you broke the board game. You scared us."

Alice looked around at the hatchet sunk into the table. "I would never. I would never hurt you."

"We know." Wren whipped around Evie and threw her arms around Alice's middle. "We know that."

But Evie looked less certain. She stepped forward and peeled Wren off their mother.

"Take Thea to your room," Evie said.

Thankfully, for once, Wren didn't object or push back. She simply released Alice and came to collect Thea.

Once they were safely down the hall, Marin walked into the library.

Alice looked bewildered and then, in a flash, angry. "How dare you make them afraid of me?"

"You did that on your own." Evie was defiant, but it was more than that. Marin heard the almost imperceptible tremble in Evie's voice. She was scared too.

"I'm exhausted," Alice said, and dropped her face into the palms of her hands. "My head aches so badly."

And then Evie approached her mother, slowly, putting

herself between Alice and the table. Evie lifted her arms and folded them around her mother. "You need to take a break, Mother. The writing can wait."

Alice shook her off.

"Everything was perfect. Everything was perfect until he died. *You* did this to me. You made me alone. You have this *gift*, Evie. And you didn't even save him. You ungrateful brat." Marin stepped closer, moving to Evie, eager to shield her from the vitriol her mother was shedding.

"You were right there, Evie. You were right there and you could have saved him, and you didn't. Why didn't you save him?"

Marin watched Evie crumble.

"He *hated* this." Evie held up her hands. "He made me pretend it wasn't real. He never would have wanted to be brought back."

"You don't know that," Alice said. "You took him from me. It should have been you."

Evie moved back as though she'd been struck.

Alice turned on her heel and swept out of the library.

Marin stood in the shadows, feeling more like an intruder in this house than ever. She went to Evie slowly, as though she were a wild creature that might startle away.

"Evie, are you okay?"

Evie sniffled, her nose bright red, and there were tears in her eyes, but she hadn't shed a single one. "I'm fine, Marin.

She's grieving. She didn't mean it."

"No, I can't imagine she did."

"She always hated that." Evie gestured at the table, where the Winterthur game still lay there with the hatchet sunk in it. "She and my grandmother, their relationship was very complicated. Besides that, I've been pulling the Tower for her all week."

"What?"

"Everyone always worries about Death. But Tower is my worst draw. And when I ask about Mother, I always turn that damned card over. Crisis. Danger. Destruction. That's all I can see for her right now."

"Evie, stop talking about the tarot cards." Marin stepped forward, but Evie stepped back, maintaining the distance between them.

"She's right, you know. I could have brought him back."

"It was just an accident, Evie. Accidents happen." Marin reached for her.

"Stop it!" Evie shouted, pulling away from Marin, crossing to the bookshelves. "I was right there, Marin. We washed ashore together. But he hated this. He told me never to use it. That it was dark and awful and unnatural. He begged me to keep it under control. And he made me swear—" Evie hiccupped and wiped furiously at her face.

Marin didn't even know when the tears had started to spill over.

"He made me swear to never bring him back."

"Evie." Marin crossed the library, but she didn't touch her. She didn't want to corner her there, but she didn't know what to say that could comfort her either.

"He died saving me," Evie said. "I wasn't wearing a life jacket. It was so stupid. I was never a strong swimmer. And he knew that. There was a storm, and I fell in. He didn't even hesitate. He jumped in, and he pushed me back toward the wrecked boat."

"You don't have to tell me if you don't want."

"I want to," Evie said. "He went under right when I turned. I couldn't reach him. When I woke up, we were on shore; he was right there, but he was gone. And I wanted to save him. I wanted to make it right, but I swore to him, Marin. I promised I would never do that."

Evie opened her eyes. They were so dark brown they nearly looked black, reminding Marin of a shark. Her gaze was dark and intelligent and shining with the threat of tears.

"You didn't do anything wrong, Evie. It isn't your responsibility to protect everyone."

"Don't be absurd, Marin. Of course it is." Evie stalked from the library, as wild and angry as the storm on the sea outside, and Marin let her go.

The hatchet was still buried in the table, the girls' board game ended midplay. It was the one their grandmother had made for them, only now it was destroyed, the blade sunk right through the center of it.

She reached for the metal game pieces and lined them up one by one on the windowsill like little tin soldiers. The dwarf. The elf. The warrior. It wasn't until all the pieces were safely stored in the window that Marin realized it.

Charles Hallowell's piece was missing. Marin would bet anything it was tucked in Wren's pocket, safely hidden from her mother.

"This damn family," she murmured, wrenching the hatchet from the table.

23

Dead Dove: Do Not Touch

———————— ❧ ————————

That night at Lovelace House, Marin fell asleep and drowned.

It began with her standing in the tide pools, a mist covering the low tide, thick enough that she couldn't see her feet. And then she felt the slide of fingers around her ankles, holding her in place.

The tide came in, too fast, and she called for help, but no one came. There was a seagull perched on a rock nearby, carefully tap-tap-tapping against a clamshell, ticking away seconds as Marin struggled to escape the tide. When the waves lapped over her face, she gasped, inhaling water.

Marin sat up in her bed, soaked in a cold sweat. Something was tapping at her window in the dark, and Marin crossed the room and unlocked it.

It was another dove. Its eyes were milk white. And when Marin lifted the bird, she saw that its entire bottom half was decomposed, down to the skeleton. She watched the delicate latticework of bones twitch in her hands. *It's another nightmare. Wake up.*

She stood there with her feet rooted to the floor. Moonlight streamed in, illuminating every grotesque feature of the bird. It called out its mourning song, just once, its final coos echoing off the tin ceiling of Marin's room.

Marin gripped its head in one hand, the top of its body in the other.

She twisted, wringing its neck, and felt the bird's jerky, unnatural twitches stop instantly. She laid it on her desk, closed and locked her window, unwilling to invite any more death into her room that night, and crawled back into bed.

In the morning, Marin hurried out of bed to the desk. There was no sign of the bird, and Marin's relief was acute.

It had been another nightmare.

Marin went to check on the girls and found their door wide-open and the room empty. But in the corner of the room was a small, boxy old television that hadn't been there before. A wire ran from the television to a video camera.

Marin turned on the camera and pressed play.

The television screen lit up with images.

There was no sound, but when Marin tried to turn the volume up, it didn't work. The camera was missing one of the connecting wires.

It was a home video.

It was taken down on the rocks, at low tide, and the

camera zoomed in on the two small figures ankle deep in the mudflats. Wren looked to be about five, and Thea no more than four. They wore swimsuits and floppy sun hats, though with the camera still zoomed in on her, Wren tore her hat off and dropped it into the water.

A tall figure rushed forward, sweeping the hat from the ocean before it floated away and then lifting Wren into her arms and spinning her.

For a moment, Marin thought it was Evie. The woman's long white-blond curls were the same as hers. But then she turned her head and the screen showed Alice's profile. She was nearly unrecognizable, her smile bright, her lipstick a summery shade of pink.

And then another girl entered the landscape. She stood back from Alice and the little girls, perched on the balls of her feet on one of the taller rocks.

The first thing Marin noticed was Evie's gloves. They went all the way up to her elbows, though one had slipped down and was scrunched at her wrist.

Suddenly Alice came running toward the camera, blocking the entire screen, a joyful laugh on her lips. The camera was jostled, and then Marin saw Charles Hallowell.

He was tall, with dark hair and a carved jawline. His gaze looked serious at first, but it softened when it fell on the woman behind the camera.

On Alice.

Charles crossed to Evie and, without saying a word, tugged her fallen glove back to her elbow.

Evie glared at him and pulled the gloves from her hands, one after the other, and dropped them pointedly into the mud before turning and making her way toward the house.

Alice filmed her walking away, filmed Neera rising from the stairs and wrapping her arm around Evie's shoulders. Alice must have stood, the camera angle shifting with her, but Neera waved her away and guided Evie up toward the house.

The camera was then set down on the rocks, facing the little girls as they played in the mud, and Marin was left wishing for that missing cord, so she could hear the conversation that took place that day between Alice and Charles.

Marin turned off the camera and knelt there.

Alice had been so different. She was laughing in that video and playing with the girls. Marin had seen the look she gave Charles when he aimed the camera at her face, the way her love for him was there in her eyes, in the easy comfort of her smile, in the lazy, happy way she approached him.

Marin sat there a moment, trying to reconcile the Alice in the home video with the one with hollow eyes and a missing smile, who had sunk her hatchet into the table next to Wren. This other Alice had been in love, and it had changed her for the better. It had brought out the light in her—the humanity. When Charles died, the darkness took over. It crept into the spaces carved out by grief like a toxic black mold.

Marin suddenly understood Alice in a way she never had before.

Alice didn't just want Charles back.

She wanted that part of herself that he took with him when he drowned.

When Marin returned to her bedroom, she noticed another rolled-up slip of paper had been slid under her door. She must have walked right over it earlier.

Marin opened the note.

Meet me in the orchard.

Before leaving, Marin tucked the note into the drawer of her side table, where she'd kept the others Evie had left for her. The tiniest little slips of paper, each one rolled tight, each one tied with a precise bow. How long had she been collecting memories of Evie? Since the very first moment?

It was a beautiful day, the storm from yesterday having cleared every cloud from sight, and if Evie was already out-side, she likely took the girls with her.

Marin gave Alice's wing a wide berth, going down the back stairs that led directly to the kitchen. After leaving the library yesterday, Marin had stood dumbly for several minutes with the hatchet in hand, trying to decide what to do with it.

In the end she'd hidden it behind her bedside table.

In the orchard, Marin found Evie in an apple tree, biting into one of the dark red fruits. She was in a violet skirt and a loose button-down oxford, and she was reading a book, held open by one gloved hand.

"Marin," she said, dropping the apple core and shutting the book.

"You should have woken me," Marin said, grabbing a branch and swinging up beside Evie.

"Why? You needed to rest. Yesterday was a lot to process."

"You need rest too," Marin said, her hand reaching out to brush against Evie's face. The dark circles under her eyes were worse than ever, and Evie was pale.

"I'm fine," Evie said.

"And the gloves?" Marin asked.

"A precaution." Evie's answer was curt and had a tone of finality, so Marin planned to let it go. But then Evie reached out and grabbed Marin's hand in her own, pulling it closer. Pulling Marin closer. The lace gloves were aged and impossibly soft. Evie squeezed Marin's hand gently.

"Vintage?" Marin asked.

"They were my grandmother's," Evie said. "Pretty, right?"

"Very." Marin gripped Evie's hand tighter. It was hard to put it all into words, but she wanted Evie to understand. Marin had waited for some new surge of anxiety after Evie's grand revelations, but it had never happened. Marin wasn't scared of Evie. She didn't think it was possible. Was it awful?

Yes. But it was part of Evie just the same.

"Where are the girls?" Marin asked.

"In the arborvitaes." Evie nodded to the row of trees in the distance that made a fort for them. "Wren is in a mood."

"Our Wren? How shocking." Marin laughed.

Evie only gave the barest hint of a smile in response. "Are you sure, Marin? You can still run. I would probably run."

In response, Marin leaned in, seeking Evie's lips and kissing her in the sunshine.

It was the least discreet they'd been, but Marin didn't care, and Evie seemed not to mind either, because she was kissing Marin back.

"I'm staying." Marin broke the kiss and jumped from the tree. "I'm not scared. But I am going to check on the girls."

She crossed the grounds with a smile on her face, and her fingers hovering just where Evie's lips had been. She'd never felt this way before. She wondered if it would always be like this.

Marin crawled into the arborvitaes, getting her knees muddy—the ground was still wet from the storms the day before.

"Hello," Wren said from the far end of the row of trees. She had a book and was sitting on a rolled-up towel to stay dry.

"How is your sister?" Marin asked.

"She's alive."

Marin rolled her eyes. "Anything else?"

"She's breathing."

"And where is she alive and breathing?"

"Don't get mad," Wren said, closing her book. "She went to Mr. Willoughby's cottage."

"Alone?" Marin asked, and Wren nodded.

Marin turned immediately around and crawled out of the trees with Wren right behind her. "It's dangerous, Wren. Something killed that deer, and we still don't know what it was. I said no woods."

"She didn't go through the woods. She took the road."

Marin whirled around, and whatever look she had in her eyes was enough to send Wren in the opposite direction, back toward the orchard and Evie. Marin took off down the road, not willing to wait for them to catch up. Not with Thea walking alone.

She reached Willoughby's cottage in record time, heaving for air in the July heat, and rapped impatiently on his door.

The door swung open and the old man looked surprised to see her there.

"Ms. Blythe, the woods aren't safe."

"Was Thea here?" she asked.

Understanding dawned on Mr. Willoughby's face, and without a word he reached for the shotgun that was propped inside his door. "Let's go," he said.

They set off together, calling Thea's name.

"She likes to visit the little graveyard in here," Marin said, veering toward the patch of woods that contained Thea's buried dolls.

They crashed through the forest, more concerned with locating the little girl than anything else that might be out there.

Then the trees began to thin.

They stepped into an area of land that looked dead. The trees were pale, stripped of their leaves. The ground beneath Marin's feet turned to soggy marsh.

"What happened here?" Marin asked.

"It's tree blight," Willoughby said. "It's salt water, climbing up into the land, killing the trees."

The dead wood stretched an acre at least.

"It's spreading," Mr. Willoughby explained. "The salt is insidious. It's been creeping into these woods for years."

Marin remembered the salt water in the kitchen faucet at the house. It had been so odd—but it had only happened the once. Neera had confirmed such. Maybe it was the same for Lovelace House as it was out here in the woods—salt water was creeping into everything, even the piping.

Marin followed, brushing her hands over the pale trunks. Compared to the lushness of the forest they'd just walked through, this land felt like a graveyard.

Then Marin saw a flash of color.

Thea.

She was crouched in the meadow ahead, her blond curls

wild. And standing in front of Thea was a doe. Thea had stretched out her hand to the animal, inviting it closer.

It was like a scene out of a fairy tale.

At that moment, Evie and Thisbe broke through into the clearing as well, on the far side of Thea. Marin felt relief until she saw the look on Evie's face.

A look of horror.

Thisbe's growl carried across the marsh, low and grave in its warning.

"Thea," Evie said, her voice shaking. "Get away from that deer."

And then Marin stepped on a branch, snapping it beneath her. The deer turned in her direction, and Marin saw what Evie had seen.

The deer's entire face was gone. Only its skull remained, bleached pearl white from the sun; it was eyeless, lifeless, and only inches from Thea's face.

Marin's eyes swept the rest of the deer, noting the places where its flesh had been ripped away. In the cavities, Marin could see glimpses of muscles and bone but also wispy tendrils of ivy, growing through the decaying skin of the creature, making the shiny swell of its liver look like a blooming flower in the greenery. Its intestines hung like pink velvet ribbons from its soft torn belly, nearly dragging on the ground.

Marin threw up on her shoes.

When she looked up, Mr. Willoughby was raising his gun,

taking aim at the deer next to Thea.

"No!" She stood up, pulling the weapon down. "Let me get her first."

He nodded but raised the weapon again, keeping it trained on the deer.

Marin hurried across the marshland, ignoring the way her sneakers sank into the wet ground. Ignoring the smell of vomit that she caught a whiff of with every step.

In a moment, she was there. Marin tried not to look at it, but up close, she could see the maggots burrowed in the dead deer's eye sockets and the stretch of dead, sinewy muscles across its back.

"No! No!" Thea protested but Marin didn't hesitate.

She lifted the kicking child into her arms and carried her to Evie.

The two older girls turned into the woods, pulling Thea away from the horrific scene behind them, ignoring her cries to go back to the deer, screaming it was hurt and needed help. When the gunshot rang as Mr. Willoughby put the creature out of its misery, Thea's screams turned to quiet sobbing. Only then did Marin feel something trickle down her cheek. She lifted a hand to wipe away her own tears.

24

Malicious Compliance

―――――――― ❧ ――――――――

Thea sobbed for most of the walk back to Lovelace.

Eventually, she stopped struggling in Marin's arms, but then she was a dead weight, limp and exhausted. Marin and Evie had to pass her back and forth twice when their muscles began to ache. At the house, Marin set Thea at the dining table and offered her cold water to sip on while they talked. Thea gulped it down, parched from her tears.

Marin ran to her room to change. The smell of vomit and death clung to her clothes, and every breath made her gag again.

In her room she went to her window, unlocking it and pressing it open for fresh air. She turned for her bathroom when a movement caught her eye. There, at the edge of her desk, blown to the edge by the breeze streaming in, was a small gray feather that she had missed that morning.

It hadn't been a nightmare.

Last night, she'd found a dove. She'd wrung its neck. She'd locked her window shut before climbing back into bed.

The feather of an undead bird on her desk.

Teeth wrapped in a sock in her drawer.

If it wasn't for the tangible evidence left behind, Marin would think it was all in her head.

When she cleaned up and returned downstairs, she clutched that feather in her palm. It was to serve as a talisman. A reminder that all of this was real.

Wren and Evie perched on stools. Thea still sat at the table, sipping at water.

"What were you doing in the woods? We told you not to go out there." Evie's voice was gentle, but it was clear she was upset with Thea.

"I wasn't in the woods. I was in the marsh."

Marin leveled Thea with a look. "Enough. You know what you did."

"I had to bury the bird," Thea said. "I'm sorry."

"What bird?" Evie asked, coming closer.

"The one on Marin's desk."

"There was a dove in my room again last night," Marin explained. "A dead one. A *not* dead one."

"I had to hide it," Thea said. "Like the others."

Evie slid into a chair beside her youngest sister and put a hand over Thea's smaller ones. "Thea, we're going to need you to tell us everything."

"It started a few months ago. When Evie came home for spring break. And then it stopped until I made her come home again," Wren said from the stool. "It took us a little while to put it all together, but they've been waking up."

"Who?" Marin asked.

"All of the dead things," Thea whispered.

Marin thought of the doves in her room.

The fawn out in the woods with its belly torn out.

The half-decomposed doe in the meadow today.

It was all Evie.

"I thought you had to be near things," Marin said.

"I thought so too," Evie said softly.

"So where can you reach?" Marin asked. "How strong is it?"

"I have no idea." Evie had already looked exhausted, but now she looked unspeakably sad too.

"Wait," Wren said, dashing from the room.

She returned just a moment later, clutching the Winterthur board game in her hands. She set it down in front of Evie.

The game worked as a map.

"How far away was it today, Evie?" Wren's voice was gentler than Marin had ever heard it before.

"The deer was in the blighted wood," Evie said, pointing to the place on the board game's surface. "So I'm waking things at least that far out. I don't know where it stops."

"That's still on Lovelace property," Wren said. "But only barely."

Wren traced the area where they had been today—right along the coast, where the salt water was seeping into the earth and killing the trees. "Just beyond that is the state park."

Wren's fingers crossed a thin line on the map, showing the edge of the Lovelace property, the start of the public grounds.

They all seemed to realize the implications at once. Evie's powers were erratic and spreading. If Evie woke things out in the park, where anyone could be wandering the trails, someone might see it.

"We didn't want you to realize how bad it was," Thea said. "Or you'd leave us again."

"I'm not leaving, Thea."

"The dolls." Marin suddenly understood what Thea had been doing with her dolls all this time. "You were burying the dolls to cover up the dead."

"We kept killing them again," Wren explained. "The doves. The rabbits. There were dead frogs hopping all over the orchard. And then we'd bury them deep, hoping they wouldn't come back again."

"And then you put the dolls over top," Evie said, catching on. "To explain all the little graves."

"We needed an excuse to be in the woods. To be digging. To be covered in mud." Wren looked like she was on the verge of tears. They'd carried this secret all summer.

"I'm sorry about the deer," Thea said. "I was all right with the others, but the deer was so beautiful. I didn't want to kill it. And it was bigger than the others."

"How many?" Evie asked. "How many have I brought

back without knowing?"

Wren and Thea glanced at each other.

"You won't leave us again?" Thea confirmed, and Evie took Thea's hands in her own.

"I'm not going anywhere," Evie promised.

"We lost count after a hundred," Wren said.

"But there were *a lot* of frogs, Evie. *So many* frogs," Thea offered, trying to soften the blow.

Evie turned to Marin, and the look in her eyes could only be described as haunted.

"I suspected," Evie said. "When we saw the little deer that first time. You were right, Marin. I saw something running away, and it looked like a coyote, but it was . . . wrong. It moved wrong. It was dead. I knew it. And I ignored what I was seeing. I just didn't want to believe it."

"It's okay, Evie."

"It's not. Whatever this is, it's out of control." Evie opened her empty hands slowly, like they contained something delicate and dangerous. "Is it getting worse? Is it spreading farther every day? What if I wake the cemetery?"

"What can I do?" Marin came to the table, taking a seat beside Evie and slipping both of her hands into Evie's empty open ones.

She wanted Evie to know that she wasn't going anywhere either.

"I need to figure out why it's doing this, and I need to figure out how to stop it," Evie said. "And there may be answers in my grandmother's journals."

"Why would your grandmother have answers?" Marin asked.

"Because she could do it too."

Wren and Thea were taken to their room and given explicit instructions to stay there.

"Do not leave the house under any circumstances," Evie said. For good measure, she made them swear on Thisbe's life to stay put before she and Marin left the room.

But Marin hesitated outside the girls' room for a moment before peeking her head back in the door. "Unless there is a fire. Please leave if there is a fire."

Downstairs, they began their search in the basement, where Evie thought her mother had possibly stored old documents. As soon as Evie opened the basement door, Marin heard a strange sloshing noise below.

"What now?" Evie whined a little as she stomped down the stairs to investigate.

Marin smiled at the sound, which was so unlike her—so unguarded and juvenile.

They went down the stairs carefully.

It wasn't until they neared the bottom that they realized the problem.

The basement was flooded.

Evie moved to step into the water, but Marin held her back.

"It could be dangerous," Marin said. They'd had flooding in the basement of one of their apartment buildings, back when Marin was five or so, and they'd lived in Louisiana for a year. "You don't know where the water came from."

"We do though," Evie said. "It's salt water."

As soon as she said it, Marin recognized the bite of brine in the air. Evie was right. The basement was flooded with ocean water. Marin shifted down the stairs closer to Evie, and her bare arm dragged against the wall.

"Dammit!" Marin pulled away, a sharp stinging sensation shooting up her arm.

Evie pulled her closer and turned her arm to look.

Marin had a dozen cuts along the back of her arm to her elbow, and blood was welling along all of them. She looked at the wall.

"Barnacles," she said, reaching out to brush her fingers over them. "That means the water has been at least this high."

Marin was still three steps up.

"Let's get out of here," Evie said. "Anything down here is ruined."

They climbed back upstairs.

Marin went to the hallway to call Mr. Willoughby. While she spoke to him, describing the state of the basement, Evie pulled down the first-aid kit to clean up the long scrapes running the length of Marin's shoulder and arm. They were shallow, but they stung, especially when Evie ran an alcohol wipe down her arm to clean the cuts.

"Where else can we look?" Marin asked as Evie turned her arm, gently wiping off the beads of blood.

"There's a closet in the hall outside of Mother's office. She keeps some family items stored in there."

Marin remembered the day she and Thea ran into Alice in that closet. She'd dropped an entire box of books.

"Do you remember what they looked like? Your grandmother's journals?"

"Old leather journals. They were dark green, with—"

"Gold lettering on the sides?"

"Yes, her initials are stamped on them."

"I saw your mother moving them, weeks ago when I first arrived here."

"Moving them where?" Evie asked.

"No idea. They were in that closet, like you said, but she pulled a whole box of them out. She said they were delicate. Where would she move them?"

"Father's study, I suppose. But my mother can't know we are going in there. She's very protective of it, ever since he died."

"I don't think I've ever seen the study."

"She keeps it locked," Evie said.

"Well, we're going now." Marin pulled Evie to her feet. She was determined to salvage the day with some answers. Though it was starting to feel like every few minutes the questions loomed larger and more complicated ahead of them.

When Marin began to step away, Evie pulled her back, and Marin turned to find she was pressed right up against her in a tight grip of a hug. It was instinct to bring her hands up to Evie's shoulders, to reassure her with a touch, and Marin saw the moment Evie recognized the feeling, saw the way Evie's shoulders slumped in relief. Then Evie leaned forward until their foreheads touched.

"I'm scared."

There was a raw vulnerability in Evie's admission.

"We'll figure it out," Marin promised. "We'll contain it."

"What if we don't? What if it keeps spreading? What if I keep waking things up?"

"It won't. You said it yourself—I worry too much, right?"

"Right."

"Well, I'm not worried, Evie. And I worry about everything. I know we will find some answers. Together. But no more secrets, okay? I can't handle any more skeletons in the closet."

A surprised laugh escaped Evie at the expression.

Marin frowned. "Sorry. That was an unfortunate choice of words."

"Okay, Marin," Evie said. "No more secrets."

Before they could break into the study, they had to steal the key from Alice's office.

Marin would have rather broken into a crypt than Alice Lovelace's sacred, *private* writing space. But she was quickly learning that she would do whatever it took to chase that fear from Evie. To help her find a way to control the strange, dark powers she possessed.

They recruited the girls for their mission. Wren and Thea knocked on their mother's door and waited until it cracked open—just a sliver of sunlight cutting across the floorboards of the darkened hallway and the shadow of Alice beyond.

Marin could only hear fragments of what the girls were saying to convince her to leave with them, but it worked.

A moment later, she and Evie were sneaking in, closing the door softly behind them.

Evie went right for her mother's desk drawers, and Marin looked around the office.

This was the first time she'd seen it in its entirety, instead of an obscured view from the doorway. She explored, tracing her hands over Alice's books. On the other side of the office, which would have normally been obscured by the open door, she paused, looking at a yellowed map on the wall.

"What's this? Places she's traveled?" she asked.

Evie barely glanced up at the map. She shrugged. "Mother never travels."

"Except the book signing."

"What book signing?"

"In California, this past spring."

"That doesn't sound right. Mother is practically agoraphobic. She rarely leaves Lovelace House anymore. Hell, she barely leaves this room."

Marin frowned. That was true. Alice had been shut up tight working almost the entire two months that Marin had lived at Lovelace House. Marin couldn't imagine her on a plane. At a bookshop. Happily greeting strangers and signing their copies of her catalog of books. But she could have sworn that the flyer she had was for a signing. She'd have to find it again to be sure.

Marin turned back to the map. There were a handful of pins—locations that seemed to have no correlation. Marin reached for a curled bit of paper pinned on the edge of the cork board and unfurled it.

She was staring at a picture of herself.

It was black and white and blotchy, an aged scrap of newspaper.

But it was her, standing next to her mother and her coach, holding up the medal hanging around her neck. The caption beneath the photo read, *"Southern Maple Middle Schooler, Marin Blythe, places 1st in meet."*

Marin remembered that day. Her mother had been so proud. After their next move, clear across the country from Michigan to Washington that time, Marin had quit competitive swimming. She was tired of having to prove herself again in every new place they went.

The dread came over her like the tide rolling in, slowly and steadily unrelenting until it settled somewhere deep inside of her. She studied the map once more, her fingers ghosting over the head of each pin. *Albany, New York. Baton*

Rouge, Louisiana. Ann Arbor, Michigan. Tacoma, Washington. San Diego, California.

"I've got it!" Evie called, victorious as she held up the key.

But Marin couldn't move.

Each pin marked a place that Marin had lived with her mother.

Alice Lovelace had been stalking them for years.

25

I've Got a Bad Feeling About This

———————— ❧ ————————

A soft cooing sound echoed up through the house. It was the call of a mourning dove, but it didn't come from a bird. It came from a little girl.

It was the signal they'd devised with Wren and Thea, to let them know when Alice was coming back.

Marin fled to the door with Evie just behind her, and they slipped out into the hall with barely a second to spare before they heard the creak on the second-to-top stair. Evie pulled Marin into an alcove just as Alice turned the corner.

In the dark niche, they were pressed up against each other, and Marin felt her chest growing tighter with each breath. It was like her heart was beating in her ears, pounding like a hammer in her skull.

She was drenched from the rain and shivering.

Let go, Marin.

She was back in that train car. Pinned by metal. She could smell something burning. She could smell blood.

Marin shut her eyes tight, willing the panic away, but it

was hopeless, and through the chaos of it, she could hear the sharp staccato of heels on hardwood. Alice's footsteps were just a few yards away, and here Marin was, about to fall to pieces and get them caught. Marin closed her eyes to stave off the panic, but it seemed hopeless. Her telltale heart would give them away in mere seconds. And then Evie's cool lips were on hers. The kiss was so gentle, so soft—so fleeting—that Marin first thought she'd imagined it.

Evie gave Marin's body as much space as possible in the cramped alcove, but her hands found Marin's shoulders and brushed across her collarbone, exposed where Marin's oversized tee had slipped down her arm. Evie's cold fingers slipped up to brush against her jaw, tucking back to pause on the nape of her neck.

The pressure and the coolness grounded her in her body like running water.

Marin focused all her attention on Evie's fingers. Followed their path as they moved from the nape of her neck and tugged gently on some of the soft, curling hairs there, the most sensitive ones. The hint of a sting pulled Marin out of the train wreck in her mind and back into the halls of Lovelace. Marin sought out Evie's lips again in earnest, eager for the distraction. Eager to find something besides fear that could make her heart feel like it might burst in her chest. And she found it with Evie, tucked away in the shadows. For as much as she hated when Evie kept secrets from her, Marin didn't mind being one of them.

For several long, precious minutes, the world was gone, her panic forgotten. Marin was encased in the moment, pressed between Evie's cool fingers and her colder lips, tasting cinnamon on her tongue.

When they finally resurfaced for air, Alice was gone, disappeared back into her office, and Marin was fully present, her grief melted back into history.

There was only now.

There was only Evie.

And Marin could have stayed longer, lost in the embrace and the comfort of it, if not for the image of that map full of pins that flashed in her mind. If not for the locked study downstairs that might possibly hold answers to Evie's questions, and maybe Marin's too.

It was time to unearth the rest of Lovelace's secrets.

Evie stood outside of her father's study.

Her hand that held the key had a slight tremor to it.

She fixed the collar of her oxford shirt and shifted her skirt until its buttons were centered and aligned with her shirt. Her hands moved to her hair, checking that the wide pearl headband she wore was still in place. And last, she tugged on the edges of her lace gloves, ensuring they were in place. Only then did she unlock the door.

It was almost as if she expected him to be waiting in there for her.

But when the heavy red oak door swung inward to an

empty, stale-smelling room, Evie stayed rooted in the door-way. Marin regarded her profile, but it could have been carved from marble in this moment. Evie was giving nothing away.

But this Marin could do.

She took Evie's hand and led her into the room.

"What exactly are we looking for?" Marin's voice was hushed, reverent. Maybe she'd expected Charles Hallowell a little too. Maybe she felt his presence in here, haunting this place through Evie's memories.

"Grandmother kept journals. Mother mentioned it once when she gave me my first one. She said it was important to keep a record of my gift. She said my grandmother had always done the same."

The room was a dark, deep green that matched the thick canopy of the Winterthur woods. Or the color of wet moss. Or the seaweed that grew in great clusters on the rocks at the shore.

There was an entire wall of books, and Marin went to that first, scanning for anything that looked like a journal.

She quickly realized her problem. *Every* book looked like one. Aged leather and browned pages. *Damn.* This would take ages.

Evie finally moved too, crossing to her father's desk. She opened and shut drawers, shuffling papers as she went and then carefully placing them back just as they had been. This entire room had been kept as a memorial.

Marin put things back exactly as they were too.

They worked in companionable silence. Marin knew this was hard for Evie, so she gave her a wide berth. She left space for all the grief that was contained in this small room, so tangible Marin felt like she could reach out and tangle her fingers in it like cobwebs.

But then Evie rattled something across the room, and Marin looked up at the sharp sound. A wooden trunk sat in the corner of the room. It was a deep walnut color, with black iron crisscrossing the wood, reinforcing it in an intricate design. It was twin to the one in the attic, the one with the braids of hair inside.

"Here," Evie said, relief hanging on the word. "Marin, come look."

She crossed to Evie and looked down at the trunk.

Across the latch of the trunk was an engraving in bold golden script on one side of the lock.

Property of Theadora Lovelace

On the other side of the lock it had the word *"ADOSSA."*

"Is this a family name?" Marin ran her fingers across the trunk, remembering the one mausoleum in the cemetery that had the same name carved into its stone.

Evie shrugged. "No, not that I know of."

Her hands joined Marin's, ghosting over the letters. "Oh, I know. It's two words. Ad Ossa. It's on an old family crest somewhere. Some ancient tapestry or heirloom plate or something." Evie waved her hand dismissively. "I think it means down to the bone."

Everything stays at Lovelace, Thea had said in the attic that day with the other trunk. The ropes of braided hair. The cemetery full of ancestors. Even Thea's little baby teeth had never been left for a fairy, only placed for safe keeping in a silver box beside her bed. *Down to the bone.*

Marin shuddered.

Family crest or not, it was creepy.

"And Theadora? That's your mother's mother?" Marin asked.

Evie nodded. "We called her Grandma Dorie. Thea's namesake." She rattled the lid again. "Damn. It's locked."

Evie pulled the key they'd used to get into the office back out of her pocket, but it was completely wrong. The door used a typical house key, and the trunk needed a skeleton key.

"Where'd they put the damned key?" Evie was feeling along the sides and back of the trunk, clearly hoping it had been left within reach of the lock.

No such luck.

"Oh, wait." Marin ducked into the hall and whistled. "Thisbe!" she called out through the house, her eagerness to test her theory momentarily drowning out any worry of disturbing Alice's peace.

After a moment she heard the click of the dog's nails on the hardwood floors, and Thisbe bounded around the corner and into the room with them.

"Good girl." Marin knelt beside the dog and reached for her collar, unhooking the key.

"Try this," Marin said. "It opens the one in the attic."

"The girls showed you the hair?" Evie asked.

"They sure did."

"And you're still here?" Evie was smiling. "I think I underestimated your bravery, Marin Blythe."

"Takes more than creepy Victorian hair murals to scare me away."

Evie slipped the key into the lock.

It didn't turn.

"Dammit, I really thought that would work." Marin couldn't hide her disappointment. It felt like they were so close.

Evie returned the key to Thisbe's collar and pet the dog's silky ears.

"What if we—"

A scratching sound interrupted her, and Marin looked around for the source of the sound. A rumble came from Thisbe's throat, and Marin followed the dog's locked gaze. The scratching was coming from on top of a cabinet. And it was growing louder, more insistent.

Marin stepped back when a small dark hand appeared over the top edge of the cabinet above them.

"Evie," she began, and Evie looked up just as it climbed over the edge and fell.

It was a raccoon, twitching, trying to crawl.

Thisbe lost her mind and went for the animal, sinking her teeth into its neck and shaking.

But no matter how she shook it, the animal kept moving.

"What the hell," Marin said.

"It was . . . it was stuffed." Evie's voice held a tone of awe as she watched the animal continue to writhe in Thisbe's jaw.

"Stuffed?" Marin didn't understand what Evie was saying. And then something else dropped from the wall.

It was some sort of cat or maybe a large rodent, and it scurried fast along the floor, heading right for Marin's feet.

Marin moved quickly out of its way, backing against the wall.

She felt a tickling sensation on her cheek and went to brush her hair back from her face. Only her hand encountered something soft and thick. Something moving.

Marin pulled her hand away, turning slightly to see what it was. The largest spider Marin had ever seen in her life was climbing onto her shoulder. She shrieked, jumping away from the wall.

The tarantula fell to the floor.

"Evie," Marin whispered, horror weaving into her voice, making it tremor.

She no longer felt brave.

"They're father's taxidermy," Evie said, and her voice was just as strained. "I don't understand how they're coming back—there's nothing *left* to them but skin and fur."

Then the other animal, the catlike creature, found Marin again, and this time it latched on, its sharp teeth digging into the tender flesh of Marin's foot.

Marin screamed, and Evie bounded across the room to her father's desk and grabbed for his letter opener. She was back in a moment, stabbing the sharp point right through the creature's neck, so hard and so fast that she pinned it to the floor.

It released Marin's foot, but it kept wriggling on the floor, desperate to free itself and oblivious to the blade through its neck. Nothing hurt it. It couldn't feel.

"Evie, what the hell is it?" Marin asked, staring down at the writhing animal. She moved away and examined her foot. There were a few long gashes across it where the creature had torn at her skin. She was bleeding enough to make a mess, but she didn't think the teeth had penetrated very deeply.

"It's a fossa. It's like—like a mongoose." Evie untied the fabric belt from her waist and waved for Marin to lift her foot. She wrapped the ivory ribbon around it, and though the first two layers soaked with blood, it didn't reach the third.

Evie tied a bow. Then she shook her head. "Sorry, force of habit." She pulled the bow loose, settling for a secure double-knot instead.

"But why did it *attack* me? Are they that aggressive when they're alive?"

The fossa was still scrambling, its claws gouging the

hardwood floors, leaving long yellow stripes in the dark wood.

Evie found a cardboard box and unceremoniously dumped its contents to the floor. She came back and unpinned the creature from the floor, shoving it into the box and folding it shut.

Then she crossed the room, lifted a large paperweight from her father's desk, and dropped it to the floor, crushing the tarantula.

Thisbe had torn the dead raccoon to pieces, although the little fingers of its hand continued to curl on the carpet. The wall still had half a dozen animals on it, stuck on their perches, but they were struggling to free themselves. A hawk that had managed to break one of its legs off was now hanging sideways, wings flapping. There was a coyote wriggling on its stand, its feet pinned in place, its mouth open unnaturally wide, its cries soundless from its gaping jaw.

"No, they aren't usually that aggressive," Evie said, staring at the wall of horror above them. "It attacked you like that because it was evil."

"What does that mean?" Marin asked.

"Sometimes they come back dark."

They used pillowcases to gather the rest of the taxidermy animals from the study wall. The largest was a deer head with ten-point antlers. As soon as Evie got near to it, the animal head began to thrash back and forth, eyes unseeing, body missing, nothing but a mounted head now freakishly reanimated by Evie's power. Marin knocked it off the wall with a shovel and wrapped it in a towel, trying to ignore the sickening thud when it hit the carpet.

It was likely that last, loud crash that summoned Neera.

Marin looked up from her grisly task to find the woman staring at her, mouth agape.

"Evie," Neera said, her eyes sweeping the room and the destruction within. "What on earth is going on in here?"

Marin's brain began to spin. How would Evie explain this? How could Marin help?

But Evie only sighed and waved her arm, as if to say, *well, what does it look like?*

"They all woke up."

"But these creatures are stuffed. Some of them have been dead for decades," Neera said. She moved into the room, picking up loose feathers from the hawk, a tuft of fur from the mangled raccoon. She dropped them into the pillowcase that Evie held open for her.

"I know. I didn't think I could wake them either."

"So your suspicions were true? Your powers are growing?"

"Not growing, exactly. Amplified in distance, yes. But it doesn't feel stronger, it feels . . . out of control. It feels chaotic."

"It's grief, my love. I've told you this."

Marin looked back and forth between Neera and Evie.

243

She'd never felt so stupid as in that moment, as she felt the puzzle pieces slowly sliding into place. Marin dropped the thrashing deer head to the floor.

"So Neera already knows?"

Neera gave Marin a look that somehow made Marin feel even dumber.

"I told you that, Marin. Neera was there when I first did it. With the mouse?"

Marin had forgotten. She'd been so caught up in Evie's ability that she'd—no, that was a lie. She could at least be honest with herself. She'd been so caught up in Evie. Kissing Evie. Imagining kissing Evie.

But Evie had told her that.

"I knew all about Theadora Lovelace, Marin. She was very honest when she hired me. Not just to caretake this house and the people in it, but to caretake this . . ." Neera gestured at the undead animals all around them. "I'm Evie's Guardian. The truth is, I've known about the curse longer than Evie's known it herself."

Marin and Evie dragged the deer head out to the older graveyard in the woods and buried it among Thea's dolls, and the frogs, and the rabbits, and the doves. It was too large to throw in the ocean and too conspicuous, mounted on its board.

They carried the pillowcases to the bluff overhanging the sea. The bay was calm today, and when the wind blew over the water, it rippled as far as Marin could see, painting the surface with an effect like a brushstroke on canvas.

One by one, they emptied the pillowcases over the cliff, watching as the undead animals thrashed for a moment before sinking into the waves. With any luck, they'd go out with the tide and stay sunk in their watery grave.

Evie reached into the pockets of her skirt and pulled out small furry objects. She tossed them into the water last. Raccoon hands. Raccoon feet. Still twitching.

When they disappeared beneath the gray-green water, Marin barked out a sharp laugh.

She clamped her hand over her mouth, trying to cover it. But that only spurred her on more, laughter pouring from her like she'd been holding it in for months and finally she'd stopped trying to contain it, and the sound ranged out across stone and sea.

When she finally caught her breath and glanced over, she found a stunned look on Evie's face, and she lost herself all over again.

She laughed until tears streamed down her face.

"I'm so sorry," Marin said between bursts. "It's just, this is all so absurd. I'm starting to feel like an extra on *Night of the Living Dead*."

"I don't understand."

"It doesn't matter. What matters is that I was so very wrong about you."

Evie looked stricken, and Marin reached out to grab her

arm, to hold her close while she regained enough control to explain herself. "Not like that, Evie. You must know that I'm completely enthralled with you. It's just that I really thought you were squeamish. *Squeamish.* About dead things."

Evie's replying laugh was dark and hollow. "Well, I'm not," she said, but the smile on her lips lingered.

"I know that *now.* You weren't avoiding dead things because they bother you. You were avoiding the dead because *you* bother *them.* You're basically their queen."

Evie tried again to pull away, but Marin held onto her.

"It isn't funny. I'm a monster," she said. She fidgeted with the end of one of her lace gloves. Gloves that were obviously pointless as her ability fractured and shifted and grew beyond the power of her touch, but Evie kept them on just the same.

"You're not." Marin pulled a gloved hand into her own. "You're not."

"I'm tired of feeling this way," Evie said.

"What way?"

"Responsible." Evie's eyes were trained on her boots like her life depended on it, so Marin's hand found her chin and lifted Evie's gaze to meet her own.

"I feel responsible too. For my mother. For the girls. For every worried impulse I don't act on. I think that's all anxiety is, really. Responsibility."

"But that doesn't make sense. You didn't cause the accident that killed your mother."

"And you aren't choosing any of this, Evie. You didn't kill your father. You need to stop blaming yourself for everything."

They stood in silence, absorbing each other's deepest guilt, hands grasped tight as the sun began to set on the dark ocean.

In this light, Evie didn't look pale or haunted. She looked so very alive, with brilliant golden light painting her face and her hair, shimmering like flecks of gold in her eyes.

"You are like Persephone and Hades all rolled into one very tired girl." Marin reached out to Evie's skirt, which was torn badly from something. Maybe the fossa's scrambling claws. Or perhaps a deer antler had snagged it. "Pretty dresses aren't very conducive for fighting the dead, you know."

"This is giving me a headache anyway." Evie pulled her pearl headband from her tangled hair and dropped it unceremoniously onto the ground between them. "The truth is, it's a control thing. The hair, the dresses . . . all of this." Evie gestured to her blouse and skirt and boots. "I'm just trying to keep myself sane. Controlling the things I can when everything else feels so utterly beyond my control. Besides, necromancers can like pretty things too."

Marin squeezed Evie's hand that she was still holding, pulled Evie a little closer. "Is that what you are?"

"I don't know what I am," Evie whispered.

"Well, whatever you are, can I keep you?" Marin whispered, her lips only millimeters from Evie's.

They sank into the kiss like a sunset on water.

Evie Hallowell was like the deep sea, her secrets chasmic and unknown, and Marin was as helpless against the pull of her as ever. Helpless when Evie's cursed hands came up to tangle in Marin's dark hair. Helpless when her mouth caught the sigh that escaped Evie's lips.

When they broke apart, Marin felt that something had changed between them. Come what may, Evie Hallowell was under her skin. And Marin knew she wouldn't change a thing about it, even if she could.

"Son of a bitch," Evie said suddenly, straightening her body and glancing toward the manor.

"What?" Marin asked.

"My grandmother's trunk." Evie took a few urgent steps toward the house and then she stopped just as abruptly.

"Oh no. No, no, no." Evie's hands came up to cover her face, worrying Marin.

"Evie, what is it? What's wrong?"

"We had *two* dogs, Marin. Not one."

"I don't understand."

"*Pyramus*. They must have kept the key to the second trunk on his collar." Evie finally dropped her hands and faced Marin. "And we buried him with it."

PART 3

The Shyness of the Crown

I shall die, but that is all I shall do for death.
—Edna St. Vincent Millay, "Conscientious Objector"

*The girl had always felt she carried tragedy in her marrow,
an unwelcome burden in an otherwise happy life. For a long
time, she tried to ignore it. She went through the motions
of normalcy. She learned to read and write. She made a
friend. She learned how to swim. But like a sickness, she
felt it always. It was as if a cancer was consuming her
from the inside out. It was a calling, dark and awful and
persistent. And it always urged her to do the same thing.
Kill, it whispered, when she was five, holding a mouse
in her little hands, poised over a bucket of water. Kill,
it beckoned, the year she turned nine. The housekeeper
found two drowned cats that month. Kill, it demanded,
when she was eleven, holding that same friend under the
waves until she stopped scratching her arms.*
—Alice Lovelace, *Drowning Games*

26

Putting the Romance in Necromancy

"Let's just break the damn thing," Wren said.

"Language," scolded Marin. She was examining the trunk, looking for screws, joints, anything that would let them take it apart.

"Mother would kill us," Thea said.

The moment the words left her lips, Evie drew a sharp breath.

An image of Alice standing in the dark library holding a hatchet over Wren flashed through Marin's mind.

"Besides, the metal casing is there to prevent that," Evie quickly explained, trying to move past Thea's innocent words. "See how it crosses all over? We wouldn't be strong enough to get through it—and even if we managed it, we'd likely destroy whatever is inside."

"What *is* inside?" Thea whined. She was bored of this game.

The game was called *Break into Your Dead Grandmother's Old Trunk to Uncover Secrets about Raising the Dead before*

Evie's Powers Are Discovered or She Wakes Something Dangerous.

They were losing the game.

Thea moved to her father's bookcase, and a small, excited cry escaped her lips.

"Shh!" In unison, Evie, Wren, and Marin all shushed her.

"I found the zoetrope," Thea whispered, and lifted a round lamp-like device from a shelf. "Watch this!"

She slid a metal lever on the bottom of the lamp, so that the lightbulb flickered on, before setting it on the very corner of the desk. It cast shadows against the wall—animal shapes. A lion, a hawk, a raccoon. When Thea spun the top, the lamp rotated on a wheel, and the shadows began to spin around the room, shifting in a kaleidoscope of colors and light.

It reminded Marin of the creatures that had climbed off these very same walls the day before, and left her feeling nauseated, with a sour taste in her mouth. Thisbe had been sleeping on the thick burgundy carpet of Charles Hallowell's study, but she lifted her head and whimpered, ears perked.

Then Marin heard it too.

Footsteps coming down the hallway.

"Out," Evie whispered. "Quickly now."

According to Alice Lovelace, the study was strictly off-limits to everyone in the household, and none of them wanted to be caught breaking her rules today. It took them all of ten seconds to slip out of the room. Evie had just turned the key in the lock and slipped it back into her pocket when Alice rounded the corner.

"Evangeline. What's going on?"

"Oh, we thought we heard something," Evie said. "But it's still locked, so it was probably nothing."

Alice stepped forward and rattled the doorknob. She swayed a bit on her feet, her fingers flying to her temple.

"Another migraine?" Evie asked softly.

"It's coming on. Vertigo. Light sensitivity." Alice briefly met Marin's eyes, and Marin saw nothing but pain and a vague look of vacancy there.

"They're getting worse. Maybe it's time to visit a doctor—"

"No." Alice's tone brooked no room for discussion on the subject.

"Then you should rest, Mother. Marin and I will get the girls through dinner and bedtime tonight."

"Yes, very well. Thank you, Evie."

Alice left slowly, one hand trailing along the wall for support. It had been almost a week since Alice had last read to the girls at night. Her headaches seemed almost constant, and when she wasn't ill, she was writing.

Alice *resting* or Alice *writing* were both fine options as far as Marin was concerned. She'd prefer those versions instead of Alice standing over Wren with a hatchet clutched in her hands.

Dinner was a quiet affair. Everyone seemed lost in their

own thoughts. Marin could guess with fair confidence that Evie was preoccupied with the trunk. Marin supposed she should be thinking about it too, how to break into it without Pyramus's key. But she wasn't. She was thinking of the pins on the wall in Alice's office. She wanted to get back in there. She wanted to find out what else Alice had known about them. To find out how long she'd been searching for them, studying them like ants under a magnifying glass.

"I'll clean up," Neera offered. Gentle as it was, her voice startled Marin from her reverie. She felt as though she'd been caught cheating on a quiz. "It is getting late."

"It's not even dark out," Wren protested, gesturing toward the sky outside. Neera was right. It was already a few minutes past eight; the summer days simply stretched on forever. The sunset filled the sky with brilliant crimson streaks that ran right to the water. It reminded Marin of the tarot card that Evie kept pulling for Alice. The tower loomed in front of a bright red sky. Everything in the background burned. *It means danger, destruction,* Evie had told her, forecasting doom with the pull of a card.

She remembered how easy it had been to say she didn't believe in it the first time Evie had read for her. Now Marin had seen things that were so dark, so inexplicable, that she had to reconsider everything she knew.

Evie could wake the dead. Anything else was possible after that. Maybe it meant Evie could read the future in her deck of cards. Maybe it meant Marin should trust every twist and tug of anxiety that she felt, following her intuition for the first time in her life.

She felt something cool on the back of her hand under the table and looked down to find Evie's hand had covered her own. Evie continued to eat, not even looking in Marin's direction.

It was a soft, mindless gesture.

Marin turned her hand, pressing her warm palm against Evie's cold one, interlocking their fingers.

Marin still wasn't sure if she belonged at Lovelace House, but she knew that she belonged here, next to Evie, and every time her worries about this place swelled up inside of her, the thought of Evie quieted that furious wave of fear.

Lovelace House might be strange and dark and possess more secrets than Marin could keep track of. But then again, the same could be said of Evie.

And Marin could never be afraid of Evie.

Marin turned her shower scalding hot before climbing in.

Evie was reading to the girls and they planned to meet in the orchard once the girls were asleep.

Tonight, they had a grave to dig up.

Marin stayed in the touch-too-hot water until she felt drowsy. Until the skin on her fingers had shriveled. She licked her lips and wondered if she tasted just the barest hint of salt. She wasn't sure.

Marin lingered in the shower. She didn't want to think about the task ahead of them. It wasn't until the water turned lukewarm that she finally shut it off and leaned her head against the tile. She watched as the water that had gathered at her feet drained slowly away.

Marin wanted to put on pajamas and crawl into bed. To be precise, she wanted to crawl into Evie's bed. She wanted to wrap her arms around her and fall asleep with the smell of her on her pillow.

Instead, Marin pulled on her jeans and glanced at the clock on her wall. She'd spent too long in the shower, gathering her nerves for what she knew they had to do, and she didn't want to keep Evie waiting longer.

She grabbed a tank top and finished dressing. Marin had already applied lipstick halfway before she remembered it was nighttime, and she was about to be robbing a grave, so the occasion didn't exactly call for it.

But then she put the rest on anyway. For Evie.

She popped her head into the girls' room on her way past to make sure they were well and truly asleep. She smiled at the light snoring from within. Thea had fallen asleep with her arms wrapped around one of her few remaining dolls.

She must still be burying them.

It was overcast and cooling quickly, so Marin grabbed Evie's cable-knit sweater from the front hall closet. The pockets were still filled with shells and sea glass, and she ran her fingers over them as she walked.

As soon as Marin set foot in the orchard, a shadow fell from the tree ahead of her.

"Shit!" Marin shouted, stepping back. She tripped on a branch and fell hard onto the ground.

"Oh my gosh, I'm sorry." Evie fell to her knees beside Marin, her hands flying up and down Marin's body. "Are you hurt?"

But Marin didn't answer. Her brain was unraveling faster than she could form new thoughts because she couldn't process what she was seeing.

Evie Hallowell was wearing jeans.

"What the hell are those?" Marin pointed, and Evie huffed.

"Marin, I thought I hurt you!"

"Well, then maybe you shouldn't be jumping out of trees onto unsuspecting victims."

"I'm sorry. I thought you saw me."

"Hey, Evie?"

"Yeah?"

"I *really* like your jeans," Marin teased.

"Shush, you." Evie kissed Marin, probably just to shut her up. But Marin was hardly going to object to her tactics.

Cinnamon.

For the rest of her life, when Marin tasted cinnamon, she would think of kissing Evie.

In that cove in the orchard, smothered in dirt and prepared to dig up a grave, Marin kissed Evie Hallowell until it was as though they no longer ended where their bodies did. Evie was the tautness of her silk chiffon blouse pulled against her ribs. Marin was the low timbre of her voice when she was tired and falling in love. Her usual dulcet voice notched deeper with Evie's name on her lips between kisses.

There was movement in the brush next to them, a crackling sound as twigs snapped, and Evie braced herself on her hands, giving Marin space to sit up.

A pair of rabbits emerged from a thatch of bramble.

They froze like stone garden statues when they spied the girls intertwined on the ground.

One was brown, rounded, and healthy, its ears twitching in alert at the sounds of Evie and Marin's orchard tryst. But the other was all black, so emaciated its skeleton was visible rippling beneath the fur. Its eyes were sunken and milk white. When it turned to rub its head against its mate, Marin saw that one of its legs was only bone, attached by a string of sinew as thin as thread, barely hanging on.

She worried at the sight.

The hares didn't bother her, but Evie would think they did. Evie would want to hide away from that rabbit she'd unintentionally brought back from the dead. But Marin watched as the rabbits nuzzled against each other. The dead one wasn't aggressive. It was . . . loving.

Evie's magic had done that. Reunited them.

Evie's foot slipped on a rotten apple, and the bunnies scattered in an instant, gone in the dark.

Marin tugged on Evie's arm so her elbow folded and she collapsed onto Marin. Evie laughed as she rolled onto her back beside her, their hands gripped tight across Marin's belly.

"We should go," Marin said. "We have work to do."

"In a minute," Evie replied. She pointed at the apple trees above them. "Marin, look at the that."

"What exactly am I looking at?"

"See those lines between the trees? They look almost like little rivers of blue-purple sky. The treetops don't *quite* touch. All through the orchard they do that. Did you know—"

"Evie, I promise you, I *never* know."

Evie smiled, eyes still on the branches above. On the little rivers of sky that ran in between them. "It's called crown shyness. They think it's to keep parasites from spreading between the trees. A little distance keeps them safe. Do you understand?"

Marin digested the words slowly. *Distance keeps them safe.* "Evie, I'm not leaving Lovelace House. Do you really want me to go?"

"*Want* isn't the right word, Marin. But it isn't safe here. And I can't bear the idea that whatever is happening could hurt you."

"It could hurt you too. And the girls."

"We're family, Marin."

"And what am I?"

"You're—" Evie cut off. She could say the words. Even for that second, as they hung unsaid in the air between them, Marin could already feel their sharp bite.

You're not part of this family.

But that's not what Evie said.

"You're too special to me, Marin," Evie said. "I like the way you look at me. And if you stay here much longer, if you see all the awful things I can do, you won't look at me like that anymore."

"Evie, none of it changes how I feel about you. Or how you make *me* feel. I know it sounds perverse, but I feel safe here with you. Which is *kind of* a big deal for me."

"Maybe for now. But we don't know what's coming. I won't be your villain, Marin. And I'm afraid if you stay, that's exactly what I'll become. The dead are rising at Lovelace, and I don't know how to stop it. Some of them will come back dark. Violent, even."

Marin thought of the dead doves in her room, the deer in the marsh, the rabbit in the brush.

"I've always played this game in my head. For as long as I can remember, I'd think of the absolute worst possible thing that could happen. I'd imagine it all the way through, the worst-case scenario, however awful it was. By the time my mom died, I'd already pictured it happening a million different ways. I think my anxiety all these years was really grief just waiting on the tragedy to strike. But thanks to you I've realized there was another half of that game that I had been missing all along."

"What was it?" Evie asked.

"If I was allowing for the thought that the absolute worst thing could happen, then I had to allow that the best possible thing could happen too. You make me imagine the best-case scenarios, Evie. So that's what we need to do here. We have to imagine the *best* version of this. So close your eyes."

"Marin—"

"Humor me. Please," Marin said.

Evie shut her eyes.

"Stop thinking of the worst that can happen. Instead, picture the best. It's a few months from now. Maybe it's winter. Is it snowing outside? Are the fireplaces lit up?"

"Mmm, yes. Hot cocoa with the girls during the first big storm of the year. It's tradition."

"What else?"

"Everyone is safe. And I've learned to control my powers."

"Hey, Evie?"

"Yes?"

"Am I there too?"

Evie opened her eyes and turned to Marin. "Yes. Of course you are there."

"I don't want to run. I think we can figure out your powers, *together.* Isn't it worth trying?" Marin hadn't even realized the truth of her words until she said them out loud. She didn't want to leave Lovelace.

"Do you really think that people like me get to live happily ever after?"

"I don't know, Evie. Are there any other people like you?"

Evie shoved at her playfully.

"But truly? I don't think happily ever after is the point," Marin said.

"You don't?"

"No. I think happily for now is pretty great too."

"You should still leave, Marin. Not because I *want* you to go. But because I want you to stay. Forever. I don't know if you've noticed, but Lovelace has trouble letting go of people."

"*Everything stays at Lovelace,*" Marin said.

"Down to the bone," Evie finished.

Maybe it was true. After all, this land contained every Lovelace buried in over a hundred years. The bones of their ancestors, their grandparents, even the dogs.

Everything stayed here forever.

Waiting to be woken up.

27

Must Love Dogs

❧

They stood side by side next to Pyramus's grave, each of them holding a shovel. Each of them dreading what came next.

"Are you sure you're okay with this?" Evie asked.

"It's just a dog. No big deal." Marin was lying through her teeth.

"Okay. Of course. You're right," Evie lied in return.

It was only polite.

Neither of them was about to call the other out. Tonight, these lies were the only things keeping them upright.

They knew that they couldn't spend much more time in the study—Alice would catch them or notice the missing key eventually. There was no time to find another way into the trunk.

Pyramus was the only way.

But they'd disagreed on who would do it.

Marin insisted she could do it alone and keep Evie away

from the cemetery, but Evie had rejected the idea outright.

Which is how Marin found herself beside a grave with night closing in around them, next to the girl she was quickly falling for, gripping a shovel like it was a lifeline, and preparing to dig up a dead dog.

"Let's get this over with." Evie sank her shovel into the ground first. They were lucky it had rained so much recently. The earth was soft and wet and gave way to their efforts.

It still took an hour, and by the end, Marin wished she'd saved her shower for after. The summer night was sticky and warm.

Then Marin's shovel struck something hard.

They cleared the soil on top of the buried dog, and Evie climbed out of the hole.

Marin reached for the edge of the crate that contained the remains of Pyramus and pried the top off.

The smell was even stronger than she'd anticipated. She held her breath and worked faster.

There was a towel covering the body, and Marin pulled it back in one swift motion before she could lose her nerve. Or her stomach.

He was more than skeleton, but not much. There were long lines of purple muscles stretching between the bones and a few lingering patches of fur. His ears and eyes were gone, and his lips had curled back as they decomposed, exposing his rows of white teeth and blackened gums.

She began to retch and turned away just in time to throw up into the dirt.

"Marin," Evie said.

"I'm sorry, I'm going as fast as I can." Marin moved back to the dog's body, reaching for his neck. Her fingers slipped under the collar, and she quickly undid the clasp and slid it from his too-thin neck, trying not to gag again when her fingers brushed against his neck and broke through the soft skin.

As she pulled the collar away, Marin could have sworn she felt the dog shift beneath her. It was subtle. No more than a shudder.

They had to hurry.

"Marin." This time Evie's tone pulled Marin's gaze from the dead dog.

Mr. Willoughby was standing on the other side of Pyramus's grave, a look of disgust twisting his features.

"I never believed it, Ms. Hallowell. The rumors about this house. I told the people in town they were nonsense. I defended you all—"

"It's not what it looks like," Marin began.

"It looks like you're playing games with the dead," Mr. Willoughby said.

"Okay, it's exactly what it looks like," Marin corrected. "But we have good reasons."

"I saw your flashlights. Thought maybe the little ones

lost something out here, and I was coming over to help."

"Mr. Willoughby," Evie began, holding up her empty hands as though they were proof of her innocence.

But then Evie slipped.

She fell into the grave and landed on Pyramus, her hands directly on his bones.

"No!" Marin was reaching for Evie, to pull her back off before—

The dog shook once violently. His body shivered beneath Evie's hands. Then Pyramus lifted his eyeless head toward them.

He struggled to rise, as though there wasn't enough tying his bones together. His feet scratched against the crate, searching for a perch. Despite the effort, he stood and leapt for the edge of the grave, pulling his undead body out.

"Ms. Hallowell, I quit." Mr. Willoughby turned without another word.

"He left us," Marin said, watching Mr. Willoughby's retreating form. He never even looked back.

Evie scrambled up out of the ground. She grabbed for Pyramus, trying to pull him back toward his grave. A low rumble sounded from what was once Pyramus's chest.

"Evie, watch out!"

The creature turned fast, its jaws snapping for Evie's hand on its hip. Evie pulled back just in the nick of time.

"Marin, throw me that shovel."

Marin grabbed for the shovel nearest to her and tossed it across the dead dog to Evie. The creature was now pacing, watching Evie's every movement.

Looking for an opportunity.

Finally, it lurched forward.

Marin screamed.

Evie moved a half step to her right, so near the edge of the grave that Marin was sure she'd topple in. But she dug in her feet and swung the shovel hard.

It struck at the base of the animal's neck, severing it completely.

The dog's body fell with a thump.

He was dead once more.

Marin finally looked over to Evie. She was completely wrecked. Her hands were covered in graveyard dirt, her hair in tangled knots, and her flushed cheeks covered in mud—except for the tear tracks running down them.

"Evie," Marin said. "I'm so sorry. I'm sorry about Pyramus."

Evie dropped to her knees in the dirt. She looked tired, and Marin ached to comfort her.

"That wasn't Pyramus," she said.

Marin was the first to move. She rose and dragged the dog's body and head back into its crate, covering it gently once more and sealing it shut with a few forceful taps of the handle of the shovel on each corner.

Evie sat quietly with her grief and her guilt while Marin

shoveled dirt in to fill the grave.

What a goddamned nightmare.

They walked wordlessly back to the house, though at some point Marin's hand slipped into Evie's, and she didn't pull away.

Marin wasn't even surprised to find Neera waiting for them in the kitchen.

"Mr. Willoughby woke me," she said.

"Is he gone then?" Evie asked.

"Yes, I think that was the limit for Mr. Willoughby," Neera said with a sad smile. "Evie, dear, did you find what you were looking for?"

"Yes, we—" Evie looked over at Marin.

Marin reached into her pocket and pulled out Pyramus's collar, key dangling from the end of it.

"Yes, we did," Evie said.

"Good. And does this have anything to do with your grandmother's things?" Neera's voice was so gentle, and she pressed lightly on the sensitive topic at hand. But it was enough.

Just like that, it all came pouring out. Evie told Neera about the search for the journals, the mutilated deer in the woods, the fact that her powers were erratic. Unpredictable. Growing more so every day.

Neera listened patiently, and when Evie was done confessing—for that's exactly what it had felt like she was doing—Neera took one of Evie's cursed hands in her own.

"Evie, I knew your grandmother better than anyone. We spent many years out here. We had so much time to talk. To learn from each other. And what I know more than anything is how much she loved and admired you."

Evie looked up, her dark eyes bright with unshed tears. "Really?"

"Oh, that woman thought the sun rose and set just for you, sweet one. She hated knowing you had the same dark ability as her. Her journals were meticulous accounts of it, and she always meant for you to have them. I have no idea why your mother has hidden them away. But I'll bet that if there are answers to be found about whatever is happening here, your grandmother will have written it down."

Evie leaned in, thanking Neera and hugging her tight.

"It's late, girls," Neera said as she released Evie. "Can you get yourselves washed up here in the kitchen so you aren't traipsing cemetery dirt all over the floors?"

Despite everything, Evie smiled.

"Of course. Thank you, Neera."

"Oh, I almost forgot. He left this for you, Marin."

She offered Marin a small slip of paper, and Marin realized she was still gripping Pyramus's collar in her hand so tight her knuckles were white. She set the collar on the counter and unfolded the note. It contained a phone number and a single line of text: *Lovelace is sinking. Get out before you drown.*

Mr. Willoughby had left her a way out. A lifeline.

Marin crumpled the note into her jeans pocket and joined Evie in saying good night to Neera. When they were alone, they stood silently in the soft yellow glow of the light hanging over the kitchen sink. The house was dark, quiet. It had grown late. Marin's bleary eyes could barely make out the time on the clock over the stove. It was a few minutes past one in the morning.

Marin's mother used to call this time of night the witching hour, though the name had never felt more apt than it did tonight, here with Evie, covered in graveyard dirt.

"Let's get cleaned up," Marin offered gently, pulling out towels and soap and starting the water so it could heat up.

Evie went first, digging each of her nails under the other to scrape the mud from beneath them. She scrubbed her hands again and again, steam billowing from the sink from the piping hot water, until Marin understood that her hands had long been clean, and Evie still didn't stop.

"Enough!" Marin pulled Evie's hands out of the scalding water, wrapped them in a towel to dry them off. "Enough, Evie."

Evie finally looked at Marin.

"You're hurt," Evie said, stepping closer, her face twisted in concern.

She reached out and ran her thumb across Marin's cheek and bottom lip.

It came away covered in blood and a streak of Marin's lipstick. They were almost identical shades of deep, dark red.

"I'm fine, Evie. It's a scratch." Marin lifted the hem of her shirt to wipe the blood off her face. Anything to make Evie stop looking at her like that.

Marin quickly finished washing up.

Evie had pulled a large bottle of alcohol from its perch in a cupboard. She swallowed a gulp of whatever it was before passing it to Marin.

Marin took a small sip. The cinnamon was so strong that she gasped, the heat of it sliding down her throat and burning as it went.

"Are you all right, Evie?" Marin returned the bottle to Evie.

"Willoughby said you could leave with him, didn't he?" Evie didn't seem sad about the idea, only thoughtful.

"He did."

"He's right to do it. It's dangerous, Marin. *I'm dangerous.* I can't control it. You should leave Lovelace. I won't keep you here."

"Oh? How noble of you," Marin said, and couldn't keep the soft laugh from her voice. Here was Evie at her lowest, most vulnerable point, and all she could think about was making sure that Marin was safe.

"Yes, I'm a goddamned saint," Evie said, pulling the bottle back to her lips for another swig.

Marin moved before she thought. It was instinct, fierce and

sure, that drove one hand to the back of Evie's head, tangling in those messy curls, and the other to her hip, pulling her closer. Her mouth was on Evie's as soon as she swallowed, the taste of whiskey hot and spicy and burning her lips.

Marin drank her up.

She was *glorious*.

A sound came from the back of Evie's throat—half hum, half surprised gasp.

Evie broke away, searching Marin's eyes.

"Can I really keep you?" Evie asked.

"I'm not going anywhere," Marin said before kissing her again.

Somehow, they made their way through the winding, heavy darkness of the sleeping house, stumbling into Marin's bedroom. The curtains were closed against the moonlight, windows shut tight against the waking dead. With no light in the room, Marin felt entirely grounded in her body, aware of every touch and movement, the nuance of a cool kiss on her collarbone. The whisper of Evie's knuckles across her bare belly when her shirt rode up.

There was a slight desperation in each of Evie's movements. Her hands were insistent, questioning. Like she was trying to atone for some imagined sin. *I've been so lonely, for so long*, Evie's touch said. And Marin's hands answered. *You aren't alone. Not anymore.*

Evie's hands on Marin's waist were cool and smooth as a wave lapping against a ship's hull, gentle and possessive.

They held each other like anchors hold the ocean floor, their weight countering the pull of the tide, their fingers gripping just shy of too tightly.

And then, as one, they gave in to the call of those unknown depths. Marin felt the very moment of capsize, going under with Evie in a way that was somehow wholly new and unpredictable and yet as familiar as breathing.

There was no great mutiny within her at the surrender, no worry or fear. It was as simple as loving Evie, and letting Evie love her in return. Marin broke to pieces in Evie's arms and found beauty in the wreckage.

28

A Pocket Full of Posies

M arin woke to the unfamiliar weight of someone beside her in bed.

At first, she didn't open her eyes. She was content, enjoying the way the early sunlight slanted into the room through a break in the curtains. It fell across her face, illuminating her closed eyelids with a soft pink glow. When she breathed in, the air brought Evie with it. Her peach and rose shampoo and her hint-of-cinnamon perfume, but also the harsher smell of soap—lemongrass and bergamot—that she'd used to clean dirt from under her fingernails when they finally returned to the house late last night.

And of course, there was one last scent.

It was the one that clung to Evie always, like a perfume worn a day ago that lingers. The smell of death. Of decay. Of unholy resurrection.

No matter how she tried, Evie couldn't wash it all away. It was part of her.

But oh, how she'd tried.

Evie had scrubbed her skin too hard last night, desperate to get rid of the evidence of their dark exhumation. Her hands had been raw, red and angry, but *clean*, when she'd finally abandoned the kitchen sink and stepped into Marin's waiting arms.

Warmth flooded Marin's whole body at the memory of Evie's fingers tangled in her hair, her lips on Marin's lips, her neck, her chest. The memory of how they almost didn't make it past the kitchen.

Marin rolled over, smothering the earnest memory of Evie by Evie herself, there beside her like some kind of angel of death, fallen and vulnerable.

At some point Evie's braid came loose—in the cemetery or later, Marin couldn't remember. The white-blond curls that had escaped now framed her face. She had dark shadows under her eyes, and Marin remembered when they first met, how she wondered what could possibly cause them. She who was born to such privilege, such security.

Now Marin knew what haunted her.

For a few soft moments, Marin watched her sleep. Could there ever be enough mornings like this one? Waking up next to Evie with the memory of her kisses still on her and the light catching in her eyelashes.

Marin tossed her arm around Evie and sank deeper into the blankets.

The room brightened quickly. The sunlight outside reflected off the ocean, amplifying it back to the house again, shimmering across the tin tile ceiling. It crossed Marin's room like the tide coming in. Steady and inevitable.

Marin wished they could stay there all day, responsibilities forsaken. Worries forgotten.

As if on cue, she heard the creak of a floorboard outside. Marin shifted away from Evie to the far side of the bed, and a half second later, the doorknob squeaked.

Thea's bare feet pattered across the hardwood floor, and she climbed onto the wide bed beside Marin.

"We need help," Thea said, neither noticing nor caring that Evie was in Marin's bed. "We need to get the costume trunk outside."

Marin was already climbing out of bed. She didn't want to disturb Evie if they could help it. It had been a long, late night, and that was before they'd even stumbled into each other's arms and Marin's warm bed together.

"Why outside?" Marin asked, keeping her voice low.

"Pirates," Thea whispered, matching Marin's volume.

Marin waited, but apparently that was all the explanation she was going to get.

"All right, let's go."

She sent Thea off to wait for her and then got dressed.

But when she turned to leave, Evie was awake, quietly watching her.

"You're so beautiful," she said, and yawned.

Marin yawned too. She smiled. They'd been caught in this loop before.

Marin bounced back into the bed and kissed Evie awake.

"So. Are. You," she said, dotting Evie's face with kisses until she giggled.

Evie didn't laugh enough.

Marin was going to change that.

"The girls want to play costumes down at the shore," Marin said. "Want to join us?"

"I'll meet you down there," Evie said. "I'll bring tea."

"Coffee."

"Sacrilege," Evie said. "But fine. Coffee."

It was the lowest of low tides down on the rocks. Evie had explained to Marin that this far north, the tide was even more susceptible to the pull of the moon, and when it was full, the tide rose higher and went out lower than any other time.

It was just two days until the next full moon, which meant that at low tide, at least twenty yards of coastal rock and tide pools were exposed. Marin wandered around, searching the mud for small treasures. She collected more smooth bits of sea glass and dropped them into the pocket of her sweater.

Well, Evie's sweater.

It was hers now.

The little girls played chase on the rocks, their laughter riotous and echoing off the stone shore. Eventually Marin circled back, joining Evie where she had perched on a rock, and they watched the girls in silence for a long time, handing them props from the trunk of costumes they had painstakingly dragged down from the house.

Evie pulled out her tin of mints, and Marin caught a whiff of the warm, sweet heat of cinnamon. As always, she offered one to Marin before taking one herself.

Marin leaned her head on Evie's shoulder.

"Why cinnamon?" Marin asked, sucking on the strong candy, gripping the coffee mug that Evie had brought down for her with both hands.

"There is this . . . smell. It's sweet. Sickly sweet. Cloying. It's almost . . . rotten. And I can smell it—nearly taste it—whenever I'm too close."

"Too close to what?" Marin asked.

"Death. It's the smell of death. It's sort of always there now. It used to only be when I brought something back, but now it never goes away. Which makes sense—I'm waking things without meaning to, without even knowing it, all the time. But the cinnamon covers it up. It's the only thing that is strong enough."

"Hence the mints. And the perfume."

"And the whiskey," Evie said.

"Oh, how could I forget the whiskey?" The tide turned while they sat there, and Marin watched the first tide pool slip under the water. She couldn't help but think about all the things that could lie hidden beneath the surface.

Pyramus's key was in Marin's pocket too, its weight shifting against the sea glass. She was so aware of it that it felt like an anchor, holding her down, reminding her that this wasn't their life. Not really. It wasn't sea glass glinting in sunlight or children's laughter echoing off the rocks. Not with the dead rising all around them every day.

But for a little while, they could pretend.

Eventually they would go to the study, but Marin didn't push the issue. Evie was exhausted. Whatever had happened last night with the dog had drained her. The trunk and all the Lovelaces' dark secrets could wait a few more hours. In fact, if it were up to Marin, they could wait forever. The thought startled her.

But it was true.

She would let all her questions go in a heartbeat if it meant saving Evie from whatever it was that was slowly consuming her. Whatever was happening, it was taking a toll on her. And as much as Marin wanted to understand *why* Alice had followed her mother all these many years, the truth was, she wanted Evie even more.

Lovelace could keep its secrets if that meant that Marin could keep Evie.

"We don't have to be gravediggers," Marin said. "We don't have to live among the dead if you won't want to."

"What else could we be?"

Marin looked out over the water.

"Pirates," she said, knocking her knee into Evie.

"Poets," Evie said, but her expression was still grim, and Marin knew what Evie was thinking.

Evie believed she couldn't have anything but death, and awakening, and death again. An endless cycle of horror and loss. Or maybe she just didn't believe she deserved anything else.

Marin set her mug down, balanced precariously on an outcropping of rock, and reached across Evie to the chest of dress-up clothes that the girls had been pulling costumes out of. She grabbed a hat, pulling it onto her own head.

"Cowboys," Marin said, and tilted her head to look at Evie from under the wide brim.

Evie smiled despite herself. "Cowboys?" she challenged.

"Together, we could." Marin's voice was whisper soft, and Evie reached out and pulled one of Marin's hands between her own, holding it tight.

Marin picked up one of the girl's discarded crowns and placed in on Evie's head. "There, now you can be queen."

"Queen of what?" asked Evie.

"Queen of the world."

"And what about you?"

"I guess I'll be king," said Marin.

Evie smiled for real and tilted her head to steal a soft, quick kiss from Marin. The crown shifted, slipped down over her forehead, and Marin gently moved it back into place.

"We could just toss it into the tide." Marin didn't have to tell Evie that she meant the key. "We could run away together."

"We could," Evie agreed.

Marin followed her gaze to Wren and Thea playing on the shore below them. "But we won't."

"No," Evie answered, her eyes never leaving her little sisters. "We won't."

"Then let's get this over with." Marin stood and brushed off her jeans, offering Evie a hand to help her stand up.

Evie stood barefoot on the sharp rocks. She still wore her nightgown, and her hair was disheveled from falling out of its braid the night before. The dark marks under her eyes were like soft purple bruises in the bright July sun.

This morning, she was a wreck, in every definition of the word. Exhausted, windswept, her lips nearly bruised from their kissing—they'd been almost frantic to lose themselves in each other. All because Evie Hallowell was cursed. Damned to raise the dead, over and over again, against her will.

But if Evie was damned, then Marin might as well have been damned right alongside her.

Because Marin was completely in love with her.

29

Love You to the Bone

———— ❧ ————

They shepherded the girls off the shore and into the kitchen for lunch. But as they walked in the side door, all four of them stopped short in the doorway.

Alice and Neera were sitting together in the conservatory, drinking glasses of champagne.

"Girls," Neera said. "Join us, we're celebrating. Your mother has just finished her twelfth novel."

Wren and Thea cheered, rushing forward to wrap their arms around their mother.

"Can we have some?" Wren asked.

"Absolutely not," Neera said, but she rose and pulled some grape juice and ginger ale from the refrigerator and poured the girls a bubbly drink of their own.

Then she poured small glasses of champagne for both Marin and Evie.

"This is your accomplishment too," Neera said. "For chasing these little heathens all summer."

"Hey!" Wren protested.

"*Adorable* heathens," Neera said.

"Why, thank you," Thea said.

Alice looked better than she had in weeks. The dark circles under her eyes weren't gone, but they were less severe. She wore a robin's-egg blue dress, and it was the brightest color Marin had ever seen on her. With sunlight flooding the room and the taste of expensive champagne on her tongue, things at Lovelace House felt almost . . . normal. Dare she say it, maybe even happy.

"Delia, my dear, when did you arrive?"

Marin looked up to find Alice studying her closely.

Delia. Cordelia.

"Do you mean Marin, Mother?" Evie asked.

A shadow crossed Alice's face, and she frowned ever so slightly at the correction.

"Marin. Of course. You look so much like your mother I confused your names." But there was a subtle change. Alice shook her head. "You know, I think I've had enough champagne."

She set her flute down on the table.

"Thea, my love. I think I've been promising to play dolls with you for months. Shall we?"

Thea leapt to her feet, reaching for Alice's hand. "Oh, this is going to be *perfect*. Let's play in the greenhouse. It's *perfect* weather for it. We just need—Wren! We need you!"

Wren rolled her eyes but obeyed her sister, trailing behind them to the next room.

"She seems . . . better?" Evie asked.

But Neera sat quietly, staring down into her champagne. "She called you Delia," Neera said.

"My mother's name was Cordelia," Marin explained. "Were you at Lovelace House when she and my grandmother were here?"

"No, I came on after them. Alice was a teenager—a very serious teenager, determined to be published before the age of twenty."

"And she did it," said Marin.

"She did. Alice has always done everything she's set out to do. Evie gets that determination from her."

"We look alike," Marin explained. "My mother and I."

"Well, then, it's no wonder she confused your names," Neera said.

"And she's so tired," Evie added, "from the migraines. I don't think she's sleeping well."

"Well, now that she's done writing, she can rest," Neera said.

But Alice didn't rest.

She was all over Lovelace House with the little girls. Thanks to Thea's directing, their games took them to all floors of the house on nothing but a whim, which meant that

Evie and Marin couldn't sneak back into Charles Hallowell's study to open the trunk.

On the other hand, this meant that they had no responsibilities toward the girls, and they took advantage of their freedom, sneaking into the orchard with a picnic blanket and eating nothing but apples for dinner, rather than join the family when Wren came to collect them.

In between bites of apples, they talked.

Marin told Evie about a childhood uprooted—moving from one place to the next, never settling. Never sitting still. As she talked about it, Marin pictured the map hanging in Alice's office at this very moment, with little pink pins marking each of those places. But why? Why would Alice track her mother so diligently over these many years? Then the conversation shifted, to the hours Evie spent in the greenhouse with her father. The botany drawings they'd made in his book. Their grand plot to bring the corpse flower to Lovelace House. They were supposed to have visitors. Her father thought people would come out to see it. He wanted to open Lovelace up, breathe some life back into it.

When they were done with talking, they began kissing. In fact, they barely surfaced for air. Marin thought she could have stayed out there the entire night, kissing Evie Hallowell under the stars.

But they knew they couldn't. And as twilight settled all around them, they rose to their feet, lazily folding the blanket before turning back for the house.

They weren't finished with Lovelace House's secrets yet. Or maybe Marin had it backward, and Lovelace House wasn't finished with them.

Alice was asleep beside Thea, book open flat against her chest to the last page she'd read. Evie snuck into the room and delicately took the book and closed it on the bedside table. Then she tugged a blanket over her mother's shoulders.

Downstairs again, in Charles's study, it took Evie all of three minutes to unlock the trunk using the key from Pyramus and retrieve her grandmother's journals. They were unmistakable. Forest green leather with gold initials embossed on the spine.

The problem was that there were so many of them.

At least a dozen.

Evie flipped through one gently.

"This one covers about two years." She paused, running a finger over the page as she scanned the words. "Starting when I was around eight." Evie looked at the stack of thick journals, all of which were filled to the brim with Theadora Lovelace's tiny, neat script. "This might take a while."

A creak of a floorboard in the hall startled both of them, and they stopped speaking.

When only silence followed, Marin tiptoed to the door and peeked out into the hallway.

"It's empty," she said, turning back to Evie. "But let's get out of here before Alice catches us."

"Agreed," Evie said. She locked up the trunk once more, and each of them took a stack of the leather journals to carry out. At the door, Evie fished the key for her father's study out of the pocket of her skirt and locked up the door. "I suppose we should put this back before she notices we've taken it."

"It's late, anyway. We can start reading the journals tomorrow. Why don't you put them in the library, and I'll take the study key back to your mother's office."

"Are you sure?"

"Of course. I'll be quick. Meet you up there."

Evie told Marin exactly where she'd found the key, tucked into the back of the bottom left drawer of Alice's desk.

Marin slipped into the office, feeling every bit a trespasser in forbidden land. She took a chance and tugged the pull chain on a small table lamp, casting a warm yellow glow in the room, and shut the door firmly behind her. It took her no time at all to return the key to its hiding spot. And then she turned in a slow circle.

The room had changed since Marin was last there.

Alice's desk was in disarray—scribbled notes and dirty coffee mugs littered the entire surface. There were throw blankets draped over the windows, blocking out the full moon and casting the room in long shadows. The small desk lamp that she'd turned on was perched so close to the edge of the desk she was surprised she hadn't accidentally knocked it off while turning it on. Marin scooted it back from the ledge.

Something about the chaos of the room left her feeling unsettled. Exposed. This room didn't feel like it belonged to Alice Lovelace.

But she couldn't leave without looking at it once more, so she went to the map behind the door. It was just as she remembered. Each location was a place her mother had moved them in childhood.

Cordelia had never even explained it to Marin. The constant moves. She'd brushed it off with soft litanies of *We only live once* and *It's just a new adventure*. For a child who was painfully shy and struggled to make friends, the constant newness was like an abrasion, scraped open and raw with each move. An island in the sea, just like Wren. Unreachable and barren.

But not anymore.

Marin went back to the desk and pulled open another drawer. There were folders filed neatly inside, and Marin paged through them, reading the small labels. They were the titles of Alice's books, with dates going back ten, fifteen years of publishing. Drafts, Marin assumed from a quick glance into a folder.

She shut the drawer and reached for the next one.

Inside was a single folder, lying flat. Its label only had three letters: *C.E.B.*

Marin flipped it open.

There was a Polaroid of two young girls inside. One was tall and thin with gangly legs and arms, and very straight blond hair stretching all the way to her waist. The other girl had dark brown hair and a soft round face.

And then she knew. C.E.B. stood for *Cordelia Elizabeth Blythe*.

She flipped the Polaroid over. ·

Alice and Delia, age 11.

Marin dropped the photo and reached for the papers beneath it. There wasn't much there—a list of locations, another newspaper clipping, this one was from some carnival outside of Ann Arbor that her mother had taken her to, and the local paper had interviewed them and taken a photo. She ran her fingers over the blotchy black-and-white newspaper print, tracing her mother's face. It just didn't make sense. A bird sang just outside, but Marin ignored it.

Under the newspaper, Marin found a page of information all about . . . her. Her date of birth and the hospital she'd been born at. Her birth heigh and weight, all printed out, line by line. The page after that had more recent information: her height, her shoe size, her grades and test scores. Every little bit of data one could find on her, printed out and tucked carefully into this folder.

Marin lifted out the entire file and saw a white corner of an envelope sticking out from the far back corner of that same drawer.

She pulled on it.

Out came a stack of envelopes, all tied neatly with a string. Marin glanced at the address.

Cordelia Blythe, and then their address in Albany.

She quickly untied the twine and checked to the next envelope. Another letter to Albany. The next one was timestamped a year later, this time to their little house in Louisiana. She flipped through the envelopes. All addressed to Cordelia. All stamped in bold red ink: return to sender.

Her mother had never even opened them.

Marin stopped on the very last one. It was dated March of this year, addressed to their little apartment six blocks from the beach in San Diego. But this time it wasn't Alice's sprawling penmanship across the front.

It was Evie's.

Outside, the bird called again, louder and closer this time. No, not outside. It was coming from the house—the sad, sweet trill of a mourning dove.

Evie was using the signal they'd devised with the girls. Alice must have woken up.

Marin shoved the stack of letters into her pocket and slammed the drawer shut. She looked around for anything else she'd left out of place, but truth be told, the room was such a mess, she couldn't tell. She hoped that meant Alice wouldn't be able to tell either.

Marin heard a creak on the top stair and knew her time

was up. She turned off the lamp and ran from the office, pulling the door shut on her way and slipping back into the alcove that she'd hidden in with Evie.

She wasn't a moment too soon. The second she ducked into the nook, she heard the shuffle of footsteps as Alice Lovelace turned down the hallway.

Once she was sure she heard the office door shut, Marin fled to the library. She was swallowing great gulps of air and trying not to panic. She pressed the palms of her hands against her eyes, but the imprint on her lids was the same—Evie's familiar penmanship, on a letter dated just weeks before her mother died.

Marin crashed through the library door, slamming it shut behind her.

"What happened?" Evie rose instantly from the table where her grandmother's journals were sprawled, almost all of them open or bookmarked.

But when she approached her, Marin stepped back in equal measure, step for step. "Marin, what's wrong? Did she catch you in there?"

"No," Marin said. She sank to her knees and pulled the envelopes from her pocket, showing them to Evie.

"You acted like you didn't know," Marin said. "About her stalking us. But you did, didn't you?"

Evie knelt in front of Marin, lifted the letters.

"Yes. I knew."

"What did she want with us?" Marin asked.

"At first, I thought it was simple: she wanted to see your mother again. They'd been dear friends for years as children, and when Cordelia's mother left her job as housekeeper here, they lost touch. Did your grandmother never even mention this place?"

"She couldn't have. She died when I was little," Marin explained. But Cordelia could have told her. She had so many opportunities to tell Marin about Alice. To warn her. Instead, she'd kept secrets.

Marin was sick to her teeth of secrets.

"What happened, Evie?"

"Well, every letter that my mother sent, your mother returned unread." Evie held up the first letter as evidence, and the second, and the third. "I didn't know about any of this until last year, after father died. I was helping sort through family records, and we found the returned letters together, in his office. Mother was furious. Father never even told her the letters came back."

"Why would he do that?"

"Because she was obsessed, Marin. It took me months to see what he must have known for years. She was *desperate* to find your mother. It didn't make sense." Evie was still flipping through the letters, one or two addressed to each place Marin had ever lived, all sent back unopened. And then Evie reached the last one.

The one with her handwriting on it.

Both girls stared down at the letter in between them.

"Did you read it?" Evie asked, turning it even as she asked.

"No," Marin said. The envelope was still sealed.

"When I came home for spring break, she was . . . different. She had renewed her search for your mother, collected all this new information about her—and you this time too. I thought I would beat her to it. I found you first. I wrote to your mom. I told her that my mother wouldn't stop looking, and I didn't know what she wanted, but that I didn't think she should come to Lovelace House. Ever."

"And then you returned to school in March."

"Yes," Evie said. "And the letter came back here, unopened. That was all she needed. Once my mother had your new city, she arranged to visit—I suppose she thought if she could only see her in person, maybe—maybe she could let go of . . . whatever was left unsaid between them."

"My mother was running from Alice. All those years. She—she uprooted us every time she got a letter, didn't she?"

"I think so, yes."

"That means we were on that train because of her." Marin remembered that gray morning in May. The flyer her mother had pulled from her book. The urgency in her voice when she'd asked if someone had mailed it to her.

"Yes, it does. I'm so sorry, Marin." Evie's voice hiccupped on her name, her tears barely in check.

"But why?" Marin asked. It didn't make sense. "What could have possibly happened between them to cause this?"

Marin stood up, gesturing to the house all around them. "Why did she bring me here?"

"I'm still trying to figure that out," Evie said, rising as well, holding the stack of envelopes against her chest like a shield. "That's why I came home right away when Wren told me you were here."

"What were you so afraid would happen?"

"Honestly? I thought maybe she was going to hurt you."

"But why? She didn't even know me."

"It wasn't logical, Marin. It was obsession. She wanted your mother back here so badly, and when that couldn't happen, she settled on you."

"But *why*, Evie? What's wrong with her? Why was she so fixated on us, for twenty years? It's so twisted . . . it's so . . . *dark*."

And there it was.

That final word was left hanging in the air, the implication of it so awful and obvious that Marin knew it was true.

"Dark," Marin repeated. "*Sometimes they come back dark.*"

Marin whirled to face Evie. "You brought her back, didn't you?"

Evie didn't have to say it.

For once, everything was written across her features. Her guilt. Her shame.

"I didn't mean to do it."

"When?" Marin asked.

"Winter break," Evie said. "I went to wake her for breakfast. I crept into her bed and laid my head on her shoulder. She was so cold, Marin. And when I looked, her lips were blue. I guess it was some kind of stroke, in her sleep. And I grabbed her. I wasn't thinking when I did it. All I knew was that I didn't want the girls to lose another parent so soon. That I didn't want to either."

"All this time. She's been dead all this time?" Marin backed away as she spoke, but the implications of Evie's words followed her. Marin wasn't sure she could outrun them if she tried.

"She seemed okay," Evie said. "At first, she seemed all right. But as time went on, especially since I got home, she's gotten worse and worse. She's slipping away, and my powers are out of control. I don't know what's happening."

"Why didn't you just tell me?" Marin had to stop backing away when met with the closed library door.

"I was trying to protect you from all of this." Evie gestured to herself, Lovelace House, all of it.

"You *promised*, Evie. You swore there were no more secrets." Marin opened the door, had one foot in the hallways when she heard Evie behind her.

"The Lovelaces will always have secrets, Marin."

Marin turned back. "Yes. I'm beginning to understand that," she said. "But I trusted a Hallowell."

30

All the King's Horses, All the King's Men

Marin slept terribly.

She blamed her pillows for being too soft. She blamed them for being too scratchy. But mostly she blamed them for smelling like Evie, which is why sometime around one or two in the morning, she hurled them across her room.

The only good thing about going to bed angry was that Marin's mind apparently had no capacity left for nightmares. Instead, she tossed and turned, both dreamless and restless, until finally giving up and rising with the sun.

She pulled on her swimsuit and collected Wren and Thea, who were eager to join her for an early morning swim. It had been some time since their last lesson.

Instead of the rocky shore behind the house, Marin led the girls out the front of Lovelace House, beelining toward the orchards.

"Where are we going?" Wren asked, her perpetual frown firmly in place.

"You'll see," Marin said.

She led them through the apple trees and along the edge of the woods. Finally, they emerged at the top of a narrow, pebbled path.

"Oh," Thea said. "I know where we are."

The girls took off running down the steep path, and Marin stumbled along behind them. At the end of the path was the wharf. It was a huge stone pier—probably a hundred years old, at least, extending out into the water.

It looked perfect for diving, and Marin had wanted to try it since she'd first arrived.

The three of them dropped their towels on the rocks.

The view from the end of the wharf was different from the rest of the shore. Out at the end, surrounded by water on all sides and stretching forever in front of them, Marin really did feel like she was on an island.

Only this time Marin wasn't alone.

She extended a hand on either side, and waited as first one and then, tentatively, another small hand each found their way into hers.

"How about a countdown?" Marin asked, looking over to Wren.

"Three!" Wren shouted, her voice echoing across the water.

"Two!" Marin yelled as loud as she wanted to despite the early hour. It felt good.

"One!" On Thea's cue, they leapt off the edge together.

It was nearly high tide, so it wasn't the fall that made it scary. The plunge itself was short.

The water was the tough part. It was so cold that it hurt Marin's entire body on impact. The air left her lungs. It was a biting, arctic cold.

It felt incredible.

All three of them surfaced screaming, laughing, scrambling for the stone stairs on the side of the wharf. Once they'd climbed back out from the glacial waters, there was a moment when they stood there, shivering violently.

"Again?" Thea asked.

"Again," Wren said, and she was already jumping.

A half dozen leaps into frigid water later, they were spent. The sun had warmed the wide quarry rocks, and they lay out like starfish across the end of the wharf, waiting for their bodies to warm and catching their breath.

Marin swiveled her head to look at Wren.

Her eyes were closed, her face so at peace that it gentled her normally sharp features. Marin was struck by how young she looked. Wren had known almost everything, all along.

All things considered, she'd carried the burden of it quite well for a little girl.

"Hey, Wren," Marin said. "I want to thank you."

Wren turned to face her. "For what?"

"For trying to keep me safe. I thought you just wanted me to leave because you hated my guts. Now I understand why you wrote to Evie. So, thank you."

"I don't hate your guts, Marin. At least, not all of them. I've been *trying* to hate you. Would make things a lot easier when you do leave. But as it turns out, I'm pretty lousy at it."

"Yeah?"

"A complete failure really, at hating your guts."

"It's a pity," Marin said.

"It is," Wren said, closing her eyes and turning back to the warm sun once more.

"Hey, Wren? I'm not leaving. Ever."

"Ah, give it time." There was an evil twist of a grin on her face. "We have loads more pranks planned for you."

They stepped into the kitchen just as the teakettle whistled. Neera greeted them with a smile.

"Perfect timing," she said. "And I just saw Evie. She went to grab me some herbs from the greenhouse."

Thea wrapped her arms tight around Neera's middle.

"Oh, what's this?" Neera laughed, holding on to her.

"I just love you," Thea said before climbing onto a stool at the kitchen island.

"And I love . . . your scones." Wren smiled as she grabbed one, and Neera winked at her.

Marin joined Neera at the stove, taking over scrambled-egg duty while Neera drizzled icing over some cinnamon rolls.

It had to be cinnamon.

Cinnamon rolls.

Cinnamon whiskey.

Cinnamon kisses.

Cinnamon *Evie*.

"Well," Neera said, her voice dropping low enough that the girls couldn't hear. "You've certainly found your place here, Marin."

Marin glanced over her shoulder. "Have I? It doesn't always feel that way."

"I think those two girls over there would disagree."

"Oh, it's not them. They've been wonderful."

The squeak of rusty door hinges called Marin's attention across the room. Evie was standing in the doorway with two fistfuls of green sprouts.

She looked as though she hadn't slept at all—her face was drawn and pale, and the shadows beneath her eyes were pronounced. And there was something else, something different about her, but it was subtle and Marin struggled to name it.

Evie was still in her nightgown, tied haphazardly in the front over her breasts. She was barefoot. Her hair wasn't pinned or twisted or curled today, merely pulled into a loose ponytail, tied just under her left ear with what Marin thought was a ribbon until she looked closer. Evie's hair was tied with a curling tendril of dark red flowers. Amaranthus, was their name. Evie liked to identify flowers for Marin when they worked in the greenhouse—especially when doing so interrupted a particularly boring problem.

They're called love-lies-bleeding, she had said of the strings of the flowers.

And Evie had tied some into her hair.

Marin could imagine it precisely: Evie, trying to pluck herbs for Neera, only to have hair falling in her face, again and again. Reaching for a hair tie on her wrist only to realize she didn't have one. Finally grabbing for anything and finding a loop of love-lies-bleeding, wrapping it around her hair to keep it contained. Using her dark powers to keep it from wilting.

Finally, Marin understood it.

This was Evie unfiltered. She wasn't put together in a dress and boots that she wore like a uniform, preparing for battle. Her hair wasn't perfectly curled. Her grandmother's pearl earrings were nowhere in sight. Evie in her natural habitat, no longer caring what anyone thought.

No more secrets. No more confessions.

The tension between them must have been more obvious than Marin realized because when Neera looked up, her gaze went back and forth quickly between the two, and she clucked her tongue at them.

"Here now, what's this somberness?" she asked.

"Mom and Dad are fighting," Wren said.

"I wish they'd sort it out already and get back to making googly eyes at each other." Thea punctuated the sentence with an enormous bite of cinnamon roll.

"Me too, but like, for *our* sake," Wren said to Thea.

"Exactly. They're no fun when they're mad at each other." Thea could barely get the words out through the pastry and icing.

"Chew," ordered Neera. "Before you choke."

Marin shook her head as Wren's words finally registered. "Wait, who is mom in this scenario and who is dad?"

"Doesn't matter." Wren shrugged.

"Interchangeable," Thea said.

"And you don't think your own mother might object?"

"Can you imagine us calling her *mom*?" Thea asked. "She's *mother*. Not mom. Not mama. Trust me. We've tried."

"And it's not like Dad can really object," Wren reasoned. "Though I suppose we have at least one way to ask him, right Evie?"

"Rowena Hallowell!" The scolding came in unison, from Neera and Marin.

For some reason, that made Neera smile.

"I'm kidding. *Sheesh*. What's the point of having a creepy family magic trick if we can't even joke about it?"

And then, to everyone's surprise, Evie laughed. "She's not wrong."

She finally crossed the kitchen, offering up the herbal sacrifice to Neera.

"Hi," Evie said to Marin. "Can we talk?"

Before Marin could answer, the girls did it for her.

"Please, take her," Wren said.

"And we don't want to see you again until you forgive each other," Thea said.

"This way." As soon as they were out of the kitchen, Evie grabbed Marin's hand and began pulling her along the winding corridors of Lovelace House.

It reminded Marin of her first day there, being led up the stairs by Thea.

But Evie was practically running, and Marin nearly tripped trying to keep up: out to the foyer, up the stairs, straight into the library. Inside, Evie spun them, pinning Marin to the door the moment it closed, one hand on either side of Marin's body.

"I should have told you about Mother. It was stupid and selfish, and I have nothing to say for myself. I've clearly lost my mind when it comes to you because last night was one of the worst nights of my life, knowing you were angry at me, and that's saying something, because I have had some truly terrible nights, Marin Blythe. As in toe-curling, hor-ror-novel-inspiring—and I mean that literally, thanks to Mother—kind of nights. So when I tell you that I had a terrible night, I really—"

Marin kissed her.

Evie pulled back instantly. "Wait, I'm not done apologizing."

"Yes, you are," Marin said, and kissed her again.

Evie must have accepted it for what it was, because then

she was kissing her back, and it felt like an atonement. An urgent repentance for her secrets.

One that Marin gladly accepted.

Her fingers found the twist of flowers in Evie's hair, tugging gently.

"Couldn't find a damn tie," Evie murmured between kisses.

"I guessed as much," Marin said. "But you should probably know that if you're going for *inconspicuousness* as a necromancer, wearing literal plants in your hair and running around braless and shoeless will only feed the rumors."

"Let them talk," Evie said.

But when she pulled away, the look on her face dropped, replaced by those same lines of worry and exhaustion that had haunted her all these past weeks.

"What is it?" Marin asked.

"Marin, I found something in my grandmother's journals."

Evie went to the table by the window and brought back three of the worn old leather books, handing them to Marin.

"Already? You must have been up all night reading."

Evie waved the question away with her hand. "Of course. Now listen. These were her journals during my mother's childhood. There aren't as many entries in these years—and some are spaced years apart. It seems like she really had her hands full with Mother."

"But did you find what you were looking for? About waking things up without meaning to?"

"No. But I found something else. I think you need to

read them. Everything is in there. I marked the pages you need to see."

"But, Evie—"

"Read them, Marin. Just, go somewhere quiet, and read them on your own. And then you can decide for yourself."

"Decide what?"

"Whether or not you can stay here, once you know what happened."

Marin began to protest again, and Evie kissed her, a quick, unsatisfying thing, meant only to keep her from objecting again.

"Take them. *Read.* They're as much your story as ours, Marin. Maybe more so."

Evie slipped away through the door, and Marin was left standing there, holding all the Lovelace's secrets in the palm of her hand.

Part of her wished she were holding Evie's hand instead.

Marin collapsed in Wren's favorite reading chair, opened the first journal to the page Evie had marked, reading quickly.

She doesn't have it. I'm sure of it. We'd have seen some sign of it by now. I checked, and there's no record of anyone developing later than eight or nine years old. I can finally breathe. What a relief! To know she won't be cursed with this dark gift. Today, we celebrate—Alice's tenth birthday, and her freedom from this Lovelace curse.

Marin found the next bookmark. She scanned the page a bit and realized that this must be about a year after the last bookmarked entry.

It's happened again. I don't know what this sickness is. I'd hoped—fervently, I'd hoped—that it would lessen with time. I thought that revealing my abilities to her would make her less curious. Would help her understand that she, my darling girl, is the lucky one, to not be able to wake things. But this darkness remains. This . . . proclivity for death. She is particularly keen on drowning. I didn't even know she'd found the feral cat and her kittens until I heard the bath running upstairs . . .

Marin had to stop reading the entry there, feeling ill at the thought of what Theadora had discovered. She was tempted to abandon the journals right then. Part of her no longer wanted to know.

But Evie had been insistent that she read these, whatever was coming, so Marin pressed on, setting that journal down and reaching for the next one. The dates in this one were much earlier than the last—dated all the way back in the year Alice was born. Marin read Theadora's words.

What have I done? What have I done? What else could I have done instead? This morning, when I went to wake her, Alice wasn't breathing. Her lips were blue. At first, I thought she was choking. But when I reached for her, I realized—she was already gone. And then, in my arms, she woke. The color rushed back to her cheeks. She cried out, screaming. God, she screamed for hours. Hours and hours, endlessly.

But she's alive. Or is she? Do I even care if there's a difference? I know we have rules. A failing houseplant, a beloved pet—these we can wake on occasion without dire consequence. But we never—never—wake people.

I didn't mean to do it. But God help me, I think even if I'd understood, I'd have done it anyway. What else could I have done?

It was awful—more awful than she'd guessed. Evie hadn't been the first to wake Alice.

Marin had seen how their dark magic worked. How some of the woken animals had come back with a mean streak. She didn't know what that meant for Alice, brought back to life not once but *twice*, but she knew it wasn't good.

Marin opened to the last bookmark and took a steadying breath. This final entry that Evie had marked was dated the summer Alice was eleven. The same summer that the photo had been taken of her with Cordelia, laughing together in their swimsuits.

Diana and Cordelia Blythe left today. They barely packed their things, and they were gone.

*I can no longer deny that there is something very wrong
with Alice. She tried to hide it. I saw her efforts. But now
I wonder if she was simply hiding it from me.*

*It was only by chance that I saw it happen, while out
for a walk. The moment looked so tender. The girls held
hands to jump from the wharf. Again, and again, into the
water.*

*And then, the last time, I watched my Alice reach for
Cordelia, watched her push her dear friend underwater.
Watched as she didn't let her up.*

Oh, I screamed, but I was too far.

I ran, but I was too late.

*When I dove in and pulled her from the water,
Cordelia was gone. Drowned. Why? I don't know. My
touch brought her back. And she looked at us like we were
monsters.*

Perhaps we are.

*They left within a few hours, and I can't blame them
for running.*

I can confess it here, though I'd never tell a soul:

Sometimes I want to run from Alice too.

31

Drowning Games

———————— ❧ ————————

Marin slowly closed the journal.

She heard a shout outside and stepped to the window. Below, the girls were playing whiffle ball, with Evie pitching. She still wore her nightgown, was still barefoot, but her hair was loose. Marin spotted a small streak of red in the grass and knew Evie's fragile hair tie had finally fallen.

Evie pitched the soft plastic ball, a low and gentle toss, and Wren's bat connected with the ball with a loud snap. Before Thea could chase it down, before Wren could even run, Thisbe shot like a rocket across the lawn, scooping the ball up into her mouth and taking off for the woods. Evie laughed, and Marin mourned the glass and distance separating her from the sound.

Evie's shoulders lifted in a shrug at the girls. There could be no game without the ball, and Thisbe had seized her bounty and disappeared.

Marin felt like her chest was cracking at the sight below. The Hallowell girls were just that—young girls—no different from her, really, though it was hard to remember that at times. They felt like an extension of Lovelace House itself: looming so large in the landscape of Marin's mind that she could no longer see anything else. There was this house and these girls, and it had begun to feel as though the rest of the world had ceased to exist.

Marin stayed in the library long after the girls had wandered back inside. She circled back to Wren's chair, where she sat for hours, legs curled up underneath her until she couldn't feel them anymore.

Evie must have warned everyone off because no one called her for lunch or dinner. The girls didn't come to bother her or beg for a game.

Marin needed some space from the Hallowell girls, to think about the confessions she had read in Theadora's journals. And to grieve, for that's exactly what it felt like.

Marin grieved her mother all over again. She grieved for the life they might have lived together if only Cordelia hadn't been running from Alice, always looking over her shoulder for the monster of her childhood.

She grieved for Theadora Lovelace, who didn't mean to do it, to bring Alice back. She'd tried so hard to protect her granddaughters from the consequences of that decision.

And she grieved for Alice too.

Whatever was driving this inside of her—the drownings, the obsession with Cordelia, the desire to wake Charles Hallowell—it was entirely beyond her control. She'd never had a choice. She'd been woken twice, by those who loved her most. A mother, a daughter. And because of that, Alice had only ever known darkness.

Now she knew the truth about Alice, Marin waited for the fear to come. She waited for that inevitable pit in her stomach that would tell her to run away. She waited for the first round of *Worst-Case Scenario* to race through her mind.

But it didn't happen.

It didn't matter that they were chasing the cause of Evie's out-of-control powers. It didn't matter that their respective mothers had a dark, intertwined history. It didn't matter that each new revelation should have pushed Marin away, should have made her want to flee like her grandmother and mother had done so many years ago.

When she closed her eyes, Marin saw Evie's face. When she touched her fingers to her lips, she felt the memory of Evie's kiss. When she drew a deep breath, she smelled the lingering notes of Evie's perfume.

There was no worry that loving Evie couldn't vanquish.

This place might not ever feel fully like a home, and in that way, Evie was nothing like Lovelace House.

Evie had always felt like home.

When the sun began to set, casting the library in long lines of red and violet light, there was a knock on the library door.

"Yes?" Marin called. Her voice cracked from hours without use.

Neera entered the library and approached her. "There you are. I've been looking for you."

"I just needed some time," Marin said.

"Yes, of course." Neera was looking at the collection of journals on the table.

"Did you know?" Marin asked. "Did you know what she is? What she did to my mother?"

"No," Neera said. "I didn't know about your mother. Evie told me today. But I guessed the truth about Alice even before her mother told me. Theadora was always so . . . *watchful* with Alice. And not like other mothers were. Most mothers are like mama bears, ready to swoop in and defend their young. But Dorie watched Alice the way one would watch a coiled snake: afraid to startle it, watching for it to strike."

"And then you took over? Watching?"

Neera nodded. "She knew Evie would need guidance. Protection. When Charles died, I knew there would be conflict, though I didn't expect Alice to blame Evie entirely. Or beg her to bring him back. That's why I encouraged Evie to go away for school. It seemed the safest choice. Distance from Alice."

"She came back for me," Marin said, guilt spiking in her chest.

"She was right to," Neera countered.

"I thought you were like me," Marin confessed.

"What do you mean?"

"Like, another person on the outside looking in at them. It made me feel less alone here."

"You have never been alone here, Marin. Not even from the first day. I've been watching out for you too. In fact, I've been thinking you'd make an excellent new Guardian for the girls."

Marin looked up, finding warmth in Neera's eyes.

You could find a home here yet, Neera had told her early on.

"But I think I have to tell you, Marin. You are not an outsider looking in on this family. Like it or not, and I suspect right now you're leaning toward *not*, but you are already part of this family. You are free to leave whenever you'd like. We'd help you get on your feet. But for whatever it's worth, I think you belong here with us."

When Marin finally left the library, it was dark outside. She found Evie in the girls' room, getting them ready for bed.

"Another migraine?" Marin asked from the doorway.

Evie looked up from where she was sitting on the floor, all her hair spread out behind her, where Thea knelt on the bed, painstakingly braiding the mass of it. Thea liked to practice braiding on her dolls, but Marin looked around the room.

It seemed Thea had finally buried the last of them.

"Yes," Evie said. "She wouldn't even get out of bed today. I tried, but . . ."

"She yelled at her," Wren said from her bed, not even looking up from her book.

"About Father," Thea added. Her little fingers twisted down Evie's back, braiding it to the end.

"She still wants . . ." Marin couldn't say it.

She imagined the state of Charles Hallowell's body by now—a year dead. There was nothing left to wake.

"Don't worry, Evie. I cheered her up."

Evie turned, pulling her long braid over her shoulder and smiling up at her sister. "Oh yeah? How did you manage that?"

"I showed her how hard I've been practicing," Thea said, her little face proud. "She was *so* happy, Evie."

"Practicing braiding hair?" Evie asked as she stood and reached for the bedside lamp.

"No, the other thing," Thea said, scooting back on the bed and under her blankets.

Evie paused, hand on the light.

"What other thing, Thea?"

Thea's voice dropped to a conspiring whisper. "You know, Evie. The *other* thing."

Her little hand reached out toward the base of the lamp, where a glass of water stood, beads of condensation running slowly down its side. There was a dead moth floating on the surface. Thea reached in and scooped it up gently on her fingers.

For a moment, there was only quiet in the room, an unnatural stillness as everyone stared at the small dead moth. And then, a flutter. Its legs twitched, and Thea placed it on the table. The moth's wings fluttered, shaking off the wetness.

"See? I've been practicing," Thea said.

The moth turned, preparing for flight.

Thea lifted Wren's book from the table and crushed the moth beneath it.

32

Memento Vivere (Remember, We Must Live)

———————— ❧ ————————

Practicing, Thea had called it.

Evie and Marin finished tucking the girls in, leaving their door open enough to let the hall light in. Suddenly Thea's nightmares made more sense.

"What do we do?" Evie asked. She was wringing her hands so hard it looked painful, and Marin covered them with her own.

"We just love her, Evie. We teach her. We watch over her. The same things we've been doing."

Evie nodded, but she looked unconvinced.

"I hate this for her," Evie said. She walked with Marin down the hall to her bedroom door, their hands still intwined.

"I know," Marin said. "But it won't be like it was for you. You'll never pressure her like Alice did. You'll help her."

"Okay. No, you're right," Evie said. She stood there awkwardly, looking like she wasn't sure how to say the next part. "I'm so sorry, Marin. I'm sorry about your mother."

"I'm sorry about yours too," Marin said. Evie's grief might even be worse than her own. At least Marin's grief was clear, warranted. Evie's was muddled by Alice's transgressions and the blame she'd placed on Evie's shoulders since her father's death.

"Okay, well. Um, good night, Marin." Evie turned for her room, but Marin didn't let go of her hand, tugging her back.

"Marin?" Evie asked. Her dark eyes were fixated on her, pulling Marin in like a black hole, consuming her.

"Will you stay with me tonight?" Marin asked.

Evie's hand tightened in hers, and Marin pulled her into her room, shutting her door tight against the world. Locking out Lovelace and its secrets.

It felt like minutes later that light spilled into her room. Marin rolled away from it, reaching for Evie. But her hands found only emptiness.

Marin sat up.

She heard noise in the hall and climbed out of bed to follow the sound.

Outside her door, she found Wren and Evie in a heated exchange. Wren had been crying. She had her hands wrapped tight around Evie's forearms, her nails digging into Evie's skin, but Evie seemed oblivious.

"I'm telling you, I've already checked, Evie. I checked the greenhouse, the kitchen. I don't know where she is."

Marin glanced back in her room at the clock, its face just barely illuminated by the hall light. Half past three in the morning. Where the hell could Thea be?

"I'll go wake Neera," Evie said. "Marin, can you peek in on Mother?"

Marin nodded, already moving down the hall toward Alice's bedroom.

It felt like a transgression, to twist the doorknob of Alice's private room in the middle of the night. But then the door swung open, and Marin looked around.

Alice was gone too.

Marin turned to leave and saw a stack of untidy papers on the small table by Alice's door. She flipped a page in. It was Alice's latest manuscript.

Marin turned to the first page and began to read.

She frowned and turned to the second page, then the tenth.

Every single page was the same.

AD OSSA. AD OSSA. AD OSSA.

The same two words, again and again. For a hundred pages, two hundred. Marin turned to the very back of the book, desperate to find something real, but there was nothing.

This was the book Alice had worked on all summer.

Marin lifted the manuscript, taking it back down the hall.

Evie and Neera were at the top of the stairs.

"She's gone, isn't she?" Neera asked.

Marin nodded, and Evie swore.

"I told Neera about Thea," Evie said.

"She'll try to use her," Neera said. "She'll try to make her wake him."

"You really think so?" Evie asked. "Thea's so young, Neera."

"I think if she were the version of herself from last summer, this would be a different story. But if she's really been woken again by you, Evie, then there's no telling what she's capable of. Think of the worst creatures you've risen. Their single-mindedness."

"Evie, you need to see this," Marin said. She gave her the book.

Evie flipped through the first few pages, and Marin saw the exact moment Evie understood. The horror that etched itself into the fine features of Evie's face.

She gasped and dropped the entire stack of papers.

They fluttered across the stairs, slipping through the wide spaces of the banister and raining down to the foyer below.

Ad Ossa. The Lovelace family motto was there in black ink a hundred thousand times, evidence of just how broken Alice was.

Evie turned to Marin. "We'll have to go in the cemetery. I don't know what will happen when I get that close to the dead."

Marin gave her hand a quick squeeze of reassurance before dashing toward her room. "I guess we'll find out. Get dressed, Evie. Hurry."

Marin moved fast, throwing on shorts and a shirt and pulling her hair back to keep it out of her eyes. Last, she moved to her bedside table, reaching down behind it.

She pulled out the hatchet and returned to the hallway.

Wren and Neera soon joined her, dressed as though they were going hiking.

Through Dante's inferno, thought Marin.

Evie came out of her room. She wore jeans and boots and a thin, off-white camisole. For Evie, this was casual and functional. Her hair was still bound in the long braid Thea had done for her before they went to bed.

One by one, each set of eyes in the hallway landed on the hatchet in Marin's hands, but no one said a word. At the bottom of the stairs, Neera veered off to the kitchen, returning with a long knife from the kitchen and a smaller one for Wren.

Outside, they practically ran. Marin and Evie were ahead, and Neera waved them on, keeping pace with Wren's shorter legs.

It was a cool night, and the sky was mostly clear except for a few strings of purple-red clouds. There was a full, heavy moon directly above them. The thin clouds gave it a hazy yellow glow.

They paused at the entrance, scanning the grounds. The cemetery looked empty. Marin felt something brush against her arm, and she yelped, backing into Evie.

320

It was Thisbe.

"Hey, Thisbe," Marin said, petting the dog's huge head. She was panting in the heat, and every hair along her spine was bristled. "Good girl."

"Here we go." Evie stepped inside.

Marin's hands shifted up the handle of the hatchet as she followed, even as she told herself she wouldn't need it.

As soon as they stepped inside, Marin understood what felt wrong. It was too quiet. For a warm summer night on the coast, surrounded by thick woods and foliage, the grounds should have been alive with nocturnal creatures. But there wasn't even so much as a cricket chirping out in the graveyard.

They crept through the cemetery, heading for Charles Hallowell's final resting place.

Marin wasn't surprised when they stopped in front of the same mausoleum she'd once found the girls hiding in.

AD OSSA, it read over the arched doorway.

But that was a Lovelace saying. Charles Hallowell didn't believe that everything had to stay at Lovelace. He wanted to move. He insisted on putting the girls in regular school. His flask was carved with a phrase that meant *remember, we must die.*

Charles Hallowell didn't believe in waking the dead.

And yet, here they were.

Thisbe growled, a deep, low threat of a sound that rumbled

in her chest. A moment later, she took off, bounding through the gravestones.

Marin was about to call her back, but Evie gripped her upper arm. "Let her go. It's probably Neera and Wren."

Marin nodded and followed Evie up the stone steps. Sure enough, the gate was unlocked and slightly ajar.

They pushed inside. It took a moment for her eyes to adjust to the dark inside. The room itself was sparse. There was only the one sarcophagus against the back wall, beneath a small diamond of stained glass that had beams of bright moonlight streaming in. The lid had been pushed off. It lay on the floor with one long crack running up the center of it.

"I can't. I can't look, Marin. I'm sorry." Evie gestured to the stone coffin with a wave of her hand.

"I can," Marin said, and stepped forward. She could face this—Charles Hallowell's drowned and decomposed body. She could do it for Evie.

Marin peered down into the sarcophagus and wrinkled her brows in confusion. "He's not here," she said.

Evie let out a soft sob behind her. "Did they already do it? Did they wake him?"

"No, I mean. I don't think he was buried here. It's stairs, Evie."

"What?" Evie came forward and leaned over to look.

There was no body—nor had there ever been. At least, not here. There was instead a narrow set of stone stairs, leading down into darkness.

Evie looked to Marin. "What do we do?"

"We find your sister," Marin said without hesitation. "Together."

Marin knew she would go the moment she realized that Thea was down there somewhere. If she could travel down these stairs into the unknown, then Marin could too.

With Evie by her side, Marin wasn't worried. She'd follow her anywhere.

Even into the dark.

33

Burn It, Drown It, Bash It Over the Head

As a child, Marin Blythe dwelled in possibility.

Even as a very young girl, she'd understood her role—she was the antithesis of her mother's rashness. The foil to her mother's bravery. A quiet companion on her mother's adventures, like a sidekick.

Marin never minded. She was content to be the reserved one, the contemplative one. The *careful* one. Besides, the world scared her. She had too much respect for its dangers to go running into them full speed like Cordelia was inclined to do.

Or so she'd always thought.

Now Marin knew, they weren't as unalike as she'd thought. Cordelia had feared things too. She'd feared drowning. She'd feared Alice Lovelace.

As Marin descended the slick, moss-covered stone staircase in the back of the mausoleum, she understood that for Alice, hardly any of her novels had ever been fiction. She'd only borrowed truths and slanted them into something slightly new.

"Oh!" Evie's soft exclamation came from below. She turned to call back up. "Hey Marin, be careful, it's full of water down here."

A moment later, Marin was beside her, wading into freezing cold water up to her shins. Ahead of them was a dark tunnel with no end in sight.

"You can go back," Evie said. Her voice was like a plea. *Go and be safe. Give me one less person I love to worry about.*

"Thea is down here, Evie. She might be hurt. I'm sure she's scared. I'm not leaving here without her."

They forged on, seawater churning around them.

Marin slipped and got a briny mouthful of salt water and scraped her hand on the wall of the tunnel, which was hard and rippled with what felt like roots, twisting on top of each other, layers deep. But the worst was the realization that came after ten minutes or so of their slow slog through the water.

It was getting higher.

They were now soaked to their knees.

"Look, there," Evie said.

There was a soft glow ahead, and Evie gripped Marin's hand tighter in the darkness. "It's almost over."

Finally, they emerged from the tunnel and stepped into a small room.

Marin noticed several things at once, and each realization made her want to turn and climb back through the dark, flooding tunnel from which she had only just emerged.

The first was Thea, unconscious on a slab of stone in the center of the room. It was an altar of some kind, and it was surrounded by a ring of candles and a few kerosene lanterns providing the only source of light, dim and flickering as it was. Marin could smell the lamp fuel from across the room, slick and oily.

The second thing Marin noticed was Alice, who stood off to the side, staring into a darkened alcove cut right into the wall of the room. There was something else just beyond her, in the shadowed archway, but Marin couldn't make out what it was.

The third thing Marin noticed was the room itself. It was covered in barnacles, and Marin felt the ground beneath her shifting as she stepped—it was mud, like the kind covering the shore.

But it was what the barnacles clung to on the walls that made Marin take two fingers and pinch tight a bit of skin on the underside of her own upper arm.

Wake up.

Wake up.

But she couldn't.

This was real.

Lining the walls from floor to ceiling were bones. They

were pressed tight together, twisted to form the archway over the alcove. Stacked to form the altar that Thea was laying on. Skulls and ribs and femurs and tiny little bones that looks like pebbles and sticks. Metacarpals and phalanges.

It was an ossuary: a room of bones. A kind of burial chamber.

Ad Ossa wasn't just a family creed. It was directions. *Down to the bone.*

"Evie," Marin whispered. "What the hell is that?"

Marin's gaze shifted back to Alice when something moved in the darkness beyond her. It shifted closer to the candlelight, which now flickered so violently that Marin feared it would go out altogether.

Alice stepped aside, and a man emerged.

Or rather, something that had once been a man.

Half of Charles Hallowell's skin was gone, split down the center line of his face. It looked as though it had been slowly peeled away, layer by layer. On the half that was facing them, there was only skull remaining, the socket dark. There were barnacles crossing the exposed bone.

He must have been buried in a suit, but the black had faded to a sickly green. Seaweed clung to the breast of the jacket in clumps.

Evie cried out—a sound that caught in her throat with a sob as she stepped closer to him, a sound that was swallowed almost instantly by the bones around them.

The dead man turned at the sound.

On the other half of his face, his skin was ashen and sagging, and his eye had a milky white film covering his iris.

She'd actually done it.

Alice had used Thea to bring Charles back.

It was more horrific than Marin could have guessed. Not even a lifetime of anxiety, nor half a decade of reading horror novels, had prepared her for the image before her.

And even worse than the grotesqueness of it was the wrongness.

He didn't *want* this.

But Evie was entranced, eyes locked on her resurrected father.

"Daddy?" Evie's voice was small and soft.

"It's not," Marin whispered. "Evie, it isn't him. Not really."

Evie's father was facing her head-on, and his hand lifted, reaching for her. Evie slipped her fingers into his, her grip gentle on the delicate, decaying skin. Even so, Marin saw where the skin broke, splitting down the soft pad of his thumb so deep the bone was visible.

A horrible gurgling sound filled the room, and Marin looked up to his face. He was trying to talk. Marin knew this because part of his throat that had been torn away, and she could see the muscles shifting and straining. His vocal cords were rotted, and the sounds he made were like drowning—wet and tortured and dead.

Evie finally addressed Alice. "Mother, what have you done?"

Alice kept her eyes fixed on Charles too, but she seemed to see none of the death. Marin recognized that same look from the home video she'd watched in the girl's room.

Her gaze held nothing but adoration.

"You could have helped a year ago, Evangeline. You refused."

"He would hate this," Evie said, her voice pleading for Alice to see reason. "I hate this. I hate this room. I hate this curse—"

"Curse?" Alice repeated, finally looking at Evie. "Darling girl, it isn't a curse. It is a gift."

"It isn't, Mother."

"How could you have this ability and deny it? You inherited this when I did not for a reason, Evangeline. And that reason was to bring back your father, and still when the moment came, you *failed*. You left him there to *rot*."

"I did what he would have wanted."

"You can't escape this, Evie. It's in your very bones."

"I can't even control it, Mother," Evie said.

"*Of course you can't,*" Alice snapped. "You've denied it your entire life. You are too emotional, Evie. If you can't control yourself, how do you expect to control your powers? Your father tried to help you, to explain to you that you had to control it, not let it control you. And how ungrateful you've been. How ungrateful you've *all* been."

Alice turned again, this time facing Marin.

"Especially your mother. She should have worshipped the Lovelace grounds. I let her in. I made her my sister. I shared all our secrets with her. And then I watched my mother break her one cardinal rule for her, after vowing to never wake a person. But was she thankful? *No.* She was a scared little mouse who ran away. I overestimated her."

"Then why did you follow her?"

"Everything stays at Lovelace, child. Except for your mother. So I had to bring her back," Alice said. "She had to recognize this, all of this." Alice turned as she spoke, arms wide, encompassing all the nightmares that Lovelace had to offer. "For the beautiful magic that it is. And if I couldn't have that from her, I'd get it from you. But you understand, don't you, Marin, dear? You aren't scared of Evie because of her gift, are you?"

Evie finally turned away from her father and looked at Marin, waiting on her answer just like Alice was.

"I'm not scared of Evie at all," Marin said.

"Do you see?" Alice whirled on her daughter, reaching for her hand. "You can use your power, keep Charlie here, we can be a *family*—"

"No!" Evie's rejection was sharp and sure as she wrenched her hands away from Alice. "*No.* Just because I can bring things to life doesn't mean I have to, Mother. It's mine and mine alone. You don't get to decide for me."

Something dark flared in Alice's eyes, and she turned back to Charles.

Marin took advantage of the moment to cross to Thea. She placed her hand against her, relieved to find a pulse, weak though it was. When Marin's hand crossed her forehead, she realized that Thea was burning up with a fever.

"You're right, Evie. I can't force you to do it. Fortunately, your sister didn't feel such qualms about her powers."

"What's wrong with her?" Marin asked.

"It would have taken a lot out of her," Evie said, watching her parents carefully. Charles was shuffling closer to the altar, and Alice fell in lockstep with him. "To wake him. It takes energy. I was always so tired when I'd accidentally used my powers."

Marin found the dark circles under Evie's eyes. No matter how much Evie rested, they never got better. Accidentally waking the dead must have been draining her all this time.

Marin tried to wake Thea, shaking her gently at first and then more urgently. As she leaned over the little girl, she felt the water lap at her waist.

Marin looked around the room. They were likely below sea level, somewhere in the depths below Lovelace House. The ocean water was coming in with the tide.

At the rate the water was rising, this entire room could be underwater in mere minutes.

Marin realized that this must be how the water was getting into Lovelace House in the basement and the pipes. It was how the teeth and mandibles were dragged out into the tide pools. The ossuary was flooding and draining with every tide.

Lovelace House really was sinking.

"Evie, the water is getting higher." Marin spoke softly, but she couldn't quite keep the high pitch from her voice as she felt on the verge of panicking. They still had to climb back through that long, dark tunnel.

It might already be too late.

But the urgency in her voice attracted Alice's attention.

"What are you doing?" Alice trained her eyes on Marin. "You can't go."

There was no denying the desperation in Alice's voice.

"Alice, she's sick," Marin said, gesturing to Thea's pale form between them. "Let me get her out of here."

"She woke him. If she leaves, he could die again."

"No, Mother, that won't happen," Evie said. "I'm here now. I can keep him awake for you. Let Marin take Thea."

"Evie, what are you—" Marin began to object, but Evie lifted a hand to quiet her.

"Marin can do it. She'll have no trouble getting Thea out through the tunnel. She's such a strong swimmer, remember, Mother?"

While Evie spoke to Alice, Marin threaded one arm under Thea's neck, the other under her knees. She lifted Thea's lithe body against her chest, clutching her tight, prepared to make a run for the tunnel.

She didn't even get a chance to try it.

Alice lurched forward, gripping Thea's thin arm in both of her own. Marin flinched at the sight of Alice's long nails cutting into the tender flesh of Thea's upper arm and inner wrist; crimson crescents of blood bloomed almost instantly.

When Thea didn't even stir at the pain, Marin knew just how dire the situation was.

They'd all die down here.

Evie moved first.

She dove underwater, rearing back up a moment later with a splintered long bone in her hand. She didn't even hesitate, swinging it at Alice and connecting with the side of Alice's head.

When Alice's grip on Thea loosened, Marin pulled the child free and began moving toward the tunnel.

Alice shoved Evie, who slipped against the altar, cracking her face against the edge of one side. Marin saw the wide cut over her eye just as blood poured down.

Marin ran then, but it wasn't enough. She felt Alice's bony hand on her arm, tugging hard enough that she lost her balance, plunging both her and Thea briefly underwater before Marin found her footing and rose again, sputtering.

For a moment, Marin felt the hot grip of Alice's hands on her again, ready to drag her under.

The next moment, Alice was gone.

Marin watched as the thing that was once Charles Hallowell wrapped its hands around Alice, pulling her back into the ossuary.

Away from Thea.

Evie wiped blood from her face and watched as her parents struggled near the altar. Alice wrenched her arms from Charles and turned to come after Thea once more. When Charles leaned across the altar to block her, Alice whirled, knocking several candles and one of the kerosene lanterns over at once.

The lantern cracked, spilling oil across the surface of the altar until it pooled beneath Charles, soaking the tattered cloth covering his outstretched arms.

A soft sizzle of a sound hissed across the room, and then flame erupted on his sleeve. Barely a moment later, his entire arm was aflame. Alice screeched, veering back toward him, grabbing for him even as the fire burned her hands and spread up his body.

Alice pushed Charles into the water, putting out the fire, but it was too late. The oil had burned fast, and whatever magic Thea had used to bring him back was spent.

His body was still once more.

"Mother, it's time to go now," Evie said, reaching for her mother.

Alice only had eyes for Charles.

"Leave me," Alice said. She reached out, her fingers intertwining with her husband's bones.

"That's ridiculous. It's flooding." Evie's voice broke on a sob, and she clutched Alice's arm, pulling in earnest now.

"Evie," Marin said. "We can't wait."

Alice shook Evie's hands off her. She dragged Charles through the water, back into the darkened alcove.

Evie turned to Marin, her face covered in blood and tears and salt water.

"I can't leave them," she said.

"I know," Marin said. "But you must."

The ossuary began to shake around them. An earthquake? Was the room collapsing? But then she heard Evie cry out, and she turned to see a skeletal hand on the wall of the ossuary, clenching and unclenching.

Reaching.

"They're waking," Evie said. "I'm waking them."

Sure enough, more of the bones of the walls were shaking, practically vibrating, trying to break free.

"Please, Marin. Get Thea out of here before we get trapped."

Marin ducked into the tunnel.

The moment the archway crowded her line of vision, she dared to glance back and saw Evie just a few yards behind her, still begging Alice to come with her before the darkness swallowed them.

Inside the tunnel, it was dark and cramped and the water was rising fast. Marin's breathing ticked up its pace, and her heart began to pound.

Not now.

Thea needed her.

She took a deep breath, even though that air was saturated with salt and blood and the scent of death behind them. She pushed everything out of her mind except putting one foot in front of the other. Instead of the ossuary behind her, Marin pictured the greenhouse and the snapdragons and kissing Evie in the dirt. She remembered the taste of the apples in the orchard, crisp and sweet and tart all at once. She locked on a memory of cinnamon kisses and stayed there, imagined how she would kiss Evie if they survived this night together.

Marin straightened her shoulders. Her breathing began to feel lighter.

She understood how her mother had pressed onward, always, into the next moment, into the next adventure. She'd done it all not because she was fearless, but in spite of her fears. She'd done it for Marin.

In that moment, Marin understood that fear had a limit. A threshold that it couldn't penetrate. There was no nightmare that Marin wouldn't face down if it meant getting Evie and Thea out of here.

It wasn't hard to be brave. Not if it was for someone you love.

Several long, cold minutes into traveling the awful tunnel, Marin heard a noise behind her.

"It's okay," Evie's voice echoed in the dark. "It's me. Keep moving, we don't have much time left."

Marin could have cried in relief, but she forged on. "Your mother?"

"I couldn't convince her, Marin."

Alice had chosen to stay. She'd chosen death with Charles over everything else.

"And your father?"

"Oh, he's very, very dead."

"Evie—"

"Marin, *go.*"

The water was at her belly now. Marin shifted Thea's weight in her arms, pushing her up onto her shoulder to keep her face out of the water.

Something moved against her leg, and she screamed.

"What?" Evie's voice called out. She was just behind Marin now, nearly within arm's reach.

"I don't know," Marin said. "I thought I felt something in the water."

"Maybe something came in with the tide. An eel."

But Marin felt the tight grasp of a hand closing around her ankle. It was followed by another on her calf, and she knew. The tunnel wasn't made of wood or roots or even stone.

It was made of bones too, and they were waking to drown her.

34

We All Fall Down

---- ❧ ----

Evie reached out in the dark, finding Marin's hand and squeezing it nearly tight enough to break something.

Marin couldn't move—there was a bony hand wrapped around the ankle of her left foot, another gripping her right thigh so hard she felt it pierce the soft skin there.

"Evie," Marin cried. "Evie, we aren't going to make it."

For a moment, there was only the sound of water and a scraping sound that Marin finally recognized as bones rubbing against each other as they woke.

It felt like the walls were closing in around her.

Suddenly, Marin was back in that derailed train car that crumpled on impact. She was drenched from the rain and shivering. She smelled something burning. Was it fuel? She tasted blood, metallic on her tongue, where she'd bitten it during the crash. And she gripped her mother's hand too tight, refusing to leave her behind.

Except it wasn't the train car at all. It was a pitch-black

tunnel filled with the waking dead. And it wasn't rainwater drenching Marin but salt water. The lingering scent of
something burning was on Evie's clothes. No, not something.
Someone. The smell of kerosene clung to Evie.

Marin shook her head as if that could clear the awful
realization.

This was her nightmare all along.

Her mother had never reached through that gap in the
seats. Had never gripped her hand tight and told her to let go.
That was impossible because Marin's mother died instantly,
her body crushed the moment it happened.

"Let go, Marin."

It was Evie's voice.

"Marin, you have to let go."

Marin realized she was free. The bones on her legs had
released her.

"I can't control it for long," Evie said, her voice strained.
"There are so many of them."

"Then how am I free?"

"She was right. Mother said I couldn't control it because
I was too emotional. The walls only began to wake once
I realized I couldn't save her. It's my grief that's been
waking the dead. It's my grief waking these bones now.
But I can control it a little. I can control it long enough
to get you out."

Marin heard Neera's voice in her head.

Everyone's grief looks different.

Evie's powers had been out of control for a year. Ever since she lost her father. Ever since Alice began guilting her for not bringing him back. And now, having left her parents back in the flooding ossuary, Evie's grief was rippling out in waves of her dark magic, ricocheting across everything around them. And everything around them was bone.

"What about you?"

"It's hard, Marin. It's like locking down everything I'm feeling all at once. I think I can only get one of us out at a time."

"Evie, no. Please. Please don't make me go."

"Marin," Evie said. Her voice was soft, right next to her ear in the dark. "You have to get Thea out. You need to let go now."

Evie dropped her hand.

It took everything in Marin not to reach for it again.

"I'm coming back for you," she promised.

She surged ahead through the tunnel. The water covered her breasts, and part of Marin knew there was no time. But if she acknowledged that now, it would break her. She'd turn back for Evie. So instead, she lied to herself with every painful step.

There would be time.

She would get Evie soon.

She just had to get Thea out first.

*   *   *

The moment they rose from the dark, slick stairs back into the crypt above, Thea's eyelids fluttered open like a spell had broken.

"Hi, sweet girl," Marin murmured as she propped Thea up against one of the stone walls. "How are you feeling?"

"I had a nightmare," Thea said. Then she opened her eyes wider as she looked around. "Or did I?"

"It's okay," Marin said. "Everything is going to be all right. But I need you to stay here, just for a minute. I need to go back."

"We're here." Neera was at the mausoleum's entrance, ushering Wren inside.

Marin could hear Thisbe barking madly in the distance.

Wren cried out at the sight of Thea, wrapping her arms around her neck tight.

"I have to go back," Marin said. She turned, preparing to climb back down once more.

There was water lapping against the stairs.

The tunnel was completely flooded.

"No," Marin said. "No, no, no."

She climbed down the stairs until she was waist-deep in the water.

"Marin," Wren asked from above. "Marin, what are you doing?"

"She's in there," Marin explained.

"Marin, you can't," Thea said. "You'll drown."

"I won't," she insisted. She drew a few deep breaths. Evie wasn't that far. She could get to her.

"Marin, you can't," Neera said. She was climbing down the stairs.

"I have to!" She was beginning to panic.

There was no *time* to debate this.

Then Neera was there, wrapping her arms around Marin, hauling her back against her own body.

"What are you doing?" Marin screamed, struggling to break free. "What are you doing, she *needs* me."

"We need you," Wren said. She'd reached her thin arm down into the stairwell and waited.

Marin grasped Wren's little hand and collapsed against Neera.

"We can't just leave her."

"We can't let you go in there," Neera said. "She wouldn't want you to."

Somehow between Neera and Wren, they dragged Marin back to the top of the steps. Marin perched on the edge of the stone, staring at the dark well of water beneath her.

A full minute passed.

She was dying.

Evie was dying, and Marin felt like she might as well be dying too. Surely this is what it felt like to stay here, to do nothing but wait.

The water splashed against Marin's sneakers, and she choked on a sob, wrapping her arms around her head.

And then she felt it.

A hand on her ankle.

For a moment, she thought it was the bones, rising from the tunnel. But a figure emerged from the black water, gasping for air.

"Evie!" Marin tackled her against the stone. "Oh my god, Evie."

Evie coughed a few times.

"Let her breathe," Neera said gently.

Marin released her, climbing from the stairs, helping Evie along with her, and then they both collapsed on the floor of the mausoleum, gasping for air. It took a few minutes, but Evie stopped coughing and her breathing steadied.

Finally, Evie turned toward Marin.

They were inches apart, and Marin could see every strand of blond hair that clung to Evie's face, and the jagged, deep cut above her eye that still trickled blood. It would leave a scar.

Her eyes were underscored by dark purple half-moons like bruises, and her skin was paler than ever, marked by black contusions where she'd fought the dead. She was weak, and tired, and whatever she'd done to get them out of that damned tunnel had cost her dearly.

If using her powers made Evie tired, then controlling them might just kill her.

And yet, despite everything, she looked less haunted than before. Her dark eyes were bright with relief as she stood on shaky legs in the mausoleum, dripping with salt water.

"Let's get the hell out of here."

"We have to figure out *how* to get out of here first," Wren said from the entrance, where she stood with her arm wrapped around Thea, staring out into the graveyard.

Marin joined them, peering out over the tops of their heads.

There were people outside, dozens of them, standing in the shadows surrounding the mausoleum.

"Who are they?" Marin asked. She had a brief, electric hope that someone had come to help them.

"Look closer," Thea said.

Marin looked again. They were thin—very, very thin—and standing so strangely, hunched over their own bodies. *Bodies.*

They were bodies, not people.

And there was no one coming.

"They're all dead," Marin said.

Marin looked around the cemetery and saw the disturbed ground at each of the headstones. The body nearest to them shifted, and Marin could see its empty eye sockets and a skull covered in barnacles and starfish.

"The ground was soft," Evie said. "I'd guess the ocean water has been flooding these grounds for some time, rotting the coffins. And then I woke them up."

The surge of emotions that Evie felt in the tunnel and ossuary must have stretched up to the cemetery. It seemed the more emotional Evie was, the stronger her powers became.

"Maybe they'll let us pass," Thea said, turning to glance at Marin.

Marin looked to Evie, who was shaking her head.

"What choice do we have?" Marin asked.

They moved out slowly, with Thea tucked in tight behind Neera and Wren doing the same behind Evie. When the gate of the mausoleum swung out, they held their breath and stood like statues on the top step, waiting to see if the dead reacted.

There was no movement below.

They began to walk down the stairs, their steps deliberate and careful.

At the base of the mausoleum, Marin noticed a glint of metal and slowly bent to retrieve the hatchet she'd dropped earlier. Together as a unit, they began to cross the cemetery, putting as much distance between themselves and the corpses as possible.

A third of the way to the cemetery's entrance, Marin's foot connected with something soft, and she swallowed the curse that nearly slipped past her lips. She looked down and found Thisbe. She was lying on her side and bleeding from her snout, her breathing fast and shallow and labored.

Evie dropped to her knees to check on the dog, and when

Thisbe saw her, she let out a low, keening whimper.

The response behind them was immediate. One moment the dead stood still, vacant eyes fixated ahead of them on nothing, and the next, their necks swiveled in their direction.

They began to swarm.

Marin pushed Wren toward Neera and Thea.

"Get to the house," she told them, turning back just as the first creature reached them.

It fell on Marin, bony hands scratching at her face and arms. Marin swung the hatchet, sinking it into the side of the monster's skull.

It fell back, only to be replaced immediately by another.

Evie leapt into action, and every skeleton she could get her hands on fell dead once more. For once, their proximity to the dead was to their advantage. It was easier for Evie to stop them if she could reach their animated bodies.

But there were so many of them.

Marin wrenched the hatchet from one skeleton and swung it toward another. But she wasn't killing them, only slowing them down. Marin paused to yank a hand from her shirt. It wasn't attached to a body but still clenched tight, dangling from her clothes.

Evie cried out.

Marin turned to see one of the undead dragging Evie by her braid. She couldn't get her hands close enough to kill it, and they were heading directly for the bluff.

Marin ran, but she had barely reached them when the skeleton began to topple over the cliffside. She swung the hatchet once more, aiming for the skeleton's arm.

She missed, and the blade caught just above Evie's head, severing her long hair.

The undead catapulted over the edge, still clutching Evie's braid.

When they rose to their feet, Marin realized they were trapped. The bodies were closing in, had fallen in line in a haphazard semicircle. The only way out was through, but they'd be overwhelmed fast by so many of them.

On the bright side, Marin saw Neera and the girls reach the gate and slip unnoticed out of the graveyard. At least they were safe.

Evie tugged on Marin. Together they shuffled back to the mausoleum. It could provide them some protection at least, until the dead broke in. They paused in the threshold of the crypt, surveying the dead. Evie stood a few steps below Marin, her hands outstretched, her stance protective. Evie couldn't fight them all.

Marin heard it before she felt it.

It was a wet snap of a sound, like teeth tearing the flesh of an apple.

She looked down at the noise almost out of curiosity.

There she found hands wrapped around her forearm, which was no longer intact. The white bone of her arm practically

347

glowed in the moonlight where it protruded through her skin. Hot blood poured out fast, dripping down her elbow, splashing against the cool white stone of the crypt's floor.

It was Alice. Her eyes were milk white. She was drenched from the tunnel she'd just emerged from—escaped from her own watery grave.

Alice Lovelace was dead, and she'd just snapped Marin's arm in half.

Marin felt like she was watching a movie when Alice's hands released her arm and rose higher. It was so unexpected and bizarre that Marin couldn't accept that it was real. It was just another of Alice's stories. Not even a very good one.

But then Alice's hands tightened on Marin's throat and began to choke the life from her.

A piercing scream echoed across the graveyard from one of the girls. Thea, perhaps, Marin thought sluggishly. Thea had always liked her.

She wondered if Thea might bury her with her dolls.

Marin's vision grew blurry, and she sank to her knees before Alice.

Something tugged on her neck painfully. It was Evie, desperate to get her mother to release her grip on Marin, but Alice was strong—so unnaturally strong, possessed by darkness that was like a void, taking everything living with it, starting with Marin.

It was hopeless, and Evie stepped back away from Alice.

She stopped at the bottom of the mausoleum stairs and stretched her arms wide. Marin looked up into Evie's eyes—the whites were all but gone. They were shiny and black from lash to lash. *Her beautiful eyes*, Marin thought as dark shadows crowded into the edges of her vision.

Evie drew her hands above her head, like the conductor of a great, terrible symphony, and then she screamed. It was a horrible sound that struck Marin like a knife. It hurt her to know Evie could feel that. Evie's scream made Marin wish she were anywhere but here—not because she was dying but because she was sure this would kill Evie, and she didn't want to watch.

Loss. Grief. *Guilt*. There in that graveyard, surrounded by the dead, Evie was doing the only thing she had refused to do before. She was feeling it. All of it.

Every sharp needle of pain she'd ever known to not be able to control her powers, her own body. The knowledge that it would cost her and Marin any dream they'd ever shared together of their future. It had never been enough to lock her emotions away—she had to unleash them.

Finally, it ended.

The last remnants of Evie's scream echoed around them, and then all was quiet.

Evie dropped her arms.

Alice instantly released Marin, and they both collapsed onto the stone steps.

All over the grounds of the cemetery, the dead fell to the earth. It was as though they'd been mere puppets, and Evie had cut all of their strings at once.

The graveyard was silent, and all the dead lay down.

35

All Right, Now Who Needs Stitches?

———————— ❧ ————————

The evening tide took the ocean's salt scent out with it, leaving only the smell of the brackish gray mud behind.

Marin stepped off the wooden stairs that led from Lovelace House down to the shore and sank her bare feet into the mud. It smelled of seaweed and earth, briny and cloying, and something else. Something that Marin now knew all too well.

She'd always recognize the scent of death.

The subtle but persistent notes of decay.

It was a smell that followed her everywhere now, just a hint of its sickly sweetness in her nostrils, on her breath—just as Evie had once described.

Marin reached into the pocket of her stolen cable-knit sweater and pulled out a tin of mints, popping one in her mouth, welcoming the cinnamon heat that crowded out the scent better than anything else did.

Perhaps that's what it meant to come back from the edge of

death—from nearly dying by Alice's hands in the graveyard. Perhaps she brought some of it back with her, and now it lingered. Perhaps it clung to her like a shadow.

Marin stayed in the mud, ignoring the numbness from the cold that stole over her toes, slowly stealing over her foot and up to her ankles. She didn't mind the cold so much now.

As the ocean withdrew, the birds swept in, feasting at their leisure in the tide pools, scooping up those creatures unfortunate enough to be stranded by the retreating tide. And strewn across the shore, already half-buried in mud that sucked hungrily at everything, even Marin's own feet as she walked, were the hollowed-out bodies of crabs, freshly picked clean.

Marin wrinkled her nose at the bodies, the concept of death too near and raw, the memory of that forever darkness too familiar. She closed her eyes, focusing instead on what she could hear.

Water lapping on rocks.

A cormorant's wings beating air.

The splash of something larger in the deeper waters.

Marin focused on what she could feel. A cool wind tugged at her hair from the loose knots on the back of her head, freeing some strands like Evie's fingers liked to do, without intention, only a gentle tug and release.

The breeze rippled across the plastic bag she'd put over her cast to keep it dry. She'd let Wren and Thea decorate it, and it was covered in their art.

Marin's feet sank farther into the mud the longer she remained still, but she didn't mind it. In her time at Lovelace, Marin had grown to love the thick mud's greedy pull. The way it squished between her toes, anchoring her to the earth, to her body, to this new home she'd found. She didn't even mind the occasional scrape of a sharp shell buried in its depths.

A few feet away, a gull landed on a rock, cawing, and Marin opened her eyes again, panic subsiding. Its gaze was fixed on a twitching fish that had breached the water's edge and was gasping for breath. Marin tugged her bare foot from the mud's grasp and nudged the fish back into the water.

"Well?" she challenged the gull.

The bird turned its gaze on her, unimpressed, then shuffled to the tide pools to swallow a different fish. Marin felt a familiar thud in her chest. She felt she'd played with death, saving one life only to condemn another. It was how Evie must feel all the time: responsible.

And on the other side of responsibility lay all her guilt—an unbearable weight she'd carried.

At least now she wouldn't have to carry it alone.

Laughter echoed down from Lovelace House, and Marin looked up to see the rest of the family joining her. Thisbe led the pack, fully healed now from her injuries.

Wren and Thea followed, with Neera right behind them, shooing them down the stairs and out in the tide pools with their buckets.

Last came Evie.

She wore her father's old mudlarking boots, several sizes too big, and her short hair tucked behind her ears even though her curls escaped almost constantly.

Marin walked back to greet her.

"Hello." Evie's face was bright, dark circles long gone in the weeks since the cemetery. She'd even gotten a bit too much sun, the pink burn streaked across her cheekbones and nose.

"How did it go?" Marin asked.

Evie had taken the girls into town that afternoon to enroll them in the local schools. Marin planned to attend the high school for her senior year and would drive the girls into town with her each morning. They'd decided, collectively, that the girls desperately needed structure, socialization, and normalcy.

"It went great. They accepted all their homeschool records. They'll start next month with you."

Evie was another story. Evie couldn't bear the idea of sitting in a classroom again and planned to get her GED instead. She would be the girls' primary caretaker and, with Neera's guidance, manage the Lovelace family estate.

And maybe, like her mother, she would write. Evie had whispered the idea like a confession one night, after she'd cried her eyes out for her lost mother.

"It's stupid," Evie had said. *"I'm mourning something she never was."*

"I think that deserves its own kind of grief," Marin whispered back.

Evie had worn black for weeks, a quiet symbol of the bereavement she'd so privately shared with Marin, but today she wore an off-white dress with a wide sash around the middle and a fitted burgundy blazer. She'd wanted to look like the epitome of responsibility while registering the girls for school.

When Evie tugged off the jacket, Marin reached for her. Several buttons along Evie's back had come undone, and Marin silently slipped them back into place.

"Thank you," Evie whispered.

The color of Evie's dress matched the walls of the foyer in the house that towered behind them. It could have been called *French Cream* or *Ivory Bone* or *Pearl Kiss*, and it ought to have washed out Evie's pale skin. Instead, it made her look ethereal and dreamy, like a Victorian ghost lingering on the rocks.

What a delightful haunting that would be, thought Marin.

"Here, this finally came," Evie said. "You should read it." Evie handed Marin a few pages, folded neatly and stapled, and Marin opened them.

CORONER'S REPORT: ALICE MARIE LOVELACE

In order to receive her inheritance, an autopsy of Alice Lovelace had been required. A crucial first step in securing guardianship of her sisters was establishing financial independence.

Marin scanned the pages in front of her, then looked up in surprise.

"Alice didn't drown?" Marin frowned. It didn't make sense.

"There wasn't a trace of water in her lungs. Look." Evie's fingers drifted down the page. "Cerebral aneurysm. And that's not all. In his notes, the coroner says there was evidence of several aneurysms in her brain—any of which should have been fatal."

"What does it mean?"

"It means she was dying, Marin. Over and over. And I kept bringing her back just by being so close to her. It's why I was so exhausted, I think. I was using my powers all the time without knowing it. Keeping her alive."

Marin thought of Alice's strange decline these last few months. She'd turned darker with each resurrection, descending into something unrecognizable at the end.

Marin folded the papers and gave them back to Evie, then pulled Evie's free hand into her own. But it wasn't enough, and Evie turned and stole a kiss instead.

"Evie!" Thea called from the tide pool. "Come look at this!"

Evie laughed. She reached into Marin's pocket, stealing the cinnamons, before taking off to join the girls and Neera out on the rocks. Marin met Evie's gaze from the edge of the water, where Thea had just swept a drowned butterfly out of the water and cradled it in her palm while it woke up. They all watched it fly away.

The days were growing shorter, the sun already casting an orange-yellow glow across the rocks. When the wind picked up, she shoved her hands into the deep pockets of the sweater she was never giving back to Evie, and her hand brushed against something. She pulled out a slip of paper, rolled neatly and tied with a bit of twine. Marin unraveled the note to find Evie's familiar, delicate script inside. She read it quietly to herself before slipping it back into her pocket and smiling.

Marin didn't mind secrets anymore.

Now she and Evie traded them like currency, leaving each other notes filled with every minor confession of their lives, until there were no more secrets between them at all, only the new ones they now kept together. Marin collected them like bits of sea glass plucked from the tide pools, their once-sharp edges long worn down.

Like all good secrets, she would take them to her grave.

Acknowledgments

First, my apologies to Marin Blythe, a character born from the question of what it would be like to have terrible anxiety and suddenly find yourself stuck in the pages of a gothic horror novel. It was rather mean of me, but quite effective at getting to the heart of my own questions about anxiety. What if the worst did happen? What is on the other side of it? What is the correct amount of worry, anyway? It seems easy enough to fall on the side of *too much*, and I'm afraid I've always defaulted to that place of constant vigilance and second-guessing myself. In turn, it was helpful to lead Marin in the direction of learning to trust her intuition and quiet the worries in her head. If there are any readers who feel similarly, I hope you didn't mind exploring those questions right alongside Marin and me.

All my gratitude to my editor, Ben Rosenthal, who trusted me to leap between genres a bit on this third book we've worked on together. Your insight remains unmatched, and my manuscripts have benefited so much from your thoughtful suggestions. Thank you for knowing what I'm trying to say even when a story is in its messy first drafts.

Forever grateful for my agent Suzie Townsend for her encouragement and steadfast advocating for my writing. Speaking of worrying, you've eased a great deal of mine by consistently reminding me of my words' worth. Thank you for that.

Thank you to Sophia Ramos and New Leaf Literary. Thank you to the publishing team at Katherine Tegen Books, and the talented and dedicated individuals who have worked on *All the Dead Lie Down*, including Julia Johnson, Jessica Berg, Allison Brown, Meghan Pettit, Gweneth Morton, Joel Tippie, Lisa Calcasola, Patty Rosati, Mimi Rankin, Christina Carpino, and Josie Dallam. Thank you to Molly Fehr for designing the book cover, and Marcela Bolívar for lending it some truly beautiful art. Thank you to Katherine Tegen for giving my books their home.

This year I'm thankful to the Highlights Foundation for providing an inspiring place for writers to gather. Thank you, Jenny, for the adventure of traveling there together, and for the adventure of writing together all these years of our friendship. Thank you to my friends in the writing community and those who graciously offered to read this book early and provide blurbs.

Andrew, Kayleigh, Katharyn, Jackson, Mom, Dad, Julie, Tom, and Susan: thank you for your endless support and love, and for your understanding when I hide away to work when I'm on a deadline. A special thank-you to my own little monsters, Rowan and Theo, as well as my nieces and nephews, Emma, Finn, Margaret, Harriet, Olive, Otto, Noelle, and Caleb, for being wonderful, mischievous inspiration while I wrote Wren and Theadora.